The Road
at My Door

Lori Windsor Mohr

Printed in the United Kingdom

First Printing, 2015 Alfie Dog Limited

The author can be found at: authors@alfiedog.com

This is a work of fiction. Although based on real places it is not the intention of the author to suggest that any of these events took place and any similarity to persons alive or dead is purely co-incidental.

Cover design: Ann Hammond

Book title: Inspired by William Butler Yeats' poem, *The Road at My Door*

ISBN 978-1-909894-29-7

Published by
Alfie Dog Limited
Schilde Lodge, Tholthorpe,
North Yorkshire, YO61 1SN
Tel: 0207 193 33 90

For Christine and Michael

CONTENTS

"Everything can be taken from a
man but one thing: the last of human freedoms—to
choose one's attitude in
any given set of circumstances, to choose one's own
way."

Viktor Frankl
Man's Search for Meaning

PROLOGUE

There's something about a secret that makes you want to keep it. This revelation came to me late in the winter of my fourteenth year. Deep down I must have known this about myself all along. It took facing a life-changing decision to make it real. My secret had the power to kill me. In the meantime, it made me sick in every way a person could be sick.

These were my thoughts as I made the three hour trip to visit my mother. The scenic route along Pacific Coast Highway to Laguna Beach added forty-five minutes to the freeway drive. It had been years since I'd thought about all that happened here and needed the solitude of a three-hour drive to prepare. As it was my arrival felt sudden.

Other than flower baskets that tourists love hanging along the main drag, the place was a virtual time warp back to 1964. The familiarity was disorienting. Shaggy Eucalyptus trees and family owned businesses retained the village character lost to urban sprawl in neighboring cities.

I turned at the Texaco station, the very one I had walked to every Saturday for the restroom rather than step inside her house with Dad. This time I drove past the lane of beach bungalows to an angular contemporary on the bluff in Emerald Bay.

The hospice nurse led me to her bedroom. Shards of afternoon sun cut across the hardwood floor. As the room came into focus my knees went weak. There she was, shrunken and flaccid in a hospital bed. A putrid odor hung in the air. The plug-in purifier was no contest for toxins oozing from her skin with the smell of old moth balls.

I stepped closer. The sight of her took my breath away. This was a death camp survivor, not the iconic beauty I had known. The contours that had once defined her voluptuous figure now protruded in bony peaks under the blanket. Her face was a tissue-thin layer over spider veins. She looked dead, a gurgling sound with each breath the only evidence otherwise.

I felt sick to my stomach.

Mom opened her eyes. I drew back, startled. They closed again before I could say hello. I found a chaise and sat down to wait in hopes the forgiveness I'd found on the road would survive the interlude, fully aware this would be our final moment.

1

GIFT HORSE

The bus driver glanced at me in the rear view mirror. My stop was next. The ride home from Saint Monica's High to Pacific Palisades took exactly forty-three minutes, including all the stops. My house was last on the route. I didn't mind riding alone with the driver once everyone else was off, as long as he didn't talk. That would've made it unbearable, having to be social, like adding forty-three minutes to the school day.

I jumped out the rear exit as soon as the door sprang open. The bus heaved a sigh and drove away. Alone at last. I stood at the gate to our backyard, a three-tiered oasis. Mom said Pacific Palisades was a Technicolor poster for California Living—beautiful people, tree-lined streets, the Ocean at our feet—and that we should thank the Soviet Union for making the move possible.

According to her, the Cold War was the best thing that ever happened to the Cavanaugh family because the defense industry had become a hotbed of opportunity. For college educated men like my father, a career in aerospace meant a "guaranteed ticket to success" in 1962.

I headed up the flagstone path to the back staircase. I felt like a foreigner in this new house in a new town in a new neighborhood, a neighborhood where yards were groomed by gardeners instead of shirtless dads on Saturday afternoon.

The surroundings looked different. That's about all

that had changed. Mom was still moody all the time, she and my older sister Kit still bickered all the time, Dad still walked on eggshells, I stayed out of the way, and Sunday mornings found Mom sliding celery sticks into the Bloody Marys Dad made before breakfast.

Geraniums spilled over the stone path. I shoved them aside with my saddle shoes, which I hoped might look better dirty. A uniform wasn't so bad. The freshman skirt and blouse I could live with. Saddle shoes were another matter entirely. A thirteen-year-old girl looked totally dorky in a bigger version of the shoes she had worn as a toddler.

In this outfit I didn't stand a chance with Greg Stewart. Blond and tan like just about everyone else in this beach town, he'd smiled at me in Honors English. I hadn't smiled back. Shyness usually prevented me from anything close to flirting, which Kit said even I could do with a well-timed smile. My sister was a lot of things. Shy was not one of them.

Daydreams about Greg Stewart would have to wait. Right now I needed to figure out how to keep my parents together. The "D" word had come through the walls of their bedroom in muffled tones as I eavesdropped at night, which was how I figured out everything that went on in my family. Divorce would mean being stuck with a mother who neither loved me nor hated me. Indifference, that's what I got from Mom.

My parents probably thought I was too young to notice tension between them. I don't think Dad's job was the real reason we came to the Palisades at all. I think 'moving up' as Mom called it was Dad's last ditch effort to save the marriage. I'd heard him say with a new job it didn't make sense to move for another year. Mom said if he really loved her they would take out a bigger mortgage and move now.

Two weeks before school started they put a down payment on a place in Pacific Palisades, and just like that we traded our post World War II tract house in the valley for an executive home near the beach.

Mom would be right about the move to Pacific Palisades. The new house wouldn't be what saved her from marital misery. It would be something else entirely. That something would become the source of my secret.

At the back door I listened for sounds of Mom and Kit fighting before going inside. There was no sign of Mom in the kitchen. That meant she was in the bedroom buried in one of her beloved novels, the closed door a message: 'Do Not Disturb'. I left my book bag on the washer and went through the laundry room door to the garage. Tennis racquet and ball in hand, I scooted under the heavy door to the other side.

It was as quiet on the street as it had been in the house. The sound of kids playing in the street after school at our old house had been replaced by the buzz of power mowers from gardeners who disappeared at five.

I slammed the ball against the door with a bounce-hit monotony that lulled me into a faraway zone. I tried to imagine divorce. Would life with a squabbling Mom and Kit be better or worse than the strain we lived with now?

"Tell me you're not on the tennis team."

I snatched the ball mid-air and spun around. Greg Stewart leaned against a sycamore with his ankles crossed. He was cuter close up than he had been across the classroom. I was still in my uniform with an untucked blouse and ponytail at half-mast. The saddle shoes might as well have been fins. "No. Just hitting."

He emerged from the shade. "I'm Greg Stewart. I live up the street. We're in Honors English together."

I managed a half-smile. "I know. I'm Reese."

"I didn't take you for one of those cheerleader-tennis-player types."

Of course not. I hadn't laughed in a hundred years. The sorry state of my family was written all over me, an automatic rule out for cheerleader. That would be Kit. Mom described me as the 'quiet, intense sister' compared with the 'high-spirited social one', a differentiation I interpreted from her tone as far less appealing. I didn't understand how belligerent and combative equaled high-spirited or how quiet intensity meant dull. That prejudice no doubt resulted from the similarity between my mother and sister. I wasn't sure whether 'quiet' was my true temperament or a way to cope with chaos without adding to it.

"You just hanging out?"

"Pretty much." I didn't want to tell him I was avoiding my mother. Or vice versa.

"Me too. Hey, you want to walk down to the empty house on the cliff, the one that's for sale? I have a couple of cigarettes. We could smoke by the pool."

"I don't really smoke." Stupid, stupid, stupid.

He looked at me dumbstruck, no doubt sizing up the first of what would become a growing list of deficits the longer he stuck around. A grin spread over his face. "I don't either. Don't tell anyone. You have another racquet?"

"No, but we have a ping pong table on the back patio. It's not real tennis like this," I said with a nod toward the garage.

"In that case I'll win. You can buy me a pack of

6

Marlborough's."

We both chuckled. A black sedan pulled up to the house.

"It must be Father Sebastian. Last Sunday he said he would be coming around to visit new families in the parish. I better go tell my mom."

"Okay, well, that old guy gives me the creeps. See you tomorrow in class, Cavanaugh."

"See you, Stewart." I watched him take off down the street in a mix of disappointment and relief.

The priest and I got to the porch at the same time. It wasn't old Father Sebastian at all. This man didn't look old enough to be a priest. He wasn't as tall as Dad and his frame was lean, unlike my bear of a father. In fact, the priest wasn't manly at all. He could've been one of the Beach Boys with hair bleached dry on top of his California Casual good looks. His smile, a grin really, made his whole body springy, as if his bones were held together with rubber bands.

He flickered with playfulness. His voice had not an ounce of mockery. "Well hello, young lady. I'm Father Donnelly, Jack Donnelly. I'm here from Corpus Christi Church to officially welcome you. Who might you be?"

"Clarice Cavanaugh."

"Whoa, doesn't that sound like a movie star name, with movie star looks to go with it. And is that what I should call you, Clarice? Or do you have a nickname?"

Mom hadn't been able to prevent Katherine from becoming Kit. I'd felt the need to make up for that by sticking with Clarice. Until this very moment. "Reese."

Father Donnelly extended his hand. No adult had ever shaken hands with me. His fingernails were immaculate, skin soft. In the less than 60 seconds it had taken to introduce himself I already liked Father Jack Donnelly.

I scooted around him to open the door. Mom. I would have to interrupt her. With my pointer finger in the air to signal a quick return, I took off through the living room to find her. I tapped before sticking my head inside. Mom was lying on the chaise. She didn't look up from her book.

"Clarice, is it absolutely necessary for you to run through the house like a wild horse?"

"Sorry. The priest is here."

"The prie—? Oh, Father Sebastian." She slapped the book closed and went to check herself in the vanity mirror. "I swear. It's always something." She brushed one side of her hair back Lauren Bacall style with a tortoiseshell barrette to hold it in place.

"Mom, he's waiting."

"First things first, dear. It never hurts to keep a man waiting. Heightens the allure."

I watched her preen for the attention she was about to get, the attention Mom always got from men. She opened her mouth to a gaping maw and glided red lipstick over it. With her little finger she dabbed each corner, then pressed her lips in a rolling motion.

If there was anything my mother loved, it was attention from men. I wasn't sure what she meant by allure. If that's what got men's attention, she had it. Dad never seemed bothered. Maybe because Mom's real talent wasn't in attracting men but in alienating them, men and women alike. She took pride in standing apart from the crowd, cool, detached, while others lived what she called mundane lives. Kit and I had long ago accepted our mother would never be like those of our friends, mothers who drove car pool and traded recipes.

Allure or no allure, it wasn't going to matter to Father

Donnelly. This was one man whose head Mom wouldn't be turning. I tried not to sound righteous. "It's not Father Sebastian. This priest is young, and super handsome." Why not rub it in?

"Well, why didn't you say so? That's a different matter entirely." Mom yanked the skirt of her dress. The loosened bodice returned to form fitting tightness under the belt. Satisfied with the total package, she swept past me into the hall. I rolled my eyes, amazed at her assumption that any man, even a priest, would fall prey to her beauty.

Mom introduced herself and motioned Father Donnelly into the living room. He took one club chair and she the other. I dropped on the couch between them.

"Don't you have homework, Clarice?"

Her tone told me I did. I headed to my room with a dejected nod to Father Donnelly.

"Not so fast, young lady." He had a devilish grin. "You're not rid of me yet, not by a long shot. Now that you and I are friends I expect you to come say hello at church."

I gawked at him.

"Well, what do you say, Reese. Deal?"

Mom did a double take at the two of us, a distinct scowl sliding over her face at his use of my nickname; more pointedly, at reference to a conversation to which she hadn't been privy. Somehow I felt both were okay with the priest, this radiant man with the great big grin. He would smooth it over with Mom.

"Deal." In that moment Father Donnelly won me over to his corner. Not only was he an adult, he was a priest—a priest who wanted to be my friend; a priest who addressed me by the name I preferred rather than the one demanded by my mother.

I retreated from the visit, not from the conversation. My L-shaped bedroom shared a wall with the living room. The one nickname Mom did find acceptable was Bionic Ears, an alias acquired from a career in eavesdropping. I pressed against the wall. *Please God, please let Mom and Father Donnelly get along.*

They covered the basics of who we were and where we had come from, and who he was and where he had come from. They moved on to Mom's favorite subject, sex. I could never understand why she always brought up sex — sex in marriage, sex outside of marriage, sex in the movies, homosexuality — sex, sex, sex. And he's a priest, for God's sake! For someone who was always quoting Miss Manners, Mom sure didn't follow her own advice. It's inappropriate to talk about money or politics, but sex is okay?

The crescendo in their voices was a familiar part of the exercise. Mom's energy would build the longer the discussion went on, as if she were momentarily released from what Kit referred to as her meatloaf life, which my sister said was the real reason Mom was grumpy all the time. At five minutes in, Father Donnelly had broken the record for talking with Mom about sex. I checked my watch to time how long he would last.

Mom's brazen manner was guaranteed to intimidate men, embarrass women. Talking about sex had turned out to be a brilliant repellent against actual connection with another human being. Ninety-nine percent of the time the conversation would have ended once it had served its purpose. Father Donnelly proved a worthy challenge. The one percent.

Their voices died down. Victory. It had taken Mom

longer than usual to get rid of the priest. I made a checkmark in the air next to Father Donnelly. His name would be included in today's count on the growing list of people Mom had alienated the first two weeks in our new town.

There was no need to listen for the familiar exit, nervous laughter followed by a closed front door. I stood to leave my post. An unusual noise caught my attention.

It wasn't nervous laughter. The front door hadn't closed. The sound on the other side of the wall was…laughter. Mom and Father Donnelly were laughing!

Thank you, God, thank you.

That's how I knew. I knew that even if she turned back into stone, Mom had come to the same conclusion I had: Father Jack Donnelly was special.

Another hour later the front door did close. I knew he would be back for another visit.

It wasn't long in coming.

*

The next morning I was first out of the house, just steps ahead of Kit. I piled into the new Ford and took my position in back. Kit sashayed across the lawn as only my sister could, assured of her status riding shotgun. This morning I didn't care. Greg Stewart might get to school early. He would see me dropped off in the Ford instead of rushing from the corner bus stop.

Kit opened the door as if it were any old car, a restraint commensurate with her sophistication as a sophomore, along with the condescension. I leaned over the front seat and twirled the steering wheel. She clicked her tongue at my imitation of the salesman on TV.

"It's a Fooooord," I howled in prolonged pronunciation of the manufacturer's name. Dad's deep voice had sounded better yesterday afternoon. He'd left work early to drive it home from the dealership so he could surprise Mom. She thought the executive perk wouldn't be available until the first of the year. Dad had led her outside with eyes closed, the Ford imitation a giveaway hint.

Kit honked the horn. "I'm going to be late meeting Jackie."

Mom checked to see if any neighbors might be watching, which Kit said was the real reason she left the Ford in the driveway instead parking it in the garage. Mrs. Ellery's wave from the kitchen window across the street proved Mom's strategy worthwhile.

Mom said new was the best smell in the world. She drove ten miles under the speed limit to make sure no one missed what Dad referred to as Mom's new status symbol. Mom insisted the new car was absolutely required if they were going to keep up with the Joneses in a neighborhood full of Joneses, all of whom drove late model cars and disappeared into an attached garage instead of parking in the driveway, direct evidence of a somebody rather than a nobody living there.

Sounds of a quarrel jarred me back to earth.

"Give me one good reason why I can't go see *Lolita* with Jackie?"

"*Lolita* is rated X in the Legion of Decency and Jackie's parents are divorced. I'm sure she has no supervision at home."

"I can't have a friend with divorced parents and the Catholic Church decides what movies I can and can't see? That's just bitchin'."

"Don't swear, Katherine. If you give me anymore sass your father will hear about it."

Kit folded her arms. "Fine. I'll go to the library after school and check out *Peyton Place*. You can't spy on me twenty-four hours a day."

Mom's hands tightened over the steering wheel.

I could've predicted my sister would find the one friend Mom wouldn't approve of. Like an automatic pool sweep, you could set Kit down anywhere and she'd gravitate to the edge.

We drove in silence the rest of the way to school.

Things at home may not have been different. School was another matter altogether. It was as if the world had closed, then opened up again, everything brand new. I had made another friend besides Greg. Francesca Cantello, or Francie as she preferred to be called, was also in first period Honors English.

I slid into my alphabetically-determined seat behind Francie, both surnames starting with 'C'. A fellow recent transplant, she and I had become instant allies. Francie with Italian coloring was an exception to the fair-haired prototype filling the halls. That alone made me like her, even though I was one of those blondes. Five minutes after meeting each other she confessed her crush on our teacher, a Jesuit brother.

The second bell rang. Greg threw me a quick nod on the way to his desk.

Brother Timothy McPherson waited at the lectern. It wasn't hard to see why Francie had a crush on the man. He was gorgeous. He looked the same age as the seniors. I was sure he had to be at least twenty-four. I wondered why he had chosen the life of a cleric instead of being ordained a priest. Francie had looked up the difference in the *Encyclopaedia Britannica*. She said it was a dumb way to get out of saying Mass if that was all he wanted, because

Brother McPherson had to take the same vows of poverty, celibacy, and obedience. I told her maybe he was escaping a torrid love affair with a married woman. This beautiful guy with hazel eyes that zoomed right into yours must've had lots of girls falling for him. If he hadn't ruined his life he could've had his pick.

Whatever his reason for entering religious life, it didn't matter to me. In two weeks Brother McPherson had become my favorite teacher of all time, which had nothing to do with his looks. There was something in his manner. I wanted to be in his presence, absorb his knowledge so I could be on the same plane; understand what he understood.

"*Fire and Ice*. Only nine lines long, this little poem, a brilliant example of Frost's concisely ironic literary style. Let's take the first two lines. Reese Cavanaugh, if you would enlighten us. What emotions is Frost referring to in this metaphor?"

"I think he's using fire to mean passion and ice to mean hatred."

"Right. He doesn't tell us which of these elements is more likely to cause destruction but tells us that in his personal experience, it will be fire. Then he goes on to tell us hate also makes a good argument for destruction of the world through ice."

A hand went up in the front row. "He didn't mention nuclear war. That'd work."

A giggle rippled through the classroom. Brother McPherson stepped away from the lectern to the desk and leaned against it.

"Ah! Andy makes an important point. But is Frost talking about the literal world? Couldn't he be talking about a relationship? Too much desire and passion can consume a relationship, while cold indifference and hate can be equally destructive. Isn't that what our narrator is saying?"

During that one hour of English, Brother McPherson took us into another dimension, a world in which literature related to real life. He spoke directly to me, I was sure of it, those hazel eyes peering deep into my soul.

In poetry he taught us words were symbols to be deciphered. Once we knew how to do that, a whole deeper meaning would be revealed, meaning you couldn't find in Webster's dictionary. Symbolism was the secret to unlocking lessons in loneliness, loss, despair, love, even if we hadn't experienced the emotions. That's how Brother McPherson made me feel like an equal. I got the sense he hadn't experienced them either.

But he understood them. That put him one step ahead of me.

That made him a mentor.

*

At home our new life was off to a bumpy start. The *Lolita* argument was ancient history, or so I thought.

Dad called me and Kit to the kitchen for lunch. The normal tension in the house had been amped up. Dad looked glum. He instructed us to be quiet and eat our Campbell's Bean with Bacon soup. My stomach tightened. The crunch of Saltines and the sipping of soup were the only sounds at the table.

Dad finished his lunch. He explained in a flat voice that after Kit and I finished ours we would be getting a whipping with his belt.

Kit shot back. "Why? What for?"

"On general principles." Dad didn't look at her.

Kit glared at Mom, who didn't look up, her Revlon lips

pursed as she tested the heat before each sip from the spoon.

"Dad, what did she tell you? Whatever she said, she's lying. Can't you see that? Mom, I didn't go see *Lolita*! And you can't spank me. I'm in high school!"

Silence.

"You're gonna be so sorry. You're gonna pay for this." Kit picked up her spoon and mimicked Mom with exaggerated sips, the chill between them cooling our steaming bowls.

My stomach churned as soup bobbed up and down with indecision. Dad nodded toward the living room. My sister calmly folded her napkin, slammed the spoon on the table, and marched with head high to the living room.

I sat transfixed at the sounds as I visualized the scene. Dad drew the drapes. Kit lowered her jeans and knelt on the floor, elbows propped on the couch. I didn't have to imagine anything for the next part. Dad yanked the leather belt from his waist with a snap.

Scccchhhlappp. Scccchhhlappp. Scccchhhlappp. Scccchhhlappp.

Kit didn't utter a sound. I held my breath until the whipping stopped. I waited for the aftermath I knew would follow. The force of the slammed bedroom door sent every window in the house rattling in synchronized anger all the way to the kitchen.

Mom didn't flinch.

My turn. I shot a silent plea to Mom. She refused to meet my eyes.

In the living room I whispered to Dad. "I didn't do anything. Why should I get punished, Daddy? You and I both know this is between Mom and Kit."

His face was drawn in torment. "Let's get this over

with, Clarice."

Tears blurred my vision. I knew pleading for exemption was useless. Had there been any way out of this spanking Kit would've been the one to accomplish a reprieve.

I tried to act brave like Kit. As soon as the bedroom door was shut, I hopped up and down from the sting. It was only after inspecting for blood and finding none that I noticed the open window.

Kit was gone.

On the ladder of rebellion sneaking out of the house even for two hours was a cut above talking back. I crossed my fingers for Kit to return before Mom found out. If my sister was going down, I would be going down with her. Our new life would be dead in the water.

That night in bed I wondered why Dad had done it. Was going along with Mom's demands the price of preventing divorce? I shivered under the covers. We were all at the mercy of Mom's whims, Dad included. Maybe Dad most of all.

I tried to remember life when I was little, a time when Dad would play his harmonica in the hallway at night until Kit and I fell asleep, a time when Mom and Dad were happy. A time when I felt safe. And loved.

2

BETTER THAN GOD

Father Donnelly began visiting on a regular basis, which improved Mom's mood far more than spanking me and Kit had. Wednesday, his day off, he showed up earlier and stayed later. Wednesday was also Greg's longest track practice. We wouldn't be hanging out playing ping pong.

Any other Wednesday I would be looking forward to seeing Father Donnelly for our regular chit-chat before getting The Look, my cue from Mom to go away and leave them to their 'adult conversation'. I assumed that meant talking about sex in some context or other. Today that was fine. I was in a rotten mood. The forty-three minute bus ride home took forever. I wanted to get the chit-chat over with and disappear in my room.

A hit to my social life paled in comparison with the prospect of divorced parents. I tried to keep some kind of perspective. That wasn't easy. Tension at home clouded my view of everything, like trying to see through dirty glasses.

I cracked open the back door. Mom's and Father Donnelly's voices carried from the living room. Time to walk the gauntlet. I gave them a breezy hello and kept walking toward the hall. Their conversation dwindled to a halt.

"Whoa, whooooaaaaaa. Hey. You don't speak to your friends anymore?"

Caught. I offered a perkier greeting.

Father Donnelly got up from the couch where he and Mom sat facing each other. "Hmmmm. Well, this won't do. Nope. This won't do at all." He took my hand and started toward the kitchen. "C'mon, Vivienne, we've got a crisis."

Father Donnelly and I sat at the table. Mom swished past in her full skirt to make a fresh pot of coffee.

Father Donnelly leaned close. "Now, you want to tell me what's happened to take the beautiful smile off your face?"

I fell into his blue ocean eyes, gold flecks flickering in the depths. Everything about Father Donnelly told me I could confide in him. *Mom and Dad are on the brink of divorce. You have to do something. Mom will listen to you. You're the only person who can help.* "Stephanie Hamilton is having a big sleepover Friday night. I mean, she invited everyone...even Francie." I bit my lip to calm the quivering.

"And she didn't invite you."

Silence.

Father Donnelly waited until Mom started the coffee grinder. He spoke in a low voice, a teasing grin of confidence rather than ridicule on his face. "This wouldn't have anything to do with Greg Stewart, would it?"

My blush was answer enough. Father Donnelly had noticed me and Greg on the back patio playing ping pong more than a few times. Since Mom had never asked me about Greg, I assumed he hadn't told her. The coffee grinder stopped. Father Donnelly shifted his voice loud enough for Mom to hear now that he had made clear we were conversing in code.

"Isn't Stephanie Hamilton that boy-crazy girl who's always cornering... what's his name... Greg something...

every Sunday after Mass? She practically throws herself at the poor guy. It's common knowledge she's been after him since they were fifth graders. He's the one feather she doesn't have in her cap."

I didn't know if it was common knowledge or not. It didn't matter. Father Donnelly knew something about everyone in the parish from what I'd gathered eavesdropping on his conversations with Mom. They were constantly gossiping about so and so. He continued.

"That girl thinks just because she's rich, she's better than everyone else. No matter how much her family donates to the Church, it doesn't give her license to be mean. And it's just plain mean spirited to exclude one person if she's invited the whole circle of friends."

Mom leaned against the fridge with a look of disinterest and studied her fingernails. Her presence felt intrusive in what was a private discussion.

Father Donnelly took a long sip of coffee. "Do you really want to be friends with someone like that?"

I grimaced at his typically-adult question. "Kind of."

Father Donnelly laughed so hard I could see his tonsils bobbing up and down. He slapped the table with a terrible thwack. "Wrong answer. But honest." He looked me in the eye. "Dear girl, I'm going to let you in on an important life secret."

I wondered how much of a secret it could be with Mom standing there.

"Real friends come to you. They may not be the people you expect, the popular kids who like everyone to think they have it all. In fact, most popular kids don't have close friends, they have a bunch of people they like one day and drop the next. Now here's the secret." He glanced beyond me to Mom, the message directed to her as much as me.

"When you're lucky enough to have a real friend, the thing that makes them real is that they want to be your friend as much as you want to be theirs."

He trapped Mom in his gaze as she handed him fresh coffee. Message sent and received.

"Now, if you're the smart girl I think you are I know how you're going to answer my next question." He sipped from the steaming mug, eyes twinkling over the rim. "Do you honestly want to be friends with Stephanie Hamilton? Or are your feelings hurt because you're left out. They're two different things."

My smile came out a conciliatory smirk. "I guess it's being left out."

"Well, young lady, you are in business. That we can fix!" He slapped the table again. "You don't need Stephanie Hamilton to have a good time. You know what we're going to do?" He looked at Mom again, this time drawing her into the plan. "We're going to have our very own party. After hearing confession Friday night, I'm coming right over here. At ten o'clock, you and I are going to watch *The Twilight Zone*. Your mom will bake us one of her famous chocolate cakes and we'll stay up until eleven watching TV, just the two of us."

"You mean it?" I sat up straight.

"I do indeed. Of course, if you want to invite your dad or Kit or your mom that's okay too. Nobody can join us unless you invite them. I promise you, we will have the best Friday night there ever was in the Cavanaugh residence."

And that's exactly what we did. Friday night FD, our new code name for him, came straight over after confession. All of us—Dad, Mom, me, even Kit—gathered in the living room, Kit and I on the floor, elbows propped, and watched *The Twilight Zone*.

It was without question the best party ever.

That's how the tradition began. Friday nights would find Mom, Dad, Kit and me in the kitchen at nine o'clock with hopes our fellow parishioners hadn't sinned too much. Mortal sins had a tendency to extend confession, which cut into our pre-*Twilight Zone* powwow. It went without saying that no one outside the family was to know about these Friday night rendezvous. Gossip in the parish would threaten future parties. We swore to keep FD's visits a secret.

For the first time I could remember, our family was united around a cause.

It would be the first in a long trail of secrets that would bring our family together. In the end those secrets would doom us—leave us pounding for shelter at a door that would be locked from inside.

*

Mom finished packing Dad's suitcase for another trip back East to update the government on his company's defense projects. The silence on her end told me Mom was in a bad mood. Big surprise. I was on the verge of ditching my eavesdropping post when Dad mentioned how he hated leaving the three of us girls alone in the house, how he would feel a lot better if a man were here. What did Mom think about Jack Donnelly spending a few nights?

The low giggling and kiss that followed told me she liked the idea.

A phone call from Dad was all it took and the sleepover plan was in place. FD joked that nosey parishioners would have a field day noticing his car parked overnight in front of the Cavanaugh's. That was easy enough to solve, Dad said. Why didn't FD keep his garage door opener? Arrival in stealth should guarantee secrecy, especially in the dark.

Dad's travel schedule added a bonus to our Friday night tradition. A half hour before *The Twilight Zone*, Mom, Kit and I took our positions in the kitchen, as usual, only now it was the hum of the automatic garage door that would announce FD's arrival. Just like Dad coming home from work, FD's Chrysler sedan would disappear inside. And just like Dad, FD would enter the kitchen from the garage. He would change out of his work clothes, just like Dad, the cassock replaced by the "civvies" he wore underneath—black pants, white tee, and a gold crucifix sliding over his tanned chest.

For a few precious hours, my mother would be happy—relaxed, radiant, giggly, affectionate. She might even pet my hair as I sat on the floor next to the couch. Instead of her face drawn in resentment, it would soften and make her look closer in age to Kit than thirty-five.

The Cavanaugh family had found a savior, a redeemer who descended not from on high, but through our garage with Dad's automatic opener.

*

Ten o'clock Friday morning. The air raid siren sent a high-pitched shriek through the classroom. On cue all twenty of us dropped to the floor and covered our heads. I said three Hail Marys. Praying wasn't included in the "Drop and Cover" exercise. I threw it in for good measure.

I peeked under my arm. Greg smiled from two rows over. I rolled my eyes and smiled back at the utter humiliation of holding the leap-frog position for three minutes. The exercise was a widely-adopted reminder that an actual nuclear attack could occur at any time. Dad joked the "Drop and Cover" exercise was pointless because if the Russians bombed us, no one would survive anyway.

In spite of Mom's facetious remark that our family had benefited from the Cold War because of Dad's job in defense, political uncertainty brought its own kind of anxiety. I asked Dad what we were fighting over with the Soviets. He explained it had to do with protecting a way of life in which Mom could buy a new car every year. Dad's teasing didn't fool me. I had overheard enough conversations at church to sense grown-ups, including my parents, were plenty worried. Tension between the United States and the Soviet Union increased every day.

It was hard to understand. We saw no soldiers on the evening news, heard no reports of civilian death. I decided anxiety over an invisible war half a world away added to the palpable one between my parents was too much. Given there was no way to avoid the latter I chose to ignore the former. Humiliation during the "Drop and Cover" exercise at school was the extent to which the Cold War had anything to do with me.

That was about to change.

The zigzag trail to the beach lay hidden behind scrub brush at the end of our street. Greg and I raced up the steep path to warm up. Two hours wading in tide pools in search of sea anemones for his biology class had left us cold and wet.

At the trailhead I staggered to the first patch of crab grass and collapsed. Greg dropped beside me. We turned our faces to the sparkling Pacific as our lungs filled.

"Mission accomplished," Greg said. He patted the rucksack.

"I'm not helping you once it starts getting cold."

He ignored my comment. "Did you know that a

fertilized egg from a sea anemone can attach itself to a rock and survive for fifty years?"

"Nope."

"If we were annihilated by an atomic bomb, sea anemones, one of the lowest forms of life, would survive."

"Without ever having done 'Drop and Cover'."

He swatted me on the head with his rucksack strap. "What that means is any surviving humans could start over."

"I thought the whole point of the drill was for everyone to survive."

"Not according to my dad. He says the only survivors will be in bomb shelters."

I propped on my elbows. "The only ones?"

"It makes sense. Look at what happened to everyone when we dropped the atomic bomb on Hiroshima and Nagasaki. That's how people will end up unless they can protect themselves underground."

"Well, that'll be me. Mom said for the price of a bomb shelter she'd rather have a pool. Besides, my dad says President Kennedy won't let things go that far with the Russians."

"My dad disagrees. That's why we built a shelter. "He broke into a grin.

"Really?"

"C'mon."

The sprint up the street helped warm us after lying on the grass in wet shorts. We tiptoed single file along the side of the house. Greg brought his index finger to puckered lips with a shooshing sound before taking a peek in the kitchen window. He signaled me to crouch and follow. I wondered why we were sneaking.

His backyard was all one level unlike my three-tiered

one. We walked past the kidney-shaped swimming pool, which didn't appeal in my damp condition. We walked past a guest house toward a clump of trees in the far corner. Greg checked to make sure no one was watching. He needed both hands on the metal ring to drag aside a 4' x 4' steel lid. He knelt down and switched on a light.

"Why are we sneaking?" I whispered.

"Dad says we shouldn't broadcast this because everyone will want us to let them in if we're attacked. You won't tell anyone though."

Another secret.

We leaned down and stared into the mouth of hell. The stairway was wide enough for one person. I wasn't sure my dad could fit with his broad shoulders. A metal grid protected the single fixture halfway down. It was too dark at the bottom to see anything. I struggled harder for breath than I had racing up the trail or sprinting to Greg's house.

He went first. Our heads bobbed as we descended the stairs. One moment we were eye level with the yard, the next we disappeared into earth. The patch of daylight above us shrank with each step. I tried to control rising panic in the hot, dense air. All I could think of was someone finding the steel plate off and shoving it back into place.

The darker it got the more tentative my steps. I felt for the edge of each stair. Greg offered me the tail of his shirt. Down, down, down we went until we stopped at a small landing. The two of us stood pressed against each other in the cramped space. Greg turned around. I could feel his breath. He brushed my bangs aside with his fingers and leaned down. His lips grazed mine in the dark.

Without warning he turned away. Neither of us said

anything. A moment later, Greg threw his shoulder against the door. It opened into total darkness. Greg switched on a light, this one a bright fluorescent.

The place looked like doom, an apocalyptic dungeon. It was about the size of our garage except for the low ceiling.

"Wouldn't you smother in here?" I waved my hands in front of my face to move the air.

Greg stepped a few feet to a panel in the wall. "Nah, there's a mechanical air circulation and filtration system. Maybe it's not on." He lifted the metal cover. "This is where we keep the key. The lid and door both lock from inside to keep people out. We'd be toast if we lost that."

My heart jumped at the idea of being trapped underground in the dark. Greg pointed out two sets of bunk beds in an L-shape, each with a blanket and pillow sealed in plastic. A bookshelf was loaded with paperbacks, playing cards, crafts and board games— Monopoly and Scrabble. A box of extra batteries next to a radio occupied the top of the bookshelf.

I didn't know what to say.

"Hey, check this out." Greg led me to the kitchen area. "Fully stocked." He flipped open one cupboard after another of canned soups, vegetables, boxes of macaroni and cheese, powdered milk, powdered cheese, Vienna Sausages, Spam, Tang—"The 'drink of astronauts,' my dad says." Greg beamed, as if he were showing me a remote mountain cabin instead of a death bunker. "A family of four could survive for two weeks. Not bad, huh?"

I stared at *Life Magazine* on the table: Fallout Shelters: A New Urgency. The cover depicted an exploding mushroom cloud superimposed over a letter from

President Kennedy with big block words in red, 'Be prepared'.

"Your dad really thinks it might happen?" I hoped the fear in my gut didn't show on my face.

Greg closed the cupboards. He smiled that sweet smile of his and took my hands. He swung my arms side to side in a gentle sway. "Hey, my dad's a Boy Scout leader, remember? He has to be prepared. Nobody knows what's going to happen. It's not like he has a crystal ball."

My shoulders loosened. Far in the distance a muffled sound caught our attention.

"Ah, jeeeez. My mom's calling." He dropped my hands. "We'd better go. And Reese, remember, you can't tell anybody about this. If we're at school just say, 'the day we had a cigarette in your backyard'. No one will get it but us."

Greg let me go first up the stairs. An ominous clunk echoed through the stairwell as the door closed. The passage felt even narrower than it had fifteen minutes earlier, cold concrete walls pressing against me. I was sure my lungs would collapse before I reached the top.

The sunlight was joyously blinding. I gulped fresh air while Greg dragged the metal plate back into place. He wiped his hands with a quizzical smile.

"See you tomorrow?"

I felt special in a way I had never felt special in my life, even with Father Donnelly.

"Yup."

I took my time walking home. There had to be a way to convince Mom we needed a bomb shelter, not a pool. That would lead her to ask why I was trying to convince her out of the blue. That would lead to questions about the bomb shelter, about Greg. She never asked what I was doing by myself all those hours after school. She must've been content having the house to herself, no doubt immersed in a fictional world very different from the one that would demand her attention by dinnertime.

3

THE NEED FOR SHELTER

As we got deeper into fall I became more excited about my upcoming fourteenth birthday in January. Fourteen was the magic number I needed for going to supervised parties. The timing was perfect for the freshman dance the Friday before Valentine's Day in February. Greg would be there. We had already agreed to dance every dance together.

I was ready to consult Kit on what to wear. Today wouldn't be a good time to ask. Kit got home late from school. I could hear her and Mom arguing in the living room followed by the stomp of footsteps in the hall. Odds were good Kit had gotten in trouble. She would be in a sour mood. The fashion consult would have to wait. I shoved Cyrano, my stuffed Spaniel, under my head and resumed reading.

"For cryin' out loud, do you always have to be in here?" Kit reached over and flipped back the cover of my book. "*Little Women*. What can you possibly learn from a book that doesn't even have sex? Real life teaches you more than you could ever learn in books. No wonder your life is a bore."

"If I want to get into a good college—"

"Another waste of time. The minute I graduate, I'm getting as far away as possible from that bitch. I'll take off with any boy I feel like. We'll shock the lipstick right off Mom."

"Why do you hate her?"

"I think you have that the other way around. And I'm not the only one she hates, or haven't you noticed? If you were smart you'd get away too."

"Dad says with my grades I can get a scholarship to any college I want."

"I swear, Clarice, you have zero chance for excitement holed up reading and studying. You'll be one of those pathetic people who go through life without anything ever happening to them."

I had no doubt lots of exciting things would happen to Kit. She was wrong about reading. Books were how I learned about everything. The characters were always someone I knew, at least in part. Kit was Lydia in *Pride and Prejudice*. She would run away with her Mr. Wickham and live out of wedlock. In contrast to fictional Lydia, Kit wouldn't care what anybody thought, least of all Mom and Dad.

Mom's character was Scarlett O'Hara in *Gone with the Wind*, Boss of the World, Breaker of Hearts. My dream dad was Atticus Finch. I had to admit mine was more like Mr. March in *Little Women*. It wasn't a real war that had taken him from his family. It was the Cold War in his own home.

I wasn't sure who my character was, not yet. The closest was Jo in *Little Women*, the sister who becomes a writer minus the tomboy, the swearing, the temper. Jo and I had the same Life Plan, a future built on writing and love. The first part I could achieve with education and hard work. Love, that part was the stumbling block. If my own mother couldn't love me, no one else could. I didn't understand what it was about me she couldn't love, so I had no clue how to change so she could. That meant the second part of my Life Plan was doomed to failure. And I had a feeling that was more important than the first.

I would keep searching for the version of me Mom could love. Until I found that character, my Life Plan was sketchy.

*

The strange sound awakened me. I whispered to Kit. No answer. I remembered she was at Jackie's. Dad was in New York. Cold fear gripped my stomach as I strained toward muffled cries from the living room. Mom was hurt, crying. No one else could help her. I had to go.

My silhouette mimicked every move down the hall. Hidden in darkness I waited for my eyes to adjust. The image that came into focus caught my breath. Mom wasn't hurt. A man was on top of her in a scene my brain refused to calculate—two bodies merged as one, groans stifled but inescapably audible.

The man tilted his head to the street light. It was Father Donnelly.

A tiny gasp flew from my soul. I steadied myself against the wall, certain they had heard me. Sounds of passion overpowered my whimper. I couldn't budge. One teetering step at a time, I commanded my body to retreat. Instead of getting back in bed, I crawled under it with Cyrano and buried my face in his flanks to silence anguish deep in my own.

That journey down the hall ended life as I had known it. An invisible threshold had been crossed, the line beyond which childhood ceased. I could never go back. Now I would wander the Land of InBetweendom, lost in a foreign place where nothing made sense.

Then and there, I knew God had abandoned me.

*

The next morning I woke up just as I had every other morning of my thirteen years. The earth had continued to roll around the sun in spite of my childhood having come to an end. Our morning routine was the same, everyone acting as if nothing had changed. Kit and I took turns in the bathroom getting ready for school. Mom buzzed around the kitchen making our lunches. They all looked normal. I was the one transformed — an alien from another planet disguised as human. I had entered my own *Twilight Zone*.

With a sick feeling in my stomach I ventured into the kitchen and perched on a stool. Mom stood at the counter with the usual assembly line of bread slices for sandwiches. She glanced at me.

"Clarice, why aren't you dressed? You'll make us late."

I faked an impassive tone. "Kit's still in the bathroom." I paused. "Would you and Dad ever get a divorce?"

Mom stopped fixing lunches. She stared at the wall, a mustard-slathered knife suspended in mid-air. Not a muscle moved. She resumed her work, mustard sliding across Weber's bread in smooth swirling motion like an ice skater doing figure-8s.

"Whatever made you ask such a question?" Her tone was dismissive.

"We were talking about it in class yesterday. I just wondered."

"If you were talking about it in class, then you know that in the Catholic Church divorce is grounds for excommunication. Now go get dressed. Kit has to be at school fifteen minutes early today."

And that was that. She was as cool as lemonade on a summer day and said exactly what she wanted me to hear, and in truth, what I wanted to hear. Even though she brushed it aside, her momentary hesitation confirmed that what I hoped had been a dream was not. It was real.

A terrible transgression had taken place last night. I knew it, she knew it, and now she knew that I knew it. However innocuous our exchange, I had crossed some boundary. I had intruded on Mom's private world, the world she now shared with FD.

Kit bolted from the car as soon as we pulled into the drop-off zone at school. I was tempted to see if I could crack Mom's icy demeanor by telling her where Kit was really going, which was behind the baseball field to smoke with her friends.

I got out and turned to say goodbye. Mom's expression made my knees buckle. There was fury in that look, cold, deadly rage. I closed the door and watched as she jerked the car away from the curb and disappeared around the corner.

I thought I knew what it meant to feel alone. I hadn't even come close. I felt constricted as I walked to class like a zombie. I was numb, a new realization sinking in with each mechanical step: I had lost everything. Kit couldn't help me, Dad couldn't help me, there wasn't a soul on earth I could confide in, and worst of all, the two people I most adored were complete strangers to me now. I was utterly and completely alone.

The world as I knew it had ended overnight. Nothing could turn back the clock.

*

School that day must have looked as normal as any other day, my classmates and teachers going about their business. I was somewhere far away, detached, separate. The clock ticked in slow motion. At the last bell I made an excuse to Francie and the others that I wasn't feeling well.

I took the early bus home.

My shoes might as well have been bricks with the effort it took making my way from the bus stop to the back stairs. Halfway up, I pressed my nose to the garage window. The black sedan was there. I gathered strength and opened the back door.

"And how is my favorite high school freshman this afternoon?"

FD and Mom sat drinking coffee in their usual places at the table, FD in Dad's place at the head. I forced a smile, mumbled something about having a ton of homework and kept walking. I was into the living room when FD called me back.

"Hey! Hold on a minute. I've been eyeing your mother's chocolate cake for half an hour, holding off until you got home. You can't tell me you're going to hit the books right away."

My stomach lurched. I backtracked to the kitchen.

"That's more like it. Come, sit. You cannot pass up this sinful indulgence."

You call CAKE a sinful indulgence? What about making love to Mom right in our house? How can the two of you sit here drinking coffee as if some seismic shift hasn't reordered the layers of the earth?

How otherworldly it felt being with the two people whose presence I had sought more than any other. Until last night. What a fool I'd been. There had never been any secrets between me and FD. There never would be. His secrets were Mom's secrets, one and the same, the way it was supposed to be with her and Dad.

It took all my effort to choke down the cake, so heavy was its betrayal, so bitter its truth. Swallowing Styrofoam would've been easier. FD and Mom resumed whatever conversation they'd been having earlier with gossip and laughter as if I weren't there.

How naive I'd been the first day they met to assume FD could stave off the power of Mom's charisma. Other men couldn't. A priest was still a man I supposed. The one man Mom shouldn't have was the one she wanted. Now she had him. Now she could thumb her nose at all the women in the parish who supposedly had a crush on Father Donnelly. She knew something they didn't—Sir Lancelot had chosen his Guinevere.

*

Dad answered the phone on the second ring. It was Father Donnelly. The calls were always for Mom. He talked for a minute to whoever answered the phone. He would ask about what was new at school—or work in Dad's case—followed by some cornball joke, the hearty laughter on our end confirming his identity.

Father Donnelly was only five years younger than Mom. His taste for lame humor sometimes made him seem like a teenager. Dad said his youthfulness came from not having to pay a mortgage, and that maybe he should've been a priest, too. He didn't hold the mortgage-free status against Father Donnelly. The two played golf every Sunday afternoon.

Dad being duped, by our family priest no less, broke my heart. My secret felt heavier than ever. At least it had put everything in perspective. Divorce wasn't the worst thing that could happen after all.

*

I paused for my routine check halfway up the back stairs. His car was there, as usual. We were the only family in the parish who understood the meaning behind the Agent 007 glued on the driver's side door above the handle. It was the code name Kit and I had assigned. My cuckold father had offered FD a legitimate avenue of deceit the night he transferred the garage door opener. Kit and I decided the secret agent code suited him. It was a prescient moniker.

My stomach was a pit of acid at the image of him and Mom making love. I didn't know how much longer I could keep the secret. It was a monster eating me up inside. There had to be someone to confide in, someone who would know what to do. Kit would be risky. She might just see it as an irresistible opportunity to blackmail Mom, get the upper hand once and for all. That was a gamble I would have to take. Once she recovered from the shock, Kit would know how to move forward.

I finished my homework and waited for her to get home from school. Kit moseyed into the bedroom an hour before dinner. She threw me a glare. This wasn't going to be easy. Kit sat cross-legged on the floor and extracted her trove of movie magazines under the bed. She flipped through each one before designating it to one of two piles.

"Whatcha doin', Kit?"

"What does it look like I'm doing? I'm sorting through these to swap with Jackie." My sister was as sassy as her ducktail haircut.

I moved to the edge of the bed. "I have to tell you something."

"You have something to tell me? What could a child like you possibly have to tell me?"

"I think—" The words wouldn't come. My throat went dry.

"You think what?"

"I think there's something going on...between Mom and FD."

Kit stopped sorting. The shock must've hit her hard.

"Well duhhh. How long did it take you to figure that one out?"

"You mean you know?"

Her voice dropped. "Yeah, I know."

"Does Daddy know?"

"No, Daddy doesn't know. And you're not going to tell him."

"But—"

Kit turned to me with squinted eyes. "Listen, Reese, and you listen good. Daddy is not going to find out. What Mom and FD do behind his back is their own damn business. As long as it keeps Mom off my case, I couldn't care less what that bitch does. So just leave it alone."

"How can we not tell Dad? He has to do something." I tried to curb a growing sense of desperation. Kit had to do better than tell me to leave it alone. How could I keep such a secret?

She cocked her head. "I swear, you're such a child. You're in such a hot hurry to tell Dad? What do you think will happen? I'll paint the picture for you. You blab to Dad. He confronts Mom. She refuses to give FD up. What's Dad supposed to do then? I'll tell you what...he shoots FD! Dad goes to prison for attempted murder of a priest. We never see him again."

My mouth fell open. She waited for the scene of disaster to sink in.

"And Dad's getting a life sentence would just be the beginning. It would be headline news in all the papers once the police figured why he felt justified shooting a priest. Mom would never forgive you for exposing the affair because then she really would have to give FD up. Father Sebastian would make sure he got transferred to a parish far away.

"Mom would be an outcast. Everyone we know would hate her...hate us...for getting the most popular priest in the world sent away. That wouldn't matter because we wouldn't be able to afford the Palisades anymore after Dad lost his job. We'd be forced to move back to our old house. Mom would be humiliated facing the neighbors she was so snooty to. She would hate you a hundred times more than she hates me.

"You would be to blame for ruining our lives...Dad's, Mom's, FD's, mine. Is that what you want? All because you can't keep a stupid secret?"

I looked at her in horror.

"Grow up, Reese. Real life isn't like *Father Knows Best* or any other show on TV. Well, maybe *The Twilight Zone.* Just keep this whole thing to yourself. I mean do not tell a living soul unless you want to destroy this family and be ostracized forever."

My sister resumed her magazines sorting. I sat on the bed, flummoxed. Kit had been my last hope, my only hope. Not only was she not going to help, she'd made it crystal clear I should do nothing. Nothing except keep the secret.

Kit was talking to me.

"It's too bad you had to find out about them. That'll teach you not to eavesdrop."

Was she really putting me down for how I found out? As if that mattered. "It's going to be hard, the secret."

"You're the one who thinks it's so bitchin' that FD sneaks over here all the time and you've kept that secret. Just think of this as an extra twist at the end. If you can keep the first part, there's no reason you can't keep the second." She tossed a magazine into my lap. "It's brand new. There's a spread on your beloved Troy Donahue."

I was too numb to speak.

Kit walked to the door. She turned to me with a soft look on her face. I thought she might say something comforting. Wrong. Whatever feeling she'd had was fleeting. "You better not cry on my magazine."

I didn't cry on Kit's magazine. I swallowed the secret, the burden of it cutting me off from whatever happiness was left in my world.

Kit kept the secret to free herself from Mom. I would keep it to hold on to her.

I would not betray my mother. I would not destroy my family. Even if it killed me.

4

SEE NO EVIL

The end of school on Monday came too soon. I leaned my head against the window in the back of the bus. The autumn sky hung low, late afternoon sun fading fast with the end of Daylight Saving Time. Greg didn't come over as much after school now that track season was in full swing. It was just as well. Faking my mood required too much effort. I was sure he could sense something different about me.

I still wanted to go to the freshman dance in February. For those few hours I would force myself to forget about Mom and FD. A miserable girl is no fun. It felt like a million years ago that Greg and I had run sprints on the beach, buried each other in sand. Now I wasn't sure I would ever smile again, much less feel playful.

Brother McPherson's class was the only time anyone talked about anything that mattered, anything that had to do with me. It was also the only time I didn't feel completely alone. I had become less aware of Greg's presence in class as I glommed on to any morsel of how to cope.

"'*The Road Less Traveled*', what can we conclude about Frost's meaning. Miss Cavanaugh?"

Greg caught my attention with the smile he'd been trying to send all period. I startled at my name and turned to Brother McPherson. What was the question? The meaning?

"I think he meant the road less traveled was the better one."

"Because—"

"Because in the last stanza, he says 'making all the difference...' the road he chose was the right one."

"Ah! But does our narrator say anything about the kind of difference? Good? Bad? What makes you say he made the 'right' choice?"

"I thought something awful must've happened in his life that made him want to be alone...I mean...made him not want to run into anybody." I slid lower in the desk. "Maybe that's wrong."

Brother McPherson gazed at me long after I answered. He spoke in a soft voice, as if he and I were the only ones in the room. "Everyone interprets poetry based on his or her own experience, Reese. There is no right or wrong answer, only the personal meaning you attribute to his words."

He could see right through me, I was sure of it. He spoke to the class. "The narrator decides to save traveling on the first road for another day, though he suspects he'll never actually come back. There's a wistful quality in choosing one road over the other. Frost is describing the nature of human experience. We all face tough choices and have to live with the consequences."

Choose the right road, Reese. If you get this wrong, you'll destroy everyone.

*

The Church welcomed qualified professionals willing to volunteer their time under the supervision of the parish priest. At FD's urging, Mom had enrolled in graduate school at Mount St. Mary's College. Successful completion of the one-year, post baccalaureate program in Marriage and Family Counseling meant Mom could be certified. If she doubled up on classes she would be eligible for the exam in six months, which meant she could help FD with people from the church and start seeing them on her own that much sooner. That was what she did, doubled up.

Dad was all for it. Whatever it took to keep Mom happy. Now when FD came over, instead of gossiping with characters in fiction as stand-ins, Mom and FD talked about the problems of real people, which always came down to one thing—sex, within the context of the Church of course. What did a bunch of celibate priests know about marriage, Mom asked him?

If you listened long enough to their conversations, you would think every problem in the world boiled down to sex. I knew that was just them. I didn't know much about war, but I was pretty sure the Russians wouldn't drop a nuclear bomb over sex.

After a while I began to understand the bantering between Mom and FD wasn't about making a point. Their sparring was a Tango, the real communication transcending words, meanings transmitted on a level having nothing to do with language. It's as if each of them had been lonely all their lives, wandering the earth in search of the one person with whom they could truly connect. Mom certainly hadn't found this extraordinary fusion in her husband. FD apparently hadn't found it in his God.

But find it they did—in each other. They knew it, and we knew it, too.

I knew it the first day they met.

*

Two weeks before Christmas, Mom announced that Father Donnelly would be treating us to *The Sound of*

Music as his gift to the family. He'd bought tickets for a Saturday night performance at the Music Center. Mom could hardly contain her excitement over an evening of culture in downtown Los Angeles. She would brag about it at church in high-brow style and a haughty tone of ho hum, like this was something we did every week, though she would leave out the best part, the part about FD.

It had never occurred to me that a priest might have a salary. I wondered how he paid for the gifts he brought us, the latest a soundtrack of the *The Sound of Music*. For two weeks, Julie Andrews had been in residence, all of us singing along when Mom put the album on the Hi Fi.

The story told in song became one more form of coded communication for Mom and FD. With his big goofy grin, FD would orchestrate, hands in the air, and croon to Mom as if she were Maria and he the widower infatuated with the would-be nun turned governess, two roles for which my mother was exquisitely ill-suited.

Our big night was central to every conversation as the date got close. The evening would begin with dinner at the Bel Air Hotel, an extravagance Dad never could have offered with me and Kit in private school. The famous restaurant was less than half an hour down Sunset Boulevard in Beverly Hills. It was hard to believe I had only seen it on the pages of Kit's movie magazines.

Three days before our extravaganza, I ran up the back stairs after school without checking the garage. There was no need. Now that Mom was in school, FD was in our kitchen by three o'clock most weekdays, the two of them drinking coffee at the table over Mom's books.

"Ah, speaking of the devil, here she is now. Would you please join us in here, Miss Cavanaugh?"

Mom and FD were ensconced on the couch in deep

conversation. They paused as I approached, FD turning his attention to me. I knew the game plan. Mom had laid it out for me not long after her return to school. Once I had said hello and exchanged chit chat, I was to disappear unless otherwise notified. The chit chat would be brief and never extend beyond the point at which Mom grew irritated, a temperamental shift FD was alert to and honored. He knew her anger would come back to me later. Today was one of those times I was otherwise notified to stay.

Something was definitely up. FD had a big prankish grin. His body twitched with the trademark springiness I'd noticed the first day we met. He was percolating with glee. It looked like he might explode unless he could open the valve to release pressure. Mom sparkled too, the way she always did at his delight in setting the scene for whatever was about to unfold.

I wasn't sure how long this would take. Instead of sitting in the club chair I balanced on the arm. Stage set.

His manner changed from playful to serious. He leaned forward on the couch with hands clasped. "A problem has come up with our outing to *The Sound of Music*."

"What? Are we not going?" Mom didn't look upset, so I guessed that wasn't it.

"Well, that all depends on you."

FD launched into his performance. "Here's the problem: You haven't got a dress classy enough for the Bel Air Hotel and the Music Center. I might have a solution." He took a long sip of coffee to pause for effect. "If you will kindly turn around, three boxes await you on the hearth."

The rectangular white boxes tied with blue ribbon stood against the wall. I registered passing irritation at the color scheme, a reference to 'girls in white dresses with blue satin sashes' from *The Sound of Music*. It was Mom's favorite song. That's how well I knew the man. Just like the big Life Secret he'd shared about real friends coming to you, this little drama was every bit as much for Mom as for me, if not more.

"Now, if you'll be good enough to open the first one, I think you'll begin to understand the predicament. I expect you to handle it without too much trouble."

He bubbled with excitement. I thought for a moment he might levitate. Mom sat with one leg tucked under her dress. She squeezed his forearm, beaming.

I untied the blue satin on the first box. There, under layers of pink tissue, lay a glorious crepe dress. I lifted it out with a gasp as the folds opened. This was no ordinary creation. A movie star would wear such a dress—black crepe in a knee-length sheath with long sleeves ending in white French cuffs. A wide ribbon of white flowed from the empire waist all the way down the front, forming a perfect inverted white V against the black.

"It's the most beautiful dress I've ever seen!"

"Well, now, you see, that's the problem. Maybe it is and maybe it isn't. You'd better have a look behind Door No. 2."

Mom giggled. I opened the second box. It was another black and white number, this one raw silk with a big white stripe running perpendicular across the bodice and another stripe down the front in the form of a giant T, very mod, very Julie Christie. I held it against my chest and rocked back and forth on my feet, unable to contain my thrill.

FD grinned at Mom. "Would you agree the client is responding rather well to therapy?"

I felt them watching as I evaluated and compared details of each dress.

"You're not done yet, young lady. You'd better open the third box."

I practically ripped the thing open. This box revealed pink mohair with a fitted bodice and three quarter length sleeves. Attached at the waist of the A-line skirt was a darker pink ribbon that tied in back and trailed to the hem.

"Do I really get to keep one?"

"You do indeed, but you certainly can't choose without trying them on. Why don't you put on a fashion show for us?"

Mom was glowing, though her eyes were on FD, not my dresses. Tucking the boxes under my arm, I rushed from the room, dresses and tissue spilling from all sides. Three minutes later I was back. I jumped up and down in the first dress.

"For gosh sakes, Clarice," Mom said, "stop bouncing and let's see how you look."

FD stroked his chin in the manner of a professor in deep thought. "Hmmmm. That certainly is pretty on you. Awfully pretty indeed. What do you think, Vivienne?"

"I want this one," I blurted before she could answer.

FD chuckled with his hand in the air, palm facing me. "Now wait. We have to proceed in an orderly fashion here. Let's at least take a look at the others."

Rather than jumping up and down in the second dress, I joined the game. I slowed my pace and sashayed across the room, nose in the air, hips jutting side to side, in a mock cat walk, the dress lining cold against my thighs.

"Oh, wow! Now, that's a statement dress. Don't you look sexy, Miss Cavanaugh!"

By the time I modeled the third one, I was immersed in the pretense. Each dress drew exaggerated praise from FD. Even Mom was having fun. It was a glorious interlude of joy.

"DA DUUMMM. Decision time has arrived."

"Oh, I can't choose! I love this one, but I love the second one, and the first one, too."

"This is exactly what I was afraid of. We have a predicament. Vivienne, do you have any idea how we can solve this dilemma?"

Mom suggested I retrieve the other two dresses and examine them again. I laid all three across the chair, one draped over each arm, the third one over the back. I stood back and tilted my head from one side to the other comparing A and B, B and C, C and A. Mom and FD giggled at the spectacle.

"I can't decide. Which one do you like best, Mom?"

FD blurted, "Now, wait, wait. There is one solution, but I'm not sure you'll go for it." He gave both me and Mom one final drumbeat in a long pause to draw out the climax. "I guess you'll just have to keep all three."

"WHAT? You mean it?"

"Absolutely. Of course you will have to choose just one to wear to the play. There won't be time for multiple costume changes." He was out and out guffawing now, clearly satisfied with how I had played my part, how the drama had unfolded exactly as designed.

I threw my arms around him. Mom grabbed his coffee just in time.

The night of the play I did look beautiful in the black crepe dress with white French cuffs. Our dinner at the Bel Air Hotel was memorable, all of us talking and laughing, the family decked out for an evening of culture in the city.

It was the most magical night of my short life—the dress, the restaurant, the theater, the music, the Cavanaugh family enjoying each other, and FD in his element as director. For a few hours Father Donnelly was as beloved by the Cavanaugh family as Gandhi had been by millions of Indians.

That night I fell asleep happy, my secret buried under fluttering layers of gossamer tissue.

*

January dragged on forever. I couldn't wait for the freshman dance. I would need to look especially gorgeous, which I most certainly would in one of my new dresses. Francie nixed that idea once I described them. She said the two black dresses were too fancy for an afternoon dance and the pink one not womanly enough for my first almost-date. Kit would never let me borrow one of hers. Besides, she was tall, whereas I was petite.

My mission was clear. I had to have a new dress. The dance was all the freshman girls could talk about, with a heavy emphasis on who would be wearing what. One of the drawbacks of a school uniform was increased pressure on personal style with few opportunities available for expression.

As soon as I got home that day, I headed for Mom's bedroom-turned-office. I popped my head inside. She didn't look up from her typewriter in spite of my coughing and wild waving gestures at the smoke. "Mom, can I ask you something?"

"Uh huh." The clack of her fingernails on the keys made me think of mice scurrying over a kitchen floor.

"The dance I've been telling you about is in two weeks."

"I already told you that you could go now that you're

fourteen."

"I know. I mean, that's not the problem." I sensed this was a bad time to interrupt, as if there were a good time. "I don't really have anything to wear. Francie is going in this really cute polished cotton dress with an empire waist. Her Mom thinks it's a perfect style for our age."

Mom looked up in a flash of anger. "Clarice, does it look to you like I have time to discuss fashion trends with you right now? Besides, you have the three beautiful dresses FD bought you before Christmas."

"I know, but those are too fancy. This dance is in the afternoon on Friday after school."

Mom stopped typing. "I swear, it's impossible to get anything done around here. Why don't you do me a favor and run up to Pronto for a pack of Old Gold's. I'll write a note for Sam."

"Okay. What about the dress?"

She resumed typing. "Find out what it costs and I'll see."

"It doesn't cost anything. Her mom made it."

"You expect me to make you a dress in two weeks? With a big paper due?"

"It's a real simple dress. And you can sew, right? I mean, you hem our uniforms."

"Hemming is not sewing, Clarice. But yes, I can sew. If you can read and follow directions, you can sew."

"So that's a yes?"

"Oh, for gosh sakes, Clarice, yes, I'll make it. Go buy the pattern and material after school tomorrow. Now, will you please go get my cigarettes and let me work?"

Francie and I half ran, half walked the eight blocks to the fabric shop. We picked out a pattern—the same one Francie's mom had used—and material in burgundy raw silk so our dresses wouldn't look too much the same. I couldn't wait to show Mom and get the project under way. I found her in the kitchen.

"For crying out loud, this is a Vogue pattern!"

"Isn't that okay?"

"I thought you were talking about Simplicity or McCall's."

Right on cue FD walked in from the garage, all smiles and good cheer. I grabbed the pattern and stuck it in his face. He jerked his head back to focus.

"Wow! You'll be a knockout. Burgundy will make your blonde hair—"

"Did you notice it's a Vogue pattern?"

FD gave me his familiar devilish grin, a signal there was nothing to worry about. Mom sat pouting at the table while I poured him a cup of coffee from the pot Mom had started fifteen minutes earlier. Even apart they were in sync.

"Now, Vivienne, you're a clever girl," he said teasingly. "I can't imagine you would let a Vogue pattern get the better of you. Anyone who can tackle grad school and take care of a home and two kids is no ordinary woman."

"Easy for you to say. I've hit a snag with my paper and I'm already pushing the deadline. This damn pattern is fitted through the bodice, calls for an empire waist, on seam pockets and the fabric is cut on the bias, for crying out loud!"

"Your point?" His grin barely shrank enough to sip the coffee.

"My point is that the difference between Simplicity and Vogue is like the difference between building a shack and a mansion."

"Then you'd better start loading up on wood because you're going to need a lot of framing. I can't help with the mansion, but I can with your paper."

The agreement transpired in an intimate gaze.

"Oh, for Chrissakes, Clarice, hand me the goddamn pattern."

FD beamed at her over his mug. "And I don't expect taking the Lord's name in vain is likely to help your cause."

Mom's irritation shifted to coquettish flirtation, sexual tension pulsing between them.

I was the one who blushed, an intruder in their tête à tête.

For the next week instead of Mom holed up in her smoky office, I would find her on the living room floor surrounded by pattern pieces like a giant jigsaw puzzle. Patsy Cline would be crooning torch songs of unrequited love in the background.

My mother was not going to be defeated by a Vogue pattern, not when the real challenge was proving to FD that she was, in fact, the extraordinary woman he had imagined her to be, the extraordinary woman he had fallen in love with.

*

Mom did a brilliant job on my dress. She even saved enough ribbon for a matching headband so I could ditch the ponytail. The day of the dance my face was framed by blonde waves falling over a burgundy ribbon.

Greg and I had agreed to meet in front of the auditorium. Halfway up the stairway entrance, I spotted him at the top. My ladylike steps became giant strides. He took two steps at a time until we met in the middle. We broke into nervous giggles at the sight of each other dressed up. He let out a long whistle. I slugged him in the arm, after which we raced up the stairs, a dressed up version of scrambling up the zigzag trail from the beach.

The dance was even more special than I'd hoped. I did forget Mom and FD. For two hours I had no horrible secret. Greg and I danced every dance. We teetered sideways during the Twist. There was no awkwardness between us. That is, not until the first slow dance. Greg held me close with his hand on the small of my back. His hair smelled like Dad's Brill Cream. I was sure he could feel my heartbeat. My face was probably the color of my dress. I was glad we weren't looking at each other.

His Mom waited outside the auditorium after the dance. Greg had asked if she could give me a ride home since we lived on the same street. It was early evening by the time she pulled into the driveway. Greg walked me to the door, neither of us missing a beat in the conversation we'd been having in the car.

We reached the porch. The talking stopped, replaced by the same awkward silence I'd felt standing at the bottom of the stairs in the bomb shelter. Greg stepped close enough for me to feel his breath. This time he was going to kiss me, I was sure of it. He brushed my bangs aside and leaned down.

The porch light went on. Greg jumped. It took me a moment to figure out what happened. Then I saw movement in the kitchen window.

"You'd better go, Greg. Your mom's waiting."

He scrunched his mouth to the side. We said goodbye. At the last second, he lunged forward. His kiss landed on my open mouth with a bump.

"Ow!"

Greg turned crimson. "Sorry."

"No, no. It's just...you just surprised me." I felt for blood. "Maybe we can try it again sometime."

His tension dissipated like carbonation from a Coke. "Woohoo!" Greg leapt over the porch stairs. He disappeared from view. Two seconds later he was back. He would call the next day, he said. He was gone before I could answer.

My insides jumped in glorious pandemonium. The front door opened.

"Come in the house, Clarice."

"Mom, it was so much fun! I danced every dance, and everyone loved my—"

She spun around so fast I nearly bumped into her.

"Who was that boy you were kissing?"

Blood rushed to my face. Had she been watching? I squinted at her in confusion. "Greg Stewart. He's in Honors English. Don't you remember my telling you a friend would be giving me a ride home?"

"I assumed you meant Francesca...and I was led to believe this dance was limited to freshmen."

"Greg is my friend too. He is a freshman. His mom drove us." I tried to sound matter-of-fact. I had witnessed Mom and Kit face off enough times to know the slightest hint of disagreement would be heard as sass and trigger an argument.

"Yes, Clarice. I can see he's your friend. I can also see you had no qualms about kissing him in front of God and everybody." That was a line from Peyton Place, "in front of God and everybody." Mom had used it to scold Kit for kissing her boyfriend in his car parked out front.

I didn't respond to the bait and kept my expression neutral.

"Aren't you a little young for French kissing?"

"Moooom. It wasn't a French kiss!"

"I have eyes, Clarice. I'm not a fool."

"It wasn't a French kiss!" So much for staying calm. How could she turn something sweet into something tawdry? "It was an ordinary kiss."

"Well for your sake, I hope it was. I'm sure you're aware the Catholic Church considers French kissing a mortal sin. If you died tomorrow you would go straight to hell."

"I know. It wasn't. Besides, there must be degrees of mortal sin. I mean, French kissing and murder aren't exactly the same." For the first time I understood how easily Kit got into it with Mom. Disagreement was belligerence. I couldn't believe Mom's one-track mind where everything had to do with sex instead of friendship or affection. Even if it had been a French kiss, it didn't make sense that God would throw me into the same mortal sin boat as murderers, or those coveting their neighbor's spouse. Or in her case, the parish priest.

"It's not up to me or you to decide what is or isn't a mortal sin. And don't talk back to me! That's all I need, you following in your sister's footsteps, sneaking around with boys, doing who knows what behind my back. I'd better not catch you ever again doing something like this. Do you understand?"

My mouth dropped open.

"Now go take off that damn dress. It makes you look cheap. And I want to see your hair in a ponytail by the time we eat dinner."

I steamed out of the kitchen. Her voice carried all the way to the bedroom hall.

"I suggest you be first in line for confession this week, young lady."

Me go to confession? Over a toothy first kiss?

Greg called the next afternoon, just like he said he would. I was hovering near the kitchen phone to get there first. No luck. Mom answered. She handed me the receiver with an ugly sneer at the disgusting sexual innuendo she was certain would transmit from one dirty mind to another over the wire.

I turned my back in some pathetic attempt at privacy.

"Hello?" My voice came out stilted. Greg and I talked for less than two minutes, awkwardly trying to establish some fleeting connection.

There was a moment of silence on his end. "Reese? What's wrong?"

It was hopeless with Mom standing there. I curled my left hand into a fist to keep from crying. "Nothing. I just have to go."

"Yeah, sure…no problem."

Mom stood with arms crossed, satisfaction all over her face. I bumped her as I pushed past. She stumbled backward. I heard her yell, but couldn't understand the words. I didn't stick around to hear the front door slam. I bolted down the street to the zigzag trail, my escape route to the beach.

At school Monday morning Greg made sure we had no opportunity to talk before class. He refused to even glance in my direction the entire period. As soon as the bell rang, I ran to catch him. In the hallway he cut through the throng of students and disappeared.

It was probably just as well. I would never be able to bring a boy, any boy, over to my house the way other girls did. No wonder Kit snuck around behind Mom's back. Our mother's imagination had both me and Kit headed for what she herself had failed to resist.

One toothy kiss. That was it. That was my big shot at romance.

Greg and I never spoke again.

5

STRANGE LAND

As the months rolled by, FD and Mom continued acting out their fantasy as husband and wife, Mom happy in the pretend version. FD was ever the supportive mate, never failing to negotiate a workable compromise for every problem, every problem being Kit.

"Mom, just give me one good reason why I can't smoke."

"Because, Katherine, you're barely sixteen."

"So what? Besides, all my friends do. Don't they, Reese?" Kit squinted at me with pursed lips, challenging me to disagree.

I ignored her and continued chopping vegetables.

Mom stopped rummaging through the spice cupboard and put one hand on her hip. "You're telling me their parents let them smoke?"

"Well, they don't actually let them—but they do it anyway," Kit leaned back against the wall until the chair teetered on its back legs, her feet dangling in front. "I just think it's childish to go sneaking around, so I thought I'd ask. I see now I shouldn't have bothered. That's fine. I can sneak around as well as the next kid."

"Now, hold on a minute, young lady, if you—"

FD walked in from the garage.

"Perfect timing," I mumbled to him in warning.

"Whooooaaaa. Is it hot in here, or am I feeling the heat of an argument?"

Kit lurched forward. The chair dropped to all fours. "Mom refuses to let me smoke, like all my friends. She wants me to sneak behind her back."

Mom stiffened. "Katherine, that is not what I—"

"Ok, ok." FD put his hands up in a stop gesture. A conspiratorial glance at Mom was all it took. "Let's sit down and talk about this. Vivienne, do I smell fresh coffee?" He threw me a wink as he and Mom joined my sister at the table.

"Vivienne," he said, turning to Mom, "I think we have to face the fact that Kit wants more freedom now that she's almost sixteen. That's certainly reasonable." He shifted his focus to my sister. "Kit, why don't you tell your mother and me what it is you feel you should be able to do, and we'll see if we can come up with some kind of compromise."

Kit plucked an apple from the fruit bowl and took a bite, talking with an air of smugness now that she had FD in her corner. "I want to wear make-up. Not to school, but when I go out with my friends."

"That sounds reasonable to me, as long as you're not going for the Dorothy Malone look with lipstick thick as greasepaint. Vivienne, what do you think?"

"I guess that's alright."

"Okay," FD said with satisfaction, smirking at Mom, signaling his pleasure that she was joining forces with him. He returned to Kit. "What next?"

"I want to stay up until eleven on weeknights, talk on the phone for more than half an hour, go to the movies, ride in Mich—"

"For the love of God, girl!" FD slapped the table, coffee slopping out of his mug. "Why don't we just hand over the car keys and credit card and be done with it?"

He spoke in the heavy brogue of Cardinal O'Malley, a fictional character whose authority he mimicked in voicing opposition without risking his status as Father Popular, Friend to All. No wonder everyone loved him.

"Now, why don't we start over, and maybe you can list these in terms of priority. And let's say, just for the sake of argument, that your list will be a bit more reasonable."

Kit crossed her arms in a mix of defiance and petulance. FD wasn't about to be derailed.

"Let's start with the easier ones. You want to stay up until eleven during the week. How are your grades?"

"Same as always. Bs."

"Okay, well, here's a thought. As long as they stay Bs, what if you're allowed to stay up until ten-thirty during the week, though not in the bedroom because Reese can't be staying up that late. How does that sound to you, Vivienne?"

"I suppose that would be alright," Mom mumbled.

"And I want to talk longer on the phone. You simply cannot have a decent conversation in thirty minutes."

"Okay, same condition, but if anyone else wants to use the phone, you have to hang up."

"That's two conditions, not one. But yeah, okay." She paused. "And I want to smoke...openly."

Mom wagged her finger at Kit. "Now look, young lady, if you think I want our neighbors seeing you with a cigarette hanging out of your mouth like some cheap—"

"Wait, wait, wait, wait, wait!" FD kept his stop-signal hand in the air until the huffing subsided. "Look, if Kit wants to smoke so badly, we have two choices. We can forbid her and she'll do it anyway. And Vivienne, she'll make sure the neighbors see her." He flashed a teasing smile at Kit. "But what if we compromise? What if Kit is allowed to smoke openly...but only in the house?"

Mom came forward and opened her mouth to say something. FD's eyes stayed on Kit as he squeezed Mom's arm signaling her to hold off. Both Mom and Kit looked at him, then at each other, some kind of truce transpiring.

"And it goes without saying that the smokes come out of your babysitting money," FD added. "Deal?"

Kit waited for Mom to object. She didn't.

"Deal."

"Well, then, as James Bond, Agent 007 would say, I believe our work here is done."

Kit popped up and ran from the kitchen. Thirty seconds later, purse in hand, she waved in our direction and was out the door.

FD looked at Mom with a big, self-satisfied grin. "I give her two weeks."

A slow smile came over her face in pure adulation.

That's when I understood. The final piece fell into place. Mom and FD weren't play acting. They had constructed a parallel universe, a world in which they were free of the responsibilities and expectations that shackled them as wife and priest in this one.

They weren't cheating anyone—not Dad, not me and Kit, not God. Father Donnelly and Mom had justified their actions in some sort of skewed conviction that God had brought them together as His way of saving our family. "The end justifies the means," Mom liked to say.

It all made sense now. She was no longer miserable with long days alone and long nights with Dad. She knew her other life, her true life, was as real to FD as it was to her. My father no longer existed. It was FD and Mom— husband and wife, parents to me and Kit.

That day in Greg's bomb shelter, I told him my dad didn't believe there would be a nuclear attack. In Dad's mind, he didn't need to protect us from what he didn't think would happen.

I didn't know who was right about the war. What I did know that afternoon while Kit was buying cigarettes was that a bomb had been dropped on our family.

Dad hadn't protected us. We were all breathing fallout. Destruction was a matter of time.

Mom was happy. That was all that mattered.

*

Kit's smoking lasted more than two weeks. As a by-product, my sister saved the red flip-top boxes from her Marlborough's. She glued them on our bedroom ceiling in the shape a giant red K. Like Kit, the letter would leave a lasting mark.

In late spring Mom finished her graduate program in Marriage and Family Counseling.

In addition to his afternoon visits, FD came over after dinner once or twice a week. He and Mom would set up camp in the living room. Dad would wink at me and say, "C'mon, Peanut. We can take a hint. We know when we're not wanted." That was my cue for our exit to the garage, Dad's escape of choice. He and I had become buddies in exile. We never talked about it out there, the soothing voice of Vin Scully announcing a Dodger game our pretext for ignoring the truth.

Mom's degree had legitimized the collaboration with FD. In her twisted universe she was serving the church like any missionary, only her cause was closer to home. The woman standing in the kitchen on this Friday afternoon, chattering with FD about some client or other, sure didn't look like a missionary to me.

This woman dripped with sensuality, from the way she carried herself to the clothes she wore. I watched Mom in operation, watched her use body language as seductive power. She poured FD a fresh cup of coffee, then leaned against the counter with hands shoved deep in her pockets, ankles crossed. In typical contradictory style for someone who considered herself both a feminist and an intellectual, Mom's cashmere turtleneck hugged the contours of her breasts, sculpted into tantalizing cones with help from a MaidenForm bra. To accentuate her hourglass figure, Mom cinched the belt of her gabardine slacks. The fabric detoured over her hips before falling in a graceful drape to her feet.

Mom considered this her new professional look. Now that she was a career woman, she said the nonconformist style of Katharine Hepburn with slacks and turtlenecks suited her better than the womanly full-skirted dresses of a housewife.

Goodbye Miss Manners. Hello Betty Friedan.

*

Spring gave way to the warm days of summer. Like most kids in town, the Pacific Ocean became my new address. As head of the Youth Group, FD often showed up at the beach. The guys treated him like a celebrity. They spent hours body surfing or lying on their towels in deep discussion about school and sports and girls, FD an expert in all three, at least as far as giving advice. The peal of raucous laughter would announce to anyone within earshot that FD had shared his latest corny joke, the hush of low voices that they were discussing Life.

Summer also meant baseball season. Dad and I had high hopes for the L.A. Dodgers. He surprised me with tickets to a Sunday game against the team's chief rival, the

New York Yankees.

Friday afternoon on game weekend, Dad walked in from work and found the usual gang of three in the kitchen— me and FD discussing the problems of high school social life while Mom whipped up a cake for *The Twilight Zone*. He set his watch and keys in their usual spot on the counter next to the mail. "Well, this looks like a happy gathering. Hi Jack, Reese, Sweetheart." Mom leaned to the side as he planted a perfunctory kiss on her cheek, the bowl of chocolate batter whirring on the Mix Master.

"I told FD that we're going to the game, Daddy. He's going to listen to the broadcast after Mass."

Dad sat down at the table. He looked down in the mouth. "Reese, about the game, I'm afraid it's off."

"Why?" Mom spun around and asked over the whirring noise.

"There's a powwow in New York with some big wigs who want to see the handle I designed for the X-15 rocket. Their endorsement could help Rezolin nail the next contract." He turned to me. "I'll have to take an afternoon flight on Saturday to get the straw out of my head before the meeting Monday morning." He sounded deflated enough for both of us, though I also knew he was excited about unveiling his latest product.

"It's okay, Daddy. Maybe we can go to another game."

"Now, wait just a minute," FD said in mock insult. "There's more than one Dodger fan in this family. What if I take Reese to the game?"

I perked up. FD and I waited for Dad to answer. Mom turned around too.

"That would be great, Jack, if you can trade with Father Sebastian for an earlier Mass. I was going to ask

Carson Williams to take my place for our golf game in the afternoon, so if you take Reese to the game you'd have to miss that."

"Truth is, Walker, I'm not any too keen about facing Murray and Giroux on the links with Williams instead of you. This change of plan would kill two birds with one stone."

That Sunday, I took my place riding shotgun in the passenger seat of FD's black sedan. We concocted crazy explanations why Reese Cavanaugh would be in Father Donnelly's car in case any parishioners recognized us. They wouldn't though. In matching Dodger hats, Father Donnelly and I could have been any father and daughter in any Chrysler.

Dodger stadium was much bigger than it looked on TV. The outer corridor to our section was thick with fans. Everyone bumped and shoved in a hurry to get seated. We peeled away toward the field. I halted, stunned by the sight.

A cathedral opened up before me, the nave a carpet of lush grass groomed to perfection in a crisscross pattern of light and dark green stripes. A swathe of combed red clay separated the infield from the outfield. In the stands the smell of Dodger dogs and beer wafted through the air to the sound of *Take Me out to the Ball Game*, the lyrics playing on a jumbo screen so everyone could sing along.

FD nudged me. I was blocking impatient fans. We moved along until we found our seats. The players warming up on the field looked like miniatures. Dad had joked that our seats were in what he called the peanut gallery. As far as I was concerned, they were box seats, front row.

It took ten innings for the Dodgers to beat the Yankees.

By then I was hoarse from cheering. I couldn't wait to tell Dad all about it when he got back from his trip. FD and I rehashed highlights during the half hour it took to inch our way out of the jammed parking lot. At last we were on the freeway, breezing toward the ocean and Pacific Palisades.

The car took a sudden veer to the right. FD rolled down his window to listen. "Jesus, Mary and Joseph, not now!" He gripped the steering wheel with both hands as the car pulled sideways.

"What's wrong?"

"We have a flat tire, that's what. I have to find a call box."

The black sedan crawled in the slow lane until we spotted an emergency callbox. FD eased onto the shoulder and parked. He told me to stay in the car.

"Well, there we are, Miss Cavanaugh," he said. "The cavalry will be along in twenty minutes or so to rescue us."

"What cavalry?"

"The Auto Club Roadside Service, that cavalry."

"Don't you have a spare tire?"

"Of course I have a spare tire."

"Can't you change it?" I paused. "You know how, right?"

His voice dripped with sarcasm through the trademark grin. "No, as a matter of fact, I don't know how to change it." He leaned over. "And I should probably warn you: I don't carry a Swiss army knife either. If you and I are stranded here we won't survive the night because I can't rub two sticks together to start a fire so I can cook the wild beast I butcher with the Swiss army knife I don't carry."

I smirked, embarrassed that I had asked.

"Disappointed?"

"No. I just thought—" What I thought was that every grown man knew how to change a flat tire. Dad could swap out a whitewall in fifteen minutes. FD read my mind.

"Not all men are like your dad, Reese. He and I grew up very differently."

"Didn't your dad teach you how to change a tire though?"

He watched out the driver's side window. The sedan rocked side to side each time a car whizzed past. "He'll be coming from this direction. I'd better put on my emergency lights." FD took a deep breath. "No, my dad didn't teach me how to change a tire. He didn't teach me much of anything. In fact, I didn't know my father. He died when I was a baby and my mother went to live with a cousin. I grew up with Aunt Amanda and Uncle Carlton in Monrovia."

"You mean… you don't know your mom?"

"She came back to get me when I was five. By then my aunt seemed more like my mother than my mother. So I stayed put. She died ten years ago."

"That's so sad."

"It would only be sad, Reese, if I wasn't happy now. Which I am. I have my God, my Church, and one very lovely young lady I consider to be a daughter right next to me."

It struck me how little I knew about Father Donnelly. His life had started the day we met. I'd never thought beyond that.

"Did your aunt and uncle want you to become a priest?"

He studied his hands on the steering wheel, those soft

hands with the impeccable fingernails. "No. That was my decision."

"What made you decide?"

"Who are you, Barbara Walters?" He chuckled. "I didn't have a clue what I wanted to do after high school. College was out. My aunt and uncle couldn't afford it. I didn't want to go into the military or learn a trade. I knew my career would somehow involve people. So I joined the seminary, just to see if I was cut out for the life. From the moment I entered, I knew I'd found my calling."

"How old were you?"

"Eighteen as a new seminarian. I was twenty-two when I took my final vows. That was eight years ago. Seems like yesterday."

"And once you're a priest, you're a priest forever, right?"

"Right."

"Are you still glad you're a priest?"

"Of course I am. God has led me to a life where I can serve Him best by counseling couples whose marriages are in trouble."

"Did you ever think about getting married?"

"No," he said dismissively. "Where's that tow truck?"

"So you've never been in love?"

He snapped around, a split second of uncertainty on his face. "No, I've never been in love. God has tested me in other ways. Through prayer and diligence I have survived His tests. Now, I hope this version of the Spanish Inquisition is over because if this Auto Club guy doesn't get here soon, I'm going to collapse from hunger. What do you say we head to Zucky's for a burger? I'll phone your mom from there, tell her about our little crisis."

For the first time since FD had come into our lives, I

was grateful Dad was my dad. As fond as I was of FD and had even wished a few times that he had been my father, I knew sitting next to him in his Chrysler on the freeway west of Dodger Stadium that the man beside me could never replace my father. Dad may not have been people smart like FD, or care about the finer things in life like wine. That was okay with me. There was something honest and true and sincere about my father. Even though FD had answered my questions, I was certain I would never really know this man.

I also knew—though he could never tell me, or maybe even admit it to himself—that in fact he had been, and still was, very much in love.

*

School started in September. I was a sophomore in second year Honors English with Brother McPherson. I was excited to tell Mom about the books on my reading list in hopes we might establish something in common.

Saturday morning was my opportunity. At exactly ten o'clock, I poured a cup of coffee and delivered it to Mom, as was my routine. On those lazy mornings she let me perch at the foot of the bed for a few minutes and talk.

Mom stretched and took the mug, which nearly spilled when I plopped on the bed. Even in the morning my mother looked beautiful with her auburn hair and cobalt eyes. In a good mood, she lit up inside and there was no one like her, the draw she had that made you want to be in her presence. I hoped this was one of those days.

"Mom, we got our reading list for Honors—"

"Hold on, Clarice. Your father and I want to talk to you and your sister."

Mom and Dad talking to me and Kit was never a good thing. My stomach tightened.

Kit walked in, huffing in annoyance. Dad filed in behind her. He yanked the chair out from Mom's desk and flipped it around, straddling the thing, arms crossed in front. His eyes were downcast, shoulders hunched. Kit positioned herself next to Mom on Dad's side of the bed. She shot a glance at me, probably thinking the same thing I was: we were in for another walloping.

"So what the hell's going on?"

"Must you swear, Katherine? It's ten o'clock in the damn morning." Mom drew her knees up under the covers and wrapped her arms around them, scowling at Dad, who didn't look up. The air was heavy with apprehension. No one made a sound as we waited for Mom.

She took a sharp breath. "Your father and I have something to tell you."

Kit burst in, "Don't tell me you're pregnant. I'll die of utter and complete humiliation!"

"Don't be ridiculous, Katherine, and get your mind out of the gutter." Another pause and another sip of coffee. "Your father and I...well...we've been having problems lately. The tension has been affecting all of us, even you girls. We can't go on living like this."

Both Kit and I visibly tightened and waited for the other shoe to drop.

"He and I are...well, the fact is...your father and I are going to separate."

My stomach flip-flopped, the same sensation I got in an elevator. "Separate? What does that mean? Like a divorce?"

Kit piped up. "No, dummy. It's a practice divorce."

"That's enough, Katherine," Dad said in a flat voice.

"Your father will be renting an apartment in Santa

Monica, closer to work."

Silence.

"What about us?" I asked.

She shot daggers at Dad. "Well, I can see your father wants me to be the bad guy here."

"Vivienne—" Dad grimaced and hung his head.

"No, it's alright. I'll tell them. I'll be staying in the house. Katherine, you'll go live with your father in his apartment."

Silence. I stared at Mom and tried not to panic. "Then I'm staying here with you, right?"

"No. Clarice. Your father and I...and Jack...are enrolling you in boarding school...in Arizona, St. Joan of Arc."

I jumped off the bed. "Boarding school? Why do I have to go away? Arizona's a whole different state! Why can't I stay here with you?" Nausea turned my stomach to mush.

"Clarice, settle down," Mom said in a measured tone. "This is for the best. Jack has offered to help your father and me during this difficult time...he's...well, he's agreed to be your legal guardian. He can support you, financially...and be in a position to make decisions about your welfare. You know how much he loves you."

"My legal guardian? FD? You can't give me away! You're my parents! How can you decide to make him my parent?"

"Don't be dramatic. It's called a conservatorship. Families do this sometimes in short-term situations, like illness, if there's only one parent, or if one parent is gone and the other has to work out of town a lot. It just means temporarily handing legal authority to a relative or a friend of the family who's willing to take over temporary custody. Jack is paying for this school, which I assure you, is not in any category even remotely feasible for us. With no family of his own, it's not a stretch for him."

My mind struggled to make sense of what she was saying.

"He wants to do this. He came up with the idea to help take the pressure off me and your father while we work things out. It has nothing to do with love, and we will still be your parents."

"You just said you wouldn't be if you give me away."

All of us jumped. Dad blasted out of his chair, catching the edge with his foot and knocking it over. He bolted from the bedroom, shoving the door aside with such force it hit the rubber wall protector and bounced all the way back, slamming shut behind him.

Mom's mouth fell open. Kit and I looked at each other in shock. I had never seen my father angry, much less violent. Kit had been right when she'd told me Dad would shoot FD if he ever found out about him and Mom. I'd had a hard time imagining such a thing. Now Dad had shown us there was rage inside him, rage that could result in violence.

Mom recovered her wits. "I see your father is leaving me to do the dirty work. That's par for the course." Her voice was taut with impatience as she continued. "Boarding school is the best solution. Think of it as an opportunity to get an excellent education."

"You said that's what we were getting at St. Monica's."

"Clarice, are you listening to me? This separation means one of you would have to go to public school. It'll be hard enough supporting two residences on what your father makes, let alone tuition for you and your sister. We can't accept a loan from Jack, and we certainly can't take his money outright. He has come up with a viable solution offering to be your conservator and footing the bill for your support. He wants to save our marriage as much as anybody."

Kit put her hand over her mouth and faked a cough. Anger flashed over Mom's face.

"Why does he have to be my conservator or whatever you call it? Why can't he just pay my tuition at St. Monica's?"

"Oh, right. That would look great, a tuition check coming into school every month with Jack's signature. You're obviously too young to understand money. It's not just the tuition. It costs a small fortune to support this house, two cars—"

"You and me could move to a smaller house." It took everything in me not to cry.

"You and me? That's what we're paying your tuition for? *You and I.*"

"You and me, you and I...who cares? Mom, this is my life we're talking about!"

"Yes, and as a minor you're not the one making this decision. You're just going to have to trust me...us...that this plan is best for everyone, including you."

Mom leaned back on the pillow and squeezed her eyes shut for a moment. "Clarice, you're fourteen. You can't raise yourself. I will be taking on more clients. Your father works long hours and travels. This was the best option we could come up with. Once you get to the school in Arizona, you'll love it. You'll see."

I jumped off the bed and clenched my fists. The corners of my mouth quivered as I fought tears. "I won't love it! I'll hate it! I already hate it! I'll run away!"

"This is hard enough on me without your getting emotional. There's a packet from St. Joan's with a brochure so you can see what the school looks like."

I shook with anger, or fear. It was impossible to separate the two. "So, that's it? It's a done deal?"

Mom sipped her coffee and didn't answer. Kit nodded toward our bedroom. I snatched the packet from St. Joan's and stormed out behind her. On my way I kicked Dad's overturned chair.

Kit closed the bedroom door and put a Beach Boys album on the record player to muffle our conversation so Mom couldn't hear. I dropped the packet and collapsed on the bed. Kit sat on hers propped against the wall. Neither of us said anything for a moment.

"I can't believe they're sending me away."

"Well, jeeezz, Reese, you sort of brought it on yourself."

I popped up. "Me? What did I do?"

"Didn't I tell you to let it go? But no…you had to press. You had to go and ask her point blank if she and Dad would ever get divorced."

"What has that got to do with the price of tea in China?" I used one of Mom's favorite expressions in the same superior, know-it-all tone she used. I thought Kit was on my side. I felt defensive and angry and confused all at once.

"You weren't exactly subtle. You might as well have announced Mom and FD were sleeping together by tying a banner to the Goodyear blimp for the whole world to see. You're such a fool. Why couldn't you just keep the secret? Now they're on to you."

"What are you talking about?"

My sister cocked her head in frustration, the futility of explaining adult manipulation to a guileless kid. "Think about it. You found out about them right before Christmas last year. Why do you think FD bought you all those dresses?"

"Because he thought I needed something fancy for *The Sound of Music.*"

Kit exhaled sharply. "You really think that's why? What about the way he jumped in for Dad and took you to the Dodger game? Has he ever shown the slightest interest in baseball? Why do you think he makes such a fuss over you every Friday night when he comes over to watch *The Twilight Zone,* going on about what good buddies you guys are? Why?"

"Because for your information, he likes me."

Kit scoffed and fell back against the wall. "I know he likes you. But he loves Mom."

I drew my knees up and leaned on them with both hands holding my head. Had I been a fool, like Kit said? I thought back over all the special times with FD.

"Don't you get it? They've been bribing you, Reese, the two of them. Mom's been feeding ideas to FD, masterminding your silence through him. She knows you adore him and would never blow his cover."

"Then why send me away to school?" I kept me head down so Kit wouldn't see I was starting to cry.

"Obviously Mom's afraid you'll spill the beans. She needs to get you out of the way. Remember what I said when you told me you knew? I warned you that Mom would never give FD up. Divorce isn't an option, not because of any church rule...because he can't support her on a priest's salary. She has to keep Dad in the dark. This way she can have her cake and eat it too."

"You also said if Dad found out he would shoot FD and go to prison. I would never let that happen. I would never tell anyone, least of all Dad!"

"Yeah...well...I know that but Mom doesn't. Even if she did, Mom doesn't trust anyone. I thought you would figure that out after she chased your boyfriend away. She doesn't trust you any more than she trusts me. Once she figured out you knew about her and FD, she wasn't about to risk your blowing it."

"What if I went to her and told her she was right, that I know but would never tell Dad?"

"Because it's not only that you know. It's that now you've got something on her, something you can hold over her head and use against her. What if you decided you wanted to get back at her for Greg? Don't you see? You're too dangerous to have around. Boarding school is the perfect solution. She's even thought of insurance with this stupid plan making FD your legal guardian."

I started crying in loud uneven breaths. "But why did Dad agree?"

Kit's tone softened. "Who knows? Maybe she threatened to leave him if he didn't. That's her trump card. He wouldn't risk taking a stand for you if it meant he might lose her."

My mind reeled, refusing to accept Kit's logic.

She stepped into the bathroom and grabbed a Kleenex. "Here, take it." She sat on the edge of my bed. "Anyway, you'll be better off in boarding school. Why would you want to be here?"

"Because this is my home."

"Well, not anymore, apparently. That bitch wants us out of the way and Dad doesn't want to think about his family breaking up. That's all he's ever wanted. It's twisted, but hey, welcome to the adult world. Besides, Dad's right, you'll probably love boarding school."

I was numb.

"Anyway, I gotta go. Jackie's picking me up." Kit started for the door. "It's a rotten break, Reese."

I grabbed Cyrano and fell back, looking at the giant K without seeing it. Tears pooled in my ears. How could they send me away? I was the good kid. Mom had to know me better than that, know I would never tell. *The quiet, intense one.*

I sat up and wiped my face, then opened the packet from St. Joan's. A glossy brochure showed an idyllic country setting with wholesome-looking girls strolling across the lawn in dappled morning light, all of them looking exceedingly happy.

Of course they were happy. They all came from normal homes with normal parents who weren't trying to get rid of them—girls who slept well at night knowing their mother and the parish priest weren't lovers, girls whose fathers would stand up for them, protect them, girls who weren't made to feel like whores over an innocent kiss, girls whose mothers would never, ever give them away.

Girls who prayed to a God who had not abandoned them.

How could I ever fit in with such girls? I was nothing like them. They would see right through me, see I wasn't normal. I could never make a real friend, a friend to confide in about everything that mattered because the only thing that mattered was too horrible to share.

My own mother didn't even want me around. Why should they? At boarding school I would be my same lonely self, only worse, cut off from my family and everything familiar, far away from Francie. Far away from Brother McPherson.

*

Monday morning, Kit got a ride to school with Jackie. It

was the first time Dad and I had been alone since the family meeting. He reached across the seat and slapped my hand, which was resting palm down between us. I returned the slap, our usual game, then withdrew my hand.

The silence between us felt strained. He was my only chance. I had to ask.

"Dad, about the whole separation thing. Couldn't you convince Mom to let me live with you?"

He straightened up in the seat. I knew he hated talking about serious stuff. "I brought that possibility up already. Mom adamantly rejected it."

"Yes, but why? As it is I take care of myself after school. It would be no different with you at work."

"She's worried Kit will be a bad influence. You'll want to bring friends over, and word will get out that your mother and I—"

"Bring friends over? Do I bring friends over now? That bus after school is a ferry taking me from the mainland to a deserted island. I wouldn't bring friends over!"

"Don't be sarcastic, Reese. We get enough of that from your sister."

"I can't believe you're letting her do this! It's so unfair! I'm being punished for nothing."

"Life isn't always fair. And you're not being punished. Your mother and I have to do what we think is best for all of us, and this is the plan we've come up with. You'll just have to find a way to live with it. We all will."

"We? You're the one who decided this with Mom and FD."

Dad massaged his neck the way he did at the end of a hard day. "Separation is the lesser of two evils. Ever since Mom earned her counseling certificate and started working with Jack, taking on her own clients, she feels...well, she feels like she's doing something that matters with her life, something meaningful." He flinched ever so slightly.

"And? She can't do something meaningful with one quiet, undemanding, self-sufficient, practically grown teenage daughter who stays out of her hair?"

"It's not that simple, Peanut. Your mother is a smart woman, an energetic woman, and she's always wanted a career. You girls came along pretty fast after we got married. Mom wants more than a family and kids."

"Dad, this isn't exactly the Stone Age. Women work and have families at the same time. Three people I know of at school have moms who work."

"I know that, but counseling is a lot more demanding than working in an office or dress shop. Your mother is high strung, easily stressed. She doesn't feel she can manage a career and a family. This separation will give her a break, that's all. It's not forever."

I stared at him as he looked straight ahead. Dad was a stranger, a different man from the one I had spent summer evenings with in the garage. We didn't talk the rest of the way to school, a first for us, in spite of his attempts to start a conversation. There was only one thing I wanted to talk about, the one thing we both knew and couldn't accept—there was nothing either one of us could do.

I got through the school day as Robot Reese, the mechanical motions familiar by now. I didn't think my life could get any worse. I was wrong.

The final bell rang. A quick stop at my locker and that would be that. I shimmied my way through the river of students flowing out of the classrooms. A squealing laugh carried down the hallway over the hum and chatter. I knew that laugh. It was Stephanie Hamilton, boy-chaser extraordinaire, head of the cheerleading squad, mean girl who had given me the cold shoulder from day one, starting with excluding me from her big sleepover.

I caught a glimpse of Stephanie at her locker, flirting with some cute guy, probably captain of the football team, a perfect match.

I stopped cold. Even from behind he was painfully familiar.

Greg.

The world around me blurred. I couldn't move. Greg and Stephanie Hamilton. My knees nearly buckled as he stepped closer and brushed her bangs aside. Students had to step around me to get by.

I gathered my wits and turned around. *The exit. Get to the exit.* I focused only on the door to freedom until I jammed my body into the metal bar and shoved it open with a loud clang. Fresh air didn't help. I had to get as far away as possible as quickly as possible and never show my face again.

The forty-three minute bus ride felt like forty-three hours. Greg and Stephanie. My Greg. The house was quiet. I stood outside Mom's door and listened to the hushed voices, the muted tones of intimacy between counselor and client.

Always the intruder, I tiptoed to my room and turned to close the door. A ball of anger burned in my gut. *Greg and Stephanie Hamilton. Are you satisfied, Mom?* I gritted my teeth and threw the door shut. The vibration jostled the dog figurines on my desk, knocking them askew with the tinkling sound of colliding porcelain.

Thirty seconds later, Mom burst in. I knew she was

seething. In the dark I held my breath and waited until she left. Hunkered deep in the closet, I clutched Cyrano and sobbed. My burgundy dress from the freshman dance swayed to and fro above me, the long satin ribbon brushing my face.

6

UNRAVELED

Two weeks went by and no one said a word about the separation. I knew we hadn't heard the last of it, could feel it in my bones. Anxiety was making it harder for me to stay focused at school. Sleeping through the night was rare. My appetite disappeared and carved my curves into Kit-like leanness.

I didn't suppose our family doctor would prescribe sleeping pills like the ones he had given Mom to take the edge off the gallons of coffee and cartons of cigarettes she consumed trying to keep up with grad school and counseling and her family. In that order.

I rang Greg's doorbell. No one answered, which was odd. We had planned to meet here after his track practice. Maybe he was in the backyard showing someone the bomb shelter. I walked around back and found the metal plate in the ground. I dragged the lid to the side, wondering why the heck the opening was closed if Greg was in there.

Down, down, down I went. It was black inside the bomb shelter. I propped the door open and flipped on the light.

The concrete bunker was empty.

"Greg?"

CLUNK!

I spun around just as the steel door fell shut and clicked. I rushed over and tried the knob. Locked. *Don't panic, don't panic.* Greg showed me a key somewhere. The metal panel in the wall. I dashed over. My fingers shook as I yanked the panel open. No key. I moved to the kitchen and started pulling open one drawer after another, sliding my hand over the contents in a circular motion. No key. I threw aside the bundles of bedding on each cot. No key.

Overhead the single bulb began to flicker. I ran to the door and grabbed the knob, pulling and twisting with my whole body. I was suffocating. Air, I needed air.

"HELP! SOMEBODY! LET ME OUT!" The light overhead flickered on and off before it died. The bunker fell into terrifying darkness.

I heard footsteps. "HELP! I'M LOCKED IN HERE!"

A hand touched my shoulder. I opened my mouth to scream.

"Reese, wake up! Wake up, Peanut."

My eyes popped open. I gasped for air and sat bolt upright.

Dad was standing over me.

"That was some nightmare! You okay?"

I nodded, none too convinced.

"Well, it's six anyway. Why don't you go ahead and get dressed. Maybe we can leave a little early for school this morning. Don't fall back asleep."

Dad closed the door. I dropped on the pillow, my nightgown damp with sweat.

*

Another two weeks went by and still no one said anything about the separation. At dinner one night Mom was especially quiet. Kit and I snuck looks at each other, waiting.

Dad cleared his throat. "So, that thing we talked about

a few weeks ago…it looks like your mother and I won't be separating after all, at least right now. Between renting a place in Santa Monica and paying the mortgage on the house, our finances just won't handle it."

"Oh, so what now? We just stay here and resent each other? Boy, that sounds bitchin'."

"Goddamit, Katherine, how many times have I told you not to swear?"

"Kit, Vi, please." Dad's face was a mix of apprehension and defeat. This wasn't the end, and he knew it.

"Does this mean I'm not going away to boarding school?"

Long pause.

Dad's voice was barely above a whisper. "No, you won't be going anywhere, Peanut."

God hadn't abandoned me altogether.

"We'll all just try to make the best of the situation. That's all we can do. Your mother and I, you girls too, we'll all have to find a way to be civil and give each other a little room to breathe."

"Room to breathe? This is such bullshit!" Kit's prospect of living in freedom with Dad was out the window.

Mom hissed. "Katherine, leave the table. *Now*."

I knew Mom's anger wasn't directed at Kit this time. It was her old anger, exhaust fumes of frustration leaving a contrail of hot vapor polluting the air we would all have to breathe.

*

Our family effort at civility only seemed to make things worse. Kit was home as little as possible and in a foul mood when she was. Dad worked longer hours than ever. Mom was tense, withdrawn. Our only relief came during FD's visits. Other than that, it was every man for himself.

A pall settled over the house.

It was late summer when the news broke. I listened from the back door before walking in. Something was up. Kit, Mom, FD and Dad were in the kitchen. Kit sounded stuffy, like she'd been crying.

"I knew I couldn't trust you for one minute out of sight. What exactly is your plan…or should I say you and this dirty Mexican?"

"Vivienne—" Dad grimaced.

"For God's sake, Mom, he's not a dirty Mexican! He's from Colombia. His family is rich. They own a huge cattle ranch outside Bogota."

"Alright. What do you and this boy plan to do about this? Or did you even bother to think about that in the heat of passion?"

Mom caught sight of me. "Go to your room, Clarice. This conversation is not for your ears."

From my post in the hallway it wasn't a leap to figure out Kit was pregnant. I made it to the bedroom seconds ahead of her after the conversation came to an abrupt halt. Kit threw the door flying shut, the windows rattling in domino effect from our end of the house to the kitchen.

The scowl was still on her face when she saw me. "You don't have to pretend you don't know, Reese."

I didn't say anything. I didn't turn away from her either.

Kit flopped on the bed and stared at the Marlborough K on the ceiling. "It's such bullshit. Mom's just worried about her reputation, what the almighty neighbors will think. Jeeezz, if I'd turned up with leprosy, at least she could say I'd been off in some God-forsaken outpost working as a missionary over the summer. But being pregnant—"

I waited a minute. "What are you gonna do?"

She walked to the bathroom and snapped a wad of toilet paper, the roll still spinning as she dropped on the bed. "I don't know. Carlos and I haven't talked about it." She blew her nose. "Mom is taking me out of school. I'm barely three months, but she says I'll start showing early because I'm skinny."

Kit seemed at a loss, her trademark cockiness replaced by uncertainty.

Mom let her stay in school for the next few weeks. She came home with me on the early bus as ordered, silent and sullen the whole way.

At the end of three weeks, Mom withdrew Kit from Saint Monica's "for health reasons." Sequestered, she stayed in our room or wandered aimlessly around the backyard. Mom let Jackie come over a few times. Kit wasn't allowed to see her other friends and was forbidden to talk on the phone.

Jackie told Kit the buzz around school was that she had "the kissing disease"—mononucleosis—which among my sister's crowd was an illness apparently conferring great status. Mom caught wind of it and was furious, saying Kit had humiliated the family because the kissing disease and pregnancy were conditions on the same spectrum, just a matter of degree. As far as I could tell, half the upperclassmen had contracted mono at some point or other.

Dad and I rallied around my sister. Two days a week, he ducked out early from work and drove Kit to Sunset Beach so she could get out of the house for an hour. They would walk along the deserted shore until it was time to come home for dinner. On weekends they reversed the routine and walked early in the morning before anyone was out, even surfers.

I jumped on board too as Kit's errand girl, sneaking around Mom and riding my bike to Pronto Market. Her reserve babysitting money that used to go for cigarettes was now earmarked for candy bars and movie magazines.

On weekends, Carlos visited. Soft spoken and intelligent, he had moved to the U.S. to live with his uncle in Santa Monica. The plan had been for him to get into a good college and study architecture before returning to Colombia. That plan was out the window now.

Dad and I both liked Carlos. As for Mom, it wouldn't have mattered how nice he was, she would never have approved of him, which is probably what drew my sister to him in the first place.

My sister wasn't the first girl to get pregnant in high school. St. Monica's seemed to have one of those girls once a year, girls who would drop out of sight and return a year later after traveling to Europe. At school we giggled about going to Europe being code for being knocked up. Now it was happening in our family, and no one was giggling.

There was no way Mom would let Kit go away to a home for unwed mothers and have the baby, give it up for adoption, which the Catholic church would've sanctioned. It wasn't about that. How would she explain such an absence to the neighbors, much less her fellow parishioners? She would be mortified once gossip took hold. That was not going to happen. Mom understood the cost and necessity of ruthlessness.

In an unlikely turn of events, Kit had leap-frogged over me as Mom's front-running liability. Sending her daughter to South America was a perfect solution, much better than boarding school in Arizona had been for me.

Mom hadn't engineered Kit's exit, but she forced it into action.

The clock was ticking. Mom pressed Kit and Carlos for specifics on their plan. One Saturday, Kit beside him, Carlos sat in the kitchen and talked to Mom and Dad like a real grown up. He described the plan in detail. His mother had sent money for the plane fare. He and Kit were leaving for Bogota and would live with her.

From the hallway where I listened, the words hit like a sledge hammer. I didn't hear anything after the part about moving to Bogota. My bet was Kit didn't either, though she sat two feet away.

My sister would be free of Mom at last, only not in the way she had planned.

It was Friday evening, three hours before FD was due to walk through the door for *The Twilight Zone*. These days Kit stayed in the bedroom until he showed up. Tonight I waited with her.

The bedroom floor was littered with scraps of paper as I sat cutting out pictures of Troy Donahue from the old movie magazines Kit had given me. She was lying on her bed, staring at the big Marlborough K in a Zen state of meditation. That was an improvement over the forlorn expression totally foreign to all of us.

"I wonder if they'll have *The Twilight Zone* in Bogata," I said, trying to cheer her up.

She scoffed. "They probably won't even have TV."

"I thought his family was rich."

"They are, but Carlos said they don't have everything in Columbia that we have here."

"Well they must have TV," I said, unable to comprehend any home that didn't in 1963.

Kit clicked her tongue. "Even if they do, everything

will be in Spanish."

"Oh yeah." I kept forgetting not everyone in the world spoke English. "I bet you learn Spanish real fast."

Kit brought both hands up and covered her face. She held perfectly still, as if she could hold back the tears. Her shoulders started shaking, confirming she couldn't.

"You'll be with Carlos, that's the important part," I said. Kit's crying cast my sister in a whole new light. For one brief moment, she was a scared little girl. I ached to hug her.

Her moment of vulnerability passed. Kit sat up abruptly, wiping her hand across her face in a rough slap." I don't want to be with Carlos. I don't want to learn Spanish. I don't want to go to Columbia, and I sure as heck don't want this baby."

"Kit…you don't mean that." It was as much a question as a statement.

"I don't know what I mean. It's all such a mess. I just wish I could have my old life back."

"Yeah." I was going to say more. A wave of emotion held me back. Kit, leaving this house. Until this very moment, it hadn't seemed real. Mom and Dad's sending me away to boarding school had turned out not to be real, just a sickening threat hanging over my head. A scare was one thing. This was reality. Unlike Mom and Dad changing their minds, Kit's fate was out of her hands. The baby was real. My sister would be leaving.

I waited for the feeling to subside. "It'll be weird not having you here anymore."

"Lucky you," she said. "You get the bedroom to yourself and—" She didn't finish. I could hear the strain in her voice as she tried to sound matter-of-fact. "I guess you can keep my record collection and purses. I was going to give all my good stuff to Jackie, but—" This time her voice broke. She waited a moment. "You might as well have it...I'll never see Jackie again."

"I can? Really?" I toned down my excitement. "I'll take good care of everything. When you come to visit, you can have it all back."

"Columbia is a long way away. South America's a whole different continent. It doesn't seem likely I'll be coming back anytime soon."

Leaving was one thing. It had never occurred to me that I might not see my sister again.

I jumped up and rummaged through the closet for my shoe box of treasures. "Here." I turned to Kit and opened my hand. "I have fifty-two dollars saved up. It's yours. You can buy a new purse and records in Bogota."

Kit stared at the money for what seemed like a long time. I felt stupid, standing there with my hand out, waiting for her to ask what I thought she could buy with fifty-two measly dollars.

I barely felt it and she might have just been holding it to take the money, but I think she squeezed my hand.

Kit and Carlos were married in a civil ceremony at the courthouse in downtown Los Angeles. That same afternoon, they left for Colombia.

Just like that, my sister's tumultuous tenure in the Cavanaugh household had come to an end.

*

Two weeks after Kit left our family problems fell to the wayside, at least for a few days.

I dropped my bike outside Pronto Market and fished in my pocket for the quarter Mom had given me to buy cigarettes. Something felt strange the moment I walked inside. Sam hovered over a radio at the counter along with several customers. They were straining to hear through the static and looked terribly upset.

I edged my way to Sam. He squeezed my arm and kept his focus to the radio. A woman cried out. A collective gasp went through the group.

President Kennedy was dead.

I pedaled home as fast as my legs would go. Dad's words rang in my ear. *There won't be a nuclear attack, Peanut. President Kennedy won't let things go that far with the Russians. The President is dead. He can't stop the Russians now. We don't have shelter. Greg. Greg and Stephanie.* My mind was a jumble of tangled thoughts.

I burst through the door, flushed and breathless. "MOM!"

We nearly collided in the hallway. Her irritation turned to concern at the news.

"Are the Russians going to bomb us?"

"No…no, of course not. Calm down, Clarice."

I was too distraught to savor the affection of her taking my hand in hers. She led me into the living room and turned on the TV. We sat on the edge of the couch and watched.

Walter Cronkite's face filled the screen. President Kennedy died an hour ago of a gunshot wound to the head. Mr. Cronkite sounded tense, not at all as he did on the six o'clock news. It seemed no one knew exactly what had happened. He kept saying, "This just in—"

The TV stayed on through dinner. Mom made sandwiches and brought them to the living room on trays. Dad filled her in every time she was out of earshot. Dallas, Texas. The President had been shot while riding with The First Lady in a motorcade.

I had never seen my parents look scared of anything.

They looked scared now.

Mom phoned the rectory every fifteen minutes. No one answered. On the fourth try the housekeeper picked up. FD was at the Church consoling parishioners who had gathered to grieve and pray for the President's family.

The weekend of November 22, 1963 crawled forward in a haze of patchy information and anxiety. Our TV stayed on whenever the news broadcast. A pall settled over the house, the neighborhood, and as I would learn later, the world. Shock and grief filled the airwaves, burned in the eyes and on the faces of every person we talked to or didn't. Uncertainty hung in the air.

I remembered as a kid thinking on any given day that the world would forever be as it was in that moment, because I was incapable of imagining it any other way. On that dark November day, I imagined the world as very different from the one I lived in today.

The fear radiating from my parents in the aftermath of President Kennedy's assassination shook me to the core. Family discord didn't matter. Nothing did. A nuclear bomb was going to wipe us off the face of the earth.

Only those with a shelter would survive.

The world was no longer safe, inside or outside my family.

At least if I was going to die, the secret was going to die with me.

*

Looking back on that year, it seems all the lines between right and wrong had blurred, our familiar landscape rearranged. Instead of the tension Kit managed to generate on a daily basis, a haunted atmosphere filled the house. That was the thing about Kit—everyone was defined by their catalytic reaction to her. The emptiness brought by Kit's absence threw me, Mom and Dad off kilter. It felt like the fourth leg of our table had broken and we were scrambling to regain balance with the remaining three. We had lost the one thing tacitly uniting us—the shared experience of surviving the tempest that was my sister.

Mom wanted all trace of Kit removed, even the family photos in the living room. She packed up the stuff from our bedroom and insisted Dad put it somewhere in the garage out of sight. He needed our tallest ladder to place the four boxes labeled with Kit's name high on a shelf behind the old camping gear.

There was nothing to be done except continue our family charade. Mom concocted a cover story for neighbors and parishioners that took on a life of its own. Kit had been accepted into an exclusive program abroad in cultural studies. Mom hadn't mentioned it before in case Kit hadn't been accepted. That's how elite it was. The high-spirited rebellion people might have seen in her daughter was borne of suppressing a keen intelligence. Kit clearly needed more than had been offered by a small private school in a provincial town.

Dad and I marveled at the stories Mom fabricated and wondered after a few weeks if she hadn't started believing them herself. Every Sunday after Mass, Mom would recount some exotic episode in Kit's travels. How exciting, the women would say, how proud you must feel. Kit is a fortunate girl indeed to have parents who understand the educational value of experiencing other cultures, parents who allow the girl to travel the world on her own with a group of strangers.

On the drive home from church, Mom would show not a shred of chagrin. Oblivious to the fact me and Dad had heard the pack of lies, she would bask in the glow of superiority over women who envied her for having such a daughter.

Dad didn't dare say anything, gob smacked though he was by her hubris. This aspect of Mom was no surprise to me. My mother was expert at creating a whole different world to ease the pain of disappointment in the real one. First she had become Maria the nun-turned-governess in *The Sound of Music*, followed by her marriage to FD, though that role may have preceded the other, and now she was the proud mother of a daughter accepted into an elite program of study in Europe.

I wondered if Mom had any idea how transparent she was spinning fantasies built on the ruins of her own dreams.

*

A letter arrived from Kit in December. I had just walked in the back door from school. Mom gave me the nonverbal cue to disappear after a quick hello to FD. The letter was on the kitchen table, addressed to me. The raised eyebrow from Mom made it clear she didn't approve of Kit's writing to me rather than to her and Dad.

November 28, 1963

Dear Reese,

Greetings from South America! I've gotten settled in Aida's house, Carlos's mom's house where we'll live from now on. So far everyone has been really nice to me. It's a good thing too. Carlos is with his dad on the ranch all week while I'm stuck here.

I'm already going crazy with boredom, doing nothing but eat, eat, eat. The baby won't be here for another four months. By then I won't fit through the door. It's a good thing the house is so big...7 bedrooms and 10 bathrooms, not counting the servants' quarters. I have my own maid, Rosa, who makes my bed, does my laundry, everything! Mom would love it here...she could wear a long poufy gown and pretend to be Scarlett O'Hara.

There isn't a thing to do. Aida and her sisters, who live around the corner, play cards and drink all day. It's a household of women during the week, going from one sister's house to the other. At least they're all excited about the baby. Everything is baby, baby, baby. I feel like a celebrity the way they fuss over me.

I've hardly even been into town. The servants do the shopping and women don't go out unescorted by a man anyway. It's pretty stupid. The last two weekends Carlos and I have gone to the movies but everything is in Spanish so even the movies aren't much fun. Carlos says after the baby comes, he'll take me horseback riding. That'll be so bitchin'!

I hope Mom isn't giving you hell without me to pick on. If she even cares, you can tell her I'm fine. Be sure to mention I have my own maid.

Give Dad my love. I miss him terribly.

Kit

I tucked the tissue-thin letter into my shoe box at the bottom of the closet. At dinner I told Mom exactly what Kit had instructed me to say and watched her face tighten at mention of the maid.

7

DOWNWARD TRAJECTORY

Kit's letter had been a surprise, since she could barely speak a civil word when we shared the same bedroom. I guessed being thousands of miles away in another country made it safe for her to be nice. The next day after school, I wrote back, hoping she would get it before Christmas.

December 15, 1963

Dear Kit,
Life in Columbia sure sounds different. I would die not being able to listen to the Beatles! Do people in South America know that President Kennedy was shot? I've never seen Mom and Dad so worried. As of this writing, we haven't been wiped out by a nuclear bomb. I sure wish we had a shelter. Lyndon Johnson is our President now. He says there won't be a war.

Things around here are pretty much the same since you left, without the fighting (no offense). Dad is busier than ever at work, which is good in case the Russians attack. FD is here all the time it seems. I bet Father Sebastian must know he has a secret life outside the rectory.

Speaking of FD, I took your advice. I'm disappearing as much as I can when he's around. I like having our bedroom to myself since I'm in exile most of the time.

The first semester of sophomore year is almost over. I love being in Brother McPherson's Honors English class again, not because of him or anything, though he sure is cute for a clergyman. We read lots of poetry and even have to write our own sometimes.

I've been going to the Bay Theater on Saturdays with Francie. I don't care that much what's playing, as long as I get to be with my friends.

Anyway, that's what's new here. I'll ask Dad to help me mail you some movie magazines. That way, your Troy Donahue education can continue.

Merry Christmas, big sister!

Love, Reese

P.S. Send me a picture so I can see what you look like fat. It's hard to imagine.

P.P.S. I included the poem I wrote about you and Mom. We were supposed to use the structure of Robert Frost's Fire and Ice. I got an A- because Brother McPherson thought I could come up with something stronger for the last word. Oh well. At least you don't have lice, which is the only other word I could think of.

Embers
Some people scream, their souls on fire,
Some freeze like ice;
From what the screaming does require
I think there's more than just the fire,
And if I were to roll the dice
Hoping it was not too late
I wouldn't find just fire or ice
But embers burning soft and bright.

*

FD started referring clients to Mom. If I heard voices in

the bedroom/office after school, I was to go straight to my room. Mom said her office had to look professional, and that included the living room, so I needed to be careful about not leaving anything around, including myself.

With Dad at work and Mom busy with clients or conferring on the phone with FD, I felt more isolated than ever. Adding to the gloom, Mom drew the front drapes by ten every morning. She said her clients didn't want to be seen by the neighbors. I wasn't sure how the neighbors would know they were clients. I also wondered how someone helping people have healthy relationships explained secretive meetings behind drawn drapes. At any rate, I steered clear of Mom and holed up in my room until Dad came home from work.

Dad came up with the idea of painting the bedroom so it would feel more like mine. One Saturday he and FD spent the day scraping the Marlboro flip-top boxes off the ceiling. By the time they finished, the only thing left was a leproscopic pattern in the shape of a K from the clumps of glue and chipped paint where the boxes resisted eviction.

The room had already felt lonely without Kit. Removing the Marlborough K was like finishing my sister off for good, as if she never existed at all. I wished we had left the K on the ceiling. Taking it down didn't make me feel it was my room. It made me feel sad.

Kit had been with me every day of my life. We were a pair, the way Mom and Dad were a pair. Her place was beside me—in the car, in church, on the floor watching *The Twilight Zone*, across the table at dinner. Now I faced an empty chair.

Mom's banishing Kit had gutted our family. She and Dad had lost a daughter. I had become an only child. We felt my sister's absence as profoundly as we'd felt her presence. Mom hadn't considered the devastating impact of such a loss, the difference between fire and ice immeasurable in destructive power.

*

Christmas break arrived, which meant I needed to disappear all day. Hiding out in my room wouldn't cut it. Sooner or later I would need to eat, which required running into clients coming, going, or waiting for their appointment.

My solution was to bundle up and head to the beach, the only soul in sight most days. Even wrapped in my towel and hooded sweatshirt, most days I froze until the sun peeked through for a few hours. By late afternoon the breeze brought fog, grey air hanging like a harbinger of doom.

The sense of dread weighing me down had grown stronger every day. I couldn't shake the feeling that something bad was about to happen. It didn't make sense though. For some reason, Mom had been in a better mood lately. Christmas was around the corner. I chalked it up to that. She loved decorating the house and playing nonstop Christmas music on the Hi Fi.

No one mentioned the fact that it would be the first time Kit wouldn't be with us. Mom didn't seem to notice. Christmas Day the house would buzz with cheer and Scotch-drinking priests the same way it had last year and the year before as FD and his friends enjoyed the holiday in our home.

Mom and Dad had planned to throw a New Year's Eve party, a three-pronged bash to celebrate Mom's thirty-seventh birthday and my upcoming fifteenth in January. Mom would cook roast beef, mashed potatoes and fresh green beans. Dad would bartend, mixing Black Russians,

FD's favorite drink. I would stay up until midnight, enjoying the late night crepes, Mom's specialty, and a glass of champagne to ring in the New Year.

The evening was a raging success. Mom's bubbly energy served as an elixir far more potent than Dad's Black Russians. Watching her work her magic from the wings, I couldn't help wonder if the dread hanging over me had been a figment of my imagination. Everything felt right. Mom was in her element, a trapped animal set free, basking in the pleasure of staying one step ahead of armed hunters.

Even Dad had a good time, the drinks no doubt boosting hope that Mom might be happy like this tomorrow and the next day and the next. Seeing her that night I could almost understand what had made him fall in love with her, him and FD both.

It was more than her beauty. Mom made the world spin.

I knew that because she affected me the same way.

*

What happened next shouldn't have surprised me. But it did.

The third of January was especially cold, even for winter. It was the last day of Christmas break and the end of my long lonely exile at the beach. I tugged the strings of my sweatshirt hood and tightened it under my chin. The folded beach towel under me hadn't helped much. The sand felt hard and cold, like sitting on the edge of a bathtub waiting for it to fill.

The ocean was turbulent, dark, the sun overpowered by a brooding sea meeting the sky in a narrow horizon. My feeling of dread had come back, worse than the hangover Dad described New Year's Day. I pushed the feeling down, returning as I had countless times since the party to the image of Mom happy.

The thin horizon disappeared into ocean as the sun dipped behind it. I broke my own rule and headed home an hour early. By the time I reached the back gate, drizzle had turned to steady rain. I could almost imagine the feel of a hot shower defrosting me.

Taking the back steps two at a time, I yanked off my soaked shoes and burst through the kitchen door. It hit the wall. I cringed, certain Mom and her client had heard it. I grabbed a tea towel from the drawer and dried off a little so I wouldn't drip on the kitchen floor. That's when I noticed the house was unusually quiet. The coffee pot was empty, clean like it hadn't been used all day. Mom and clients and coffee went together.

I tiptoed into the living room. The drapes were open, which was odd for a weekday, a client day. I returned to the kitchen to strip out of my wet clothes and toss them in the washer. I would have to sneak by Mom's room in my bra and underwear.

A patch of white on the kitchen table caught my eye. It was a letter with no address, only a name—Dad's. I didn't move a muscle. The same fear and confusion that had overwhelmed me the night I discovered Mom and FD washed over me now.

I walked through the living room and kept going to Mom's office. As I had a thousand times, I pressed my ear to the door, willing the murmur of voices to come through. Nothing. I slowly pushed it open.

Mom's typewriter wasn't on the desk. The shelf above had been cleared of books and client folders. I stood in front of the double closet doors and tightened my hands on the knobs, preparing for the worst, then pulled. Empty.

Mom was gone.

I sat on the sofa bed, my thoughts connecting in slow motion. The sense of foreboding I had carried so long had finally revealed its source. For two years I had felt the low rumble of warning, like the build-up of stress at a fault line. For two years I had known it would only be a matter of time before the surface cracked and the earth beneath my feet would crumble.

I returned to the kitchen on wobbly legs and opened the letter.

January 3, 1964

Dear Walker,

I'm leaving you because I have to. This has been a long time coming. You and I are strangers to each other and I cannot, will not, live my life this way. You work long hours and even when you're home, you don't have the slightest interest in me or my work. I've thought about leaving for a long time. With Kit gone and Clarice old enough to take care of herself, the time is right. I will die if I have to go on like this. Please don't try to find me. In time you'll see this is best for both of us.

Vivienne

My eyes glazed over as I stared at the kitchen cabinets, wondering how Mom had decided on the particular shade of yellow.

It was after six. I folded the thing and shoved it back in the now-unsealed envelope. The house had grown dark and I was still in my wet clothes, numb to the cold.

My fragmented thoughts no longer collided in a jumble of confusion. They came to me in the straight lines of deductive reasoning. If only I had looked more closely, I would've seen it. The truth had been there all along, obscured enough to keep me from seeing what I didn't want to see—Mom would leave us.

She would bolt from her life as a housewife, her mind spring-loaded for escape like a Jack-in-the-Box just waiting for the right moment to burst free. That moment had come.

How sanctimonious I'd felt, accusing Dad of sticking his head in the sand. The signs had been obvious if we'd chosen to read them—Mom's restlessness, wanting to be anywhere other than with us—first in her novels, then grad school, then work; the dichotomy between who she was as a housewife and who she was as a career woman tearing her apart; her gradual progression away from what she had to do toward what it was she loved. It all made sense now.

It wasn't that she couldn't choose. It wasn't that she couldn't handle both. Mom was the most capable woman I knew. It was that she had married and started a family right out of college. In 1950 that's what women did. She had chosen Dad based on the strength of their physical attraction, hoping it would be enough. Dad had been the first to admit he had never understood his wife emotionally or intellectually.

Had the Pill been available Mom never would have chosen motherhood. She was no good at it and smart enough to recognize that. The life she had lived up to now had been chosen by default.

What my mother dreamed of was the fantasy life she had created for Kit built around career and travel and a man with whom she felt deeply connected. A life with FD.

Dad walked in the front door. "Hey, where is

everybody? Peanut? Why are you sitting in the dark? The back door is wide open. Did you push it all the way closed when you came in? It's colder than an ice bucket in here!"

He flipped on the light and walked past me to close the back door. A feeling of panic far worse than being trapped in Greg Stewart's bomb shelter hit me. I had to give Dad the letter.

He took off his watch and set it in its usual place on the counter. "What's the matter? Where's your mother?"

"She's not home."

"She leave a note? You're soaking wet. How long have you been sitting here?"

I gave him the letter.

He held it for a long time, just looking at his name in her handwriting. "I'm going to change," he said in a flat voice. "You should get out of those wet clothes."

I didn't move. Couldn't move. I sat and waited for my father's reaction to the end of the world. What would happen now? Ten minutes later, he came back to the kitchen and opened the cupboard. "What do you want for dinner?"

WHAT DO I WANT FOR DINNER? "Dad, what's going on? Where's Mom?"

He stood with arms outstretched holding the cabinet doors. From behind he looked like a man who'd been crucified and left hanging on the cross. I repeated my question. Dad walked to the table where I sat like a lump and dropped in the chair, rubbing his forehead as if the answer could be massaged out. "Mom isn't coming home, Peanut. I mean…not tonight."

"Where is she?"

"Reese, your mother and I…these last few weeks I had no idea she was so unhappy. This is all my fault."

"Where is she, Dad?" I felt sick. Why didn't he know? "You must have some idea."

"Jack must know. I'll call after dinner."

"Call now!"

"He'll be in the middle of evening vespers. What do you want to eat?"

He could've spoken in Russian from the way I gawked at him. "I'm not hungry."

"Well, we have to eat something."

But we didn't. We sat and stared at our food. Two bowls of Campbell's Split Pea soup stared back.

RIIIINGGG!

Dad and I jumped at the phone ringing. My heart stopped. *Mom.* It was a wrong number.

Dad retreated to the bedroom and shut the door. I followed and pressed my ear to the door, hardly able to hear over my own heartbeat.

"She has to have gone somewhere she can stay a while, Jack. She's taken all her clothes, toiletries, books, even her typewriter. I don't even know if she has any cash. The checkbook's in the drawer. What is she doing for money?" Dad's voice cracked. He sounded more distraught than I'd ever heard him, even when he found out Kit was pregnant.

"She must've confided in you. Who else would she turn to? I have to twist her arm twice a year to call her mother in Canada. Where could she be? I'm sure she made you promise not to tell me, but you have to, Jack. You can't leave me out of this. I'll go crazy not knowing if she's alright."

But FD didn't know. Dad didn't come out of the bedroom, so I took a shower and got into my pajamas. Thirty minutes later, he was sitting on the couch in the dark. I sat down next to him. Neither of us said a word. An hour later I said goodnight. He didn't answer.

The next morning I got up for school and Dad was still slumped on the couch, his face unshaven and drawn. He startled and looked confused, disoriented. A mosaic of red had turned his brown eyes muddy.

"I'm not going in to the office today. You go ahead and catch the bus with Francie."

"Okay. You going to eat something?"

"I'll have a bowl of cereal later."

We had this same brief exchange every morning for a week. Dad called Rezolin and explained he needed to take a few days off.

*

"Reese. Reese. Reeeese, wake up!" Dad stood over me, shaking my shoulder. The light in the hallway cast a shadow distorting him into a faceless hulk from the netherworld.

I sat up abruptly. "What's wrong? Is Mom home?"

"No. But I know where she is. I don't know why I didn't think of it sooner. She's in San Francisco. I'm sure of it. Her college roommate lives there, Jane Sommers. I dug through the Christmas trash and found her card. She wrote in her note that Mom could visit any time. C'mon, get dressed." He turned on the desk lamp and tossed my jeans on the bed.

"It's the middle of the night, Daddy. Shouldn't we wait until morning?"

"The sooner we get going, the sooner we'll find Mom. If we drive all night, we should get there around nine tomorrow morning."

"You haven't slept much. Are you sure it's a good idea for you to be driving?"

"I'm not going to. You are."

"Me! I don't know how to drive! I'm not even old enough to get my permit yet!"

"There's nothing to it, just put your foot on the gas and steer. I'll bring a cushion so you can see better and reach the pedals. I'll be right beside you. It's a straight shoot all the way up and this time of night the coast highway will be deserted. I've made sandwiches and a thermos of coffee in case you get sleepy."

Fifteen minutes later I met Dad in front. He sat with the car idling, pointed in the right direction. I climbed in beside him. I put my foot over his on the accelerator like he said. He withdrew his and released the emergency break, then slid to the passenger side.

I drove up the street to Sunset Boulevard and turned left. Two minutes later we reached the ocean. A right onto Pacific Coast Highway and just like that we were on our way to San Francisco at one-fifteen in the morning.

It was a chilly, clear night, a half moon flickering in ribbons of silver on the water. I was grateful having the moon to keep me company. We hadn't been on the coast five minutes before Dad rested his head on the window and fell asleep, right after telling me San Francisco was just shy of four hundred miles from Los Angeles, a seven hour drive with no traffic.

Dad probably got more uninterrupted hours of sleep than he'd had in weeks. I kept my eye on the gas gauge like he'd told me. Once it got below a quarter tank I took the off ramp into downtown San Luis Obispo and pulled into the Texaco station. Dad's wallet was on the seat.

Our headlights woke the attendant, who didn't look much older than me. I smiled and faked a confident air. While he pumped gas and cleaned the windshield, I went to the restroom and slapped cold water on my face. The crisp night air also perked me up. I took my time walking back to the car.

I paid the attendant, who threw me a questioning look. He eyed Dad, then me, then Dad again. I thanked him and pulled away from the pump and tried to calm my nerves. The engine revved in excitement when I pushed too hard on the gas. I let up and pressed again. The car lurched its way onto the on ramp. I could hear Dad's head bounce against the window as the right wheels kicked up dust on the shoulder. I steadied the car and lined it up with the road until all four touched pavement. He didn't wake up.

I watched for San Francisco on the highway signs overhead. Traffic picked up with morning commuters the closer we got to San Jose. I stayed in the slow lane and an hour later poured into downtown San Francisco with the flow.

It was almost nine o'clock. The streets were choked with traffic—cars, buses, taxis—nothing like Pacific Palisades, even at its busiest. A big truck honked and I was forced to change lanes. I veered left without looking and got another honk. The sudden swerve and second honk managed to wake Dad.

He said he was too groggy and would direct me through the congestion. It was a miracle we made it without crashing or killing a pedestrian. We snaked along streets left dark in the shadow of glass and concrete monoliths in search of a phone booth. Dad groaned as I passed the first one. The parking space seemed too small and I didn't know how to parallel park. The second phone booth had a space nearby wide enough that I could slide most of the Ford off the street. As it was I hit the curb, scraping the front whitewall tire.

I watched Dad from the rear view mirror. He closed the booth and flipped through the phone book. A few minutes later he came back. There was no number listed under Jane Sommers. We would go straight to the address on the Christmas card. He popped open the glove box and rifled through the Auto Club maps.

Drawing a line with his finger, he directed me across the city. We parked in front of Jane's apartment on Presidio Avenue. Dad tucked in his sleep-wrinkled shirt. He surveyed the old Victorian house, then walked up the stairs and knocked.

A man answered. Dad shook his head, gesturing with his hands. The door closed. She didn't live here anymore. There was no forwarding address.

Dad stretched his neck side to side. Disappointment dwarfed him as he slumped in the seat. I suggested we go home. He wanted to find another phone booth and call FD.

On the phone with FD, Dad ran his fingers through his hair and shuffled his feet in the cramped booth. A few minutes later, he hung up. He stayed inside with his back to me. I was about to get out when I saw his shoulders shaking. He covered his face.

I felt totally helpless. There was nothing I could do, nothing anyone could do. Except Mom.

Dad tightened his trench coat against the wind and walked toward the car. I opened the map and stuck it in front of my face so he wouldn't know I'd seen him cry.

"Jack doesn't know anything. He suggested we find a motel and come home tomorrow."

"I want to go home now, Daddy." My heart was breaking at the sight of him.

He leaned against the window. "You've been up all

109

night, Reese. You shouldn't drive. And I shouldn't either."

"I'm okay. If I get tired, we can stop and sleep for a couple of hours."

He nodded wearily, grateful not to have made the decision. I pulled away from the curb and did whatever I could to keep from making a three-point turn. I fumbled my way through the city. Dad wouldn't be any help at this point. Besides, he had fallen asleep. It was just as well. Between being scared to change lanes and getting caught in the quagmire of one-way streets, it didn't take long before I was totally lost.

An hour later, I spotted a green sign in the distance. Like a beacon in the night, I followed it to the highway heading south.

I stayed in the slow lane and watched for cities I'd noted going north. Four hours later, I could hardly keep my eyes open. A sign for Pismo Beach appeared.

I figured this was as good a place as any and it looked like an easy off and on the highway. The fewer people who saw me the better. Sooner or later someone was going to notice my driving. I turned toward the ocean and found my way to an empty beach. In no time I was asleep.

In my dream I heard kids yelling and the sound of skateboards clacking over a wooden boardwalk. I struggled to wake up. The dream pulled me down. A while later I was jarred awake by two surfers running past the car.

I shivered and turned the heater on high. I did a double take. Dad was awake. The ocean was dazzling in the afternoon sun. I lowered his visor to block the glare, breaking him out of a stupor.

"It's hard to imagine anything can be this beautiful when—" He choked up. "I'm sorry, Peanut, sorry I dragged you all the way up here for nothing. I don't know what I was thinking. You've done a pretty good job behind the wheel though. Reminds me of myself at your age, driving a tractor back home in Texas. Where are we anyway?"

"We're in Pismo, halfway home I think. Let's drink that thermos of coffee."

We ate our sandwiches in silence. It was the first thing I'd eaten since last night's grilled cheese dinner. I didn't want to disillusion Dad with how scared I'd been driving in the city, lost with no clue how to maneuver the car to get from Point A to Point B without lane changes and left hand turns. If I hadn't noticed the southbound sign, we would still be trapped on one-way streets going nowhere.

Dad insisted I drink the whole thermos of coffee, fully aware how long I'd been driving.

Revived with caffeine and a two-hour nap, I backtracked to the highway and headed home.

8

A NEW ORDER

The next morning Dad called his office again, this time claiming a stubborn case of flu. It felt like winter inside and outside the house, cold as a tomb. If I forgot to turn on the thermostat before leaving for school, it wouldn't be on when I got home. Most days I walked in to a cold house and Dad lost somewhere between wake and sleep, oblivious to the temperature.

I stumbled through school, using every ounce of strength to act normal. Nights were the worst. After tossing and turning half the night, I would drift off to sleep in the wee hours. At seven the alarm would blast and I would wake up exhausted. Dad slept on the couch most nights, if you could call it sleep. He ventured into his and Mom's bedroom for a shower and fresh clothes every few days after I'd reminded him.

It was hard to squeeze more than a small bag into the basket of my bike, so trips to Pronto Market for groceries were frequent. Dinners consisted of Kraft macaroni and cheese, raw carrots and celery, sandwiches, soup, hard boiled eggs, and the occasional hamburger patty. Dad ate only half of what I put on his plate.

My schedule remained the same to fend off suspicion. I came right home after school. Dad would usually be in the same spot in the kitchen staring into space or on the couch doing the same. I'd force myself to chatter about my day and he would respond with vague eyes and a monotone voice. "That's good, Peanut."

FD showed up every few days those first few weeks. As the weeks melted into one indistinguishable block of time, his visits withered to phone calls. The conversation was always the same.

Witnessing Dad deteriorate before my eyes was slow torture. There was nothing I could do for him, nothing I could say. He was beyond consolation. I wasn't much better off. It was like trying to slow a fast moving freight train, plummeting out of control down the mountain.

I wasn't afraid the crash would kill me. I was afraid it wouldn't.

February 4, 1964

Dear Kit,

I'm writing with bad news. A month ago, Mom left me and Dad. Just upped and went. We have no idea where she is. FD doesn't even know. Daddy hasn't been going to work. All he does is sit and stare at the walls. I have to bug him to eat and shower.

When FD calls, Dad begs for information, but he's in the same boat as us. Anyway, it's horrible and I don't know what to do about Daddy. If you have any advice, I sure could use it. If I mail this today, you should get it in ten days. Please answer fast because I'm pretty desperate here.

We sure are living in two different universes, you and I. You're having a baby and I've lost a mom.

Love, Reese

It was almost the end of the second month. Dad had started going into the office for a day here and there. I had no idea how he functioned or what his colleagues thought. He looked sick, that's a fact. His clothes were baggy, his face haggard. It was obvious he couldn't concentrate and he couldn't have been much use at work. His boss encouraged him to take extra sick time if needed. I knew my dad. This effort was for me. He was trying to pull his weight at home, not at work. Even the few days a week he went into the office I took as a good sign.

As time went on we began to assume some semblance of normal life. Dad dropped me off at school on the mornings he went into work. On weekends, I did laundry and he mowed the lawn, keeping the house up to avoid drawing attention. He explained to his golfing buddies that a new project demanded he bow out for the time being.

One night I made spaghetti and meatballs, a favorite of Dad's. We ate in silence, as we usually did, avoiding conversation about the only thing on our minds. I stayed in the kitchen after doing dishes and finished my homework, then joined Dad in the living room. It was dark. I didn't bother turning on a lamp. Dad stared blankly into the fire, its light accentuating the dark circles under his eyes. I threw on another log and plopped next to him on the couch.

"I finally finished memorizing *The Raven*."

He sounded wistful, as if recalling a life long since gone. "I read Poe in college. Why don't you recite it for me? We'll see if you've got it."

"It's not exactly the most uplift—"

"No, I want to hear it."

Why did he want to hear this depressing poem? Darn Poe. Why couldn't he write about something happy? I slumped in the couch, wishing I were anywhere other than in the dark with my father, about to tell him a bedtime story of utter despair.

Once upon a midnight dreary, while I pondered, weak and weary,

Over many a quaint and curious volume of forgotten lore—

Halfway through I paused. Dad was resting his head on the back on the couch.

"Go on."

Ah, distinctly I remember it was in the bleak December;

And each separate dying ember wrought its ghost upon the floor...

I finished reciting. At first I thought Dad had fallen asleep. I looked closer and saw his wet eyelashes. My bear of a father lay broken before me. No wonder he'd wanted to hear *The Raven*. Poe was despondent in the poem, a friend in the same boat with Dad.

I accepted that Dad needed Mom. He needed me, too, needed me to give him a reason to get through each day. And I needed him. As long as we were together, I could keep going. I made a promise that no matter what, I would never desert my father. I would never break his heart the way Kit and Mom had.

In the silence I longed to curl up in my Daddy's arms, both of us reassuring each other that everything would be okay. Instead, I stifled the sob in my chest and sat with him in the semidarkness. His hand flopped around in search of mine. He squeezed it. I was glad his eyes were closed so he couldn't see the tears in mine.

This was the closest we had come to talking about Mom, the agony of not knowing where she was, or if we would ever see her again. After a while he released my hand with a pat. I kissed him on the cheek and went to bed.

*

Almost three months after Mom had disappeared we still had no clue as to her whereabouts. Dad looked like a different man, all life drained from his face and twenty pounds from his frame. Other than showing up at work two days a week, he didn't leave the house. We settled into an existence of parallel solitude.

It was a Tuesday, a workday for Dad. I was going to surprise him with baked chicken and steamed asparagus for dinner, a level up from macaroni and cold vegetables. A quick trip to Pronto and I had the goods.

Blocked from view by the grocery bag, I didn't see Dad at first. I put the bag on the counter and jumped. He was at the kitchen table with a face full of misery.

"Dad! You scared me. Why are you home so early?"

He didn't look at me. "Reese, come sit down. I have something to tell you."

"Is it Mom? Has something happened?"

Dad swallowed like his throat was sore. "Jack called me at the office and asked me to meet him here."

My whole body tightened.

"Mom is in Laguna Beach."

"Laguna Beach? What's she doing there?"

"She's living in a cottage Jack rented for her."

"You mean...you mean he knew where she was this whole time?"

"Mom swore him to secrecy."

But he knew all this time? "Well, what is she doing? When is she coming home?"

"Not for a while yet. Last fall... when Mom was seeing a client, one of the parishioners Jack referred...he raped her."

"Raped her?" My mind reeled. "Why would Mom

leave us if she'd been hurt? Is she hiding from him...is that why she left? I mean...isn't he in jail?"

"No. Jack has taken action within the church. He won't hurt her again...but for the sake of everyone's reputation...ours as well as the parish...because Mom was counseling him as a church volunteer...she and Jack both thought it best if we keep the whole thing quiet."

"She let us go through hell all this time for the sake of a stupid reputation? We would've kept it quiet! We could've avoided everything we've gone through these last three months! Why would she not tell us?"

"Because that's not why she left. There's more to it." He ran both hands over his face, as if he might see a different reality after clearing the haze. He finally looked at me. "Your mother's pregnant."

"Pregnant? But—" I shook my head in confusion, turning the word over in my mind. I couldn't fathom it. "Well...what happens now? Is Mom going to stay there with the baby?"

"No. She's not keeping the baby. Jack has arranged with the local parish to find an adoptive family."

"She's going to have it and give it to some family? Like make them conservators?"

"No, she's giving the baby up. It's a private adoption. They'll be the legal parents."

"I don't understand. Why is she even having it? Every birthday she brings up the story of how she almost died having me, how the doctor said she should never have another baby because it could kill her. Why would she have this baby if it might kill her?"

"I don't have all the answers yet. I'm still trying to absorb this myself. All Jack said was that she's having this baby. Then afterward...when she's up to it...she'll come home."

"Come home? You mean... just reappear after all this time? I thought she wanted to be separated. Why can't she stay there? We won't worry now that we know where she is, know she's okay."

"Reese, your mother has been through a terrible ordeal. And it's not over. The baby is due in August. Her health is in danger. In the meantime, Jack will relay my message that you and I will visit."

"Visit? Are you kidding? I'm not going to visit her!" I stared at him, my mouth agape.

"Reese, listen, this was not her fault. She was raped. Can you imagine what she's been through?"

Every muscle in my body tightened. "Daddy, for almost three months you and I have been struggling to make it from one day to the next. She didn't care one bit about what we were going through. Maybe you can ask her to imagine what it's been like for me having my mother...or for you, having your wife...disappear into thin air, not knowing whether she's dead or alive!"

"Look, it's not that simple." I turned my face away. "Reese... Peanut...this is what we've been waiting for, to find out where she'd gone and why."

"So now that we know, that means everything is hunky dory? You're just going to let her come home?"

"Everything is hardly hunky dory. But she is your mother. She is my wife. We will go visit her. And after the baby's born she will come home."

For once in his life, my impassive father had taken a stand. Or had he? Like the random spanking of me and Kit, was he Mom's proxy? It wasn't a stand at all was my guess. This was the plan she had laid out for Dad to follow. Master puppeteer that she was, Mom had reached all the way up the coast from Laguna Beach to pull his strings.

"This is going to work out, honey. Once Mom comes home everything will go back to normal, you'll see."

The voice that came out wasn't my own, its tone dark with malice. "Nothing will ever be normal again. Mom's ruined everything."

"Reese, please—"

"I have no choice but to go to Laguna Beach with you, but I'm not setting foot in her house or speaking to her. Can I go now?"

Dad reached out to touch my arm. I pushed my chair back with a loud scrape and stomped out, tempted as I'd ever been to slam the bedroom, Kit-style. Instead, I blew off steam with a letter to her.

March 28, 1964

Dear Kit,

Well, everything here is a big, fat mess. We found out Mom is in Laguna Beach living in some cottage that FD rented for her. He knew the entire time! And you're not going to believe this part...she's pregnant! She was raped (!) by one of her clients. She's going to have the baby and give it away to a family in the parish down there. FD arranged the whole thing.

Dad says Mom is coming home after the baby. He actually wants us to go visit her until then. I can't believe he's willing to let her come home after what she's put him through, us through.

Sometimes I think I'll explode if I have to keep one more stinking secret! And now I guess I do. The biggest one of all.

Please write back soon.

Love, Reese

Kit's reply didn't reach me for over two weeks, the turnaround time reminding me once again of the distance between us.

April 12, 1964

Dear Reese,

Mom's pregnant! Wow! Even I would never have guessed that. Rape? Is she kidding? You know as well as I do who the father is. That bitch is lying through her teeth. Dad may be willing to buy it, but we know the truth. No wonder she wants to go ahead and have the baby...it's his. She finally got to have her cake and eat it too.

When Mom comes home, she'll be back to her old self. Believe me Reese, don't have any illusions about who Daddy will stick up for if push comes to shove. Whatever you and Dad have been through, it's no contest compared to his having the bitch home.

I think I can help you. Why don't you come down here and live with us? Carlos loves the idea and said he'd arrange for your flight and everything. Aida loves the idea too. The house is so big and Carlos is hardly here. You could finish high school here. Aida would pay for private school (all girls, unfortunately) but at least I would have some company...English speaking at that!

The baby will be here any day now. I'm excited and scared. At least I'll have something to do. I'm going crazy waiting, waiting, waiting, doing nothing but eating and living in total boredom. In the meantime, I have a huge favor. I have a bunch of books in the closet, up on the highest shelf. Herzog and Roth, and be sure to send Atlas Shrugged. I know it's asking a lot, but would you send them? Think about what I said and write soon.

Kit

I read the letter again. FD the father of the baby? I shoved away the image of him and Mom on the couch. Of course, it all made sense. I felt stupid not having figured it out myself. It must've been easy for her to leave us, knowing they could be together with no pesky kid to interrupt them, no husband.

As for moving to Columbia, that was impossible. Fool that I was, I could never leave Dad, or Brother McPherson. His class was my only salvation every day.

April 26, 1964

Dear Kit,

You must be right about it being FD's baby. I just didn't want to believe it. Dad sure is clueless though, because he and FD talk on the phone. I can't imagine how he envisions things working out when Mom comes home. You're wrong about him not sticking up for me. Not after what we've been through. He'll find out once Mom's home that it's no good. Maybe he and I will move to an apartment in Santa Monica like you were going to during the separation. Mom could have the house to herself, which is what she's wanted all along.

I thought about your offer to come live with you in Columbia. There's no way I can. Dad needs me now more than ever. Who will he turn to when Mom comes home and he sees the marriage is dead? She might even leave again. Daddy is not the strongest person in the world. I found that out the hard way. Maybe I can visit this summer.

Anyway, I'll keep you posted. Good luck with the baby! Write as soon as it's born.

Love, Reese

Mom Visit Day finally arrived. On Saturday morning Dad was up before seven drinking his coffee. By eight we were on the road, driving on Pacific Coast Highway, the road connecting the one miserable experience we'd had in the north of the state to what promised to be another in the south. Dad's spirits were high as he sang from *The Music Man*.

At first I felt relief at his high spirits, Dad's return to his old self. One of my parents was present and accounted for. Relief turned to resentment. It wasn't hard to figure out the reason for his sudden cheer after three months of misery. Whether or not she was in the house, Mom had been controlling his life, our lives. The rest was geography.

Two hours of Dad's singing on Pacific Coast Highway brought us to Laguna Beach. My body tightened. We followed Dad's directions to a narrow lane of big trees and small bungalows perched on a cliff. Mom's was at the end of the lane on a corner.

Our tires crunched over the long driveway. Dad switched off the ignition and looked around for a moment before getting out. It was a beautiful setting. The white cottage with blue trim had a front porch the width of the house, its deck an oasis of potted flowers and weathered Adirondack chairs. Bright cushions added a finishing touch to the picturesque scene.

I could imagine an artist living in such a storybook cottage, setting up an easel in the cool breeze to capture the exquisite light, not my mother clacking away on client notes in a haze of cigarette smoke.

"Peanut, I wish you'd come inside. You'll be awful lonesome out here by yourself."

I crossed my arms and turned my head the opposite

direction. My father obviously had no clue most of my life outside school was spent feeling lonesome—the physical loneliness of confinement in my bedroom or staying outside until dinner; the emotional loneliness of carrying Mom's secret. Either way, Dad wouldn't understand lonesome had become my natural state.

"Suit yourself," he said, "I'll be back in a couple of hours."

He stood on the front porch opening and closing his fists before he raised his hand to knock. I strained for a glimpse of Mom. The door closed before I got a chance.

I walked around the detached garage to the backyard. What a sight! The entire Pacific Ocean spread out before me. It was clear enough I could make out dirt roads crisscrossing Catalina. The island seemed only a few strokes away rather than twenty-four miles. A wooden staircase zigzagged down the cliff to the beach where glassy water swooshed over pebbles before retreating back to sea. The place was deserted.

I checked to make sure Mom and Dad couldn't see me from the window where they sat on the couch in silhouette. The beach called me. So did my bladder. I doubled back to the car and retraced our route to the Texaco station in town. I felt liberated by anonymity. This was one place I wouldn't have to fake acting normal. I could be me, whatever was left of me anyway, at least for the walk to Texaco and back.

By the time Dad came out of the house three hours later, I had finished my weekend homework and written a poem.

Thus began this new phase of hell. Every Saturday Dad and I were on Pacific Coast Highway by eight o'clock driving to Laguna Beach. And every Saturday I waited outside. My routine was always the same—I would trek into town and use the Texaco station restroom before taking the wooden stairs to the beach and collecting tiny shells for an hour. Had I not been worried about Dad finding me gone, I could've stayed longer. Once I got a better sense of his timing that would be my plan. For now I was conservative and returned to the car after an hour to finish my homework or read.

In the beginning I would ask if Mom had mentioned me. Dad's response was always the same. Mom was preoccupied with the baby. He was sure she would want to see me. She did eventually include me for lunch, emerging from the cottage with a sandwich, usually cheese, half an orange or apple, and a glass of milk. It had been my choice to stay outside. I couldn't help feel like the dog she would've fed if she hadn't protested it was enough taking care of a house and two kids.

My mother never once glanced in the direction of the car. I saw her though. She looked younger, her auburn hair tucked behind one ear like Veronica Lake, an un-Veronica Lake-like maternity blouse draped over her bulging belly.

Dad never said what they talked about, and I didn't ask. I already knew Mom hadn't been sorry leaving us for a new life in her storybook cottage while we floundered in misery in the dark on our own. I already knew she'd expressed her anger letting Dad believe her disappearance had been his fault, a neglectful husband absorbed in work finally getting his due.

The resentment lumped in my gut, a dense dumpling refusing to digest and pass. The more I envisioned the three of us living together, the more I became convinced we could not. Dad's optimism was a gossamer dream to keep his family together.

*

May 30, 1964

Dear Reese,

Say hello to your new nephew, Carlitos (photo enclosed). He was born April 17th. That's why I haven't written. It's been pretty busy around here, even with a maid. Don't ever have one, little sister. (A baby, not a maid). I'm kidding. Carlitos is so cute and good natured, like his father thank God! But all he does is eat, sleep and poop. I'm trying to breast feed but it's harder than you'd think. When I'm not feeding him every few hours, I'm eating or sleeping. So far it doesn't feel much different from being pregnant.

You wouldn't believe the fuss Aida and all of them make over the baby. They totally ignore me now that he's here. So much for being treated like a celebrity.

I was so looking forward to horseback riding after a month or so, but that doesn't look like it will happen. Cattle ranching is hard work. The last thing Carlos wants on the weekend is to get back on a horse.

This is worse than being grounded. I'm surrounded with books I can't read, music I don't like, movies I can't understand, no one to talk to about anything but the baby, and a culture that forbids me to go anywhere on my own. It's hell.

Anyway, you've got problems of your own. I'm enclosing a photo of the baby so you can see for yourself how adorable he is! I don't mind if you show Daddy.

Write soon.

Kit

Saturdays in Laguna Beach got a lot easier the deeper we

got into summer. Now I brought my bathing suit and retreated to the little cove beneath Mom's cottage. Lying on the sand reading was a better way to pass the time than being holed up in the car. If I closed my eyes, I could almost imagine I was on our beach at home.

My pleasurable interlude was short-lived. Dad seemed distracted during the ride home one Saturday. There was no singing, or even humming. We didn't play the hand-slap game on the seat between us. Instead he was quiet, a sure sign of tension.

"Peanut, you know now that it's early August the baby is due any time."

I didn't answer. The sense of dread that I thought had dissipated the day I came home from the beach and Mom was gone returned with a punch.

"Your mother will be coming home afterward. She came up with this idea for what to tell people about her…her reappearance. It's really pretty clever. We're going to say she's been in France all this time taking care of an elderly aunt."

I rolled my eyes. "Oh, sure, they'll buy that. Maybe I'll call her 'Aunt Bordeaux'? Dad! Who's going to believe Mom suddenly had to move to France for seven months to take care of some never-as-yet-mentioned aunt?"

"Don't be smart, Reese."

"Dad, since we're on the subject…how do you see this working, the three of us together in the same house?"

"For one thing you can start by knocking that chip off your shoulder. I know we had a rough go of it, but that's behind us now. We can start with a clean slate. It'll take time, but we'll adjust. With Kit gone Mom won't be so stressed. She'll be able to focus on her work, which is what she really wants. That's what the need for a separation was about. This… other situation has actually been an opportunity for her to have a breather and sort a few things out for herself."

"Like how to ditch her husband and kids?"

"That kind of sarcasm doesn't accomplish anything, and in Mom's defense, she did wait until you kids were grown before going back to school and starting her career."

"I'm fifteen. That's hardly grown."

"Hey, you didn't eat that sandwich Mom left on the porch. What do you say we swing by Tops and get a couple of pastramis, forget cooking tonight?"

He reached over and slapped my hand. I didn't slap his back. That was the extent of anger I could bear to levy on my father.

The following Saturday we were on the road as usual by eight. These early morning drives were beautiful, quiet, the world still in pajamas drinking coffee instead of going somewhere on Pacific Coast Highway.

Two hours later the ocean was still glassy, the beach below Mom's cottage pristine. Not a soul was in sight. The whole world opened up as I stood on the cliff. I wondered if this was how Jose Carrillo had felt taking it in from his sailing vessel at the turn of the eighteenth century, the entire California coast one flawless beach from San Diego to Crescent City.

I checked to make sure Mom and Dad hadn't seen me, then wound my way down to the beach. Crisp sand cracked under my feet. I dropped my towel and kept going, right into the water. My body went rigid at the first feel of cold, an exhilarating shot of adrenaline propelling me forward. I plowed against the current until it was waist high, then dove. The Pacific Ocean swallowed me.

All became silence. In a salt water baptism of renewal I passed through the portal to another world, a magical place separate and apart from the oxygenated one above. Here only the physical dimension existed, sensory receptors recalibrated to screen out concerns of life above water.

I popped up for air, Catalina the only thing other than ocean in sight. Rolling swells lifted and carried me. I flipped over on my back, weightless and free, and drifted with the current.

A nearly imperceptible noise compelled me to lift my head and look. I had passed a buoy, the bobbing ball marking the distance from shore. That was okay. At home I'd swum past the buoy countless times and was proud of my strength as a swimmer. I hadn't been far behind Greg most times the two of us raced side by side to our buoy at home.

I dropped my head back on the water and closed my eyes again. A sense of total peace came over me as I half swam, half drifted. I heard nothing but my heart beat decreasing in proportion to muscles freeing from tension.

A second buoy bobbed in greeting. I lifted my head and squinted toward shore, cottages on the cliff tiny in the distance. What a surreal feeling, my parents visiting in that strange house, Mom about to give birth to Traitor FD's baby, and Dad deluded in some fantasy that could only end tragically.

It didn't seem possible I was connected to such a life. Maybe it had all been a dream. Maybe I would wake up and everything would be the way it was before we moved to the Palisades, before FD had come into our lives. Simple anxiety over the prospect of divorced parents would be a welcome price to pay given the present reality.

I shoved that wish out of my mind and focused on the effortless pleasure of drifting with the current, vaguely aware I was now far beyond the second buoy. The water lulled me, rocking me and whispering there was no need to worry about anything. Not Mom, or her baby, or Dad, or FD, or school. My only sensation should be the feeling of floating in this moment, the experience of unencumbered serenity. It wouldn't matter if I vanished into oblivion. For the first time in months I was at peace.

"HEY, YOU!"

A distant voice carried through the air. My half-submerged ears couldn't have heard right. No one else could possibly be out this far past the second buoy.

"HEY, YOU...STOP!"

The voice sounded louder this time, breaking the bliss of my watery nirvana. I opened my eyes to a cloudless blue sky and kept drifting.

The voice yelled loud and clear. I looked up to see a man racing toward me on a paddleboard. I rolled onto my stomach and swam hard to keep my distance from him. He kept gliding straight toward me.

"I'M A LIFEGUARD! STOP SWIMMING!" His muscular shoulders powered the board as he paddled furiously, closing the gap between us with frightening speed.

I quickened my strokes. He pulled beside me. I slowed and turned around, dogpaddling in place. I told him I was fine.

In a flash he was in the water, his massive hands clutching me around the waist. "Get on." I shook my head in protest. His size and strength negated any protest. He hoisted me onto the board, then jumped behind and paddled toward shore in fierce sweeping strokes.

My head rested on the board. I watched the world slide by sideways, just like Gidget after Moondoggie rescued her from strangling kelp in Malibu. But I wasn't Gidget and this was no Moondoggie saving his future girlfriend.

Mom's cottage grew bigger. I prayed the lifeguard wouldn't stop right in front of it. Too soon we reached shallow water. He jumped off the board, grabbed my arm with one hand and dragged the board behind him with the other. We sloshed through foam past the wet sand and kept going. He didn't say a word, just traipsed to the lifeguard station with me stumbling in tow. Sunbathers turned to the sound of his heavy paddleboard hitting the sand. The balled up towel coming at me nearly hit my face.

"Anybody ever tell you not to swim alone and not to swim out, but across, parallel with the beach? There's a strong rip current out there today. You were well beyond the buoy. Another hundred feet and I might not have seen you at all! You're lucky I noticed a fresh towel on the beach with no one on it or you'd be half way to Catalina...or gotten exhausted and pulled under by the rip tide."

I busied myself wrapping up in the towel and didn't look up or answer.

"How old are you? Twelve?"

That I couldn't ignore. "Fifteen. And I'm a good swimmer."

"Is that so? Then you should've known good swimmers don't swim out, they swim across. Didn't you realize how far out you were? Why didn't you stop when I called?"

I cleared sand with my foot.

"You live around here? I know most of the locals."

"No, I'm...visiting an aunt. She lives a few blocks up."

After rubbing a towel over his hair he flicked it over his head and grabbed the ends. "I won't call your aunt this time, but I will have to fill out a Rescue Card in case you pull this stunt again. Don't move."

In three strides he bounded up the ladder to the lifeguard station and disappeared inside. Thirty seconds later he was back with a clipboard. It was easy enough coming up with a fake name for the aunt—unfortunately the only one I could think of was 'Bordeaux'— along with the only address besides Mom's I had noticed. I figured he wouldn't find out Aunt Bordeaux lived at the Texaco station in town. No, I couldn't remember her phone number. He finished the paperwork and tossed the clipboard on the sand.

"Alright, kid. You can go. But next time, swim across, not out. Got it?"

"Got it." I turned and started toward the stairs.

"You're welcome for the rescue and holding off on the phone call."

I pretended not to hear. At the stairs I waited for a family of four to reach the bottom. The kids charged across the beach. The parents followed, dropping their gear close to the water. The mom laid out a blanket while the dad opened an umbrella and stuck the post deep in the sand. The kids rummaged through a beach bag and retrieved plastic shovels and buckets before scrambling to the water, squealing with delight as their parents watched.

If only I belonged to them.

9

FAMILY OF ONE

Mom gave birth to a healthy boy in early August. She would be home mid-month after her body had regained some semblance of her pre-pregnant shape.

It was getting harder every day to hide my depression beneath the mounting weight of this new secret on top of the old one. Maintaining a low profile with a few friends during summer was a far cry from fooling the masses, which was exactly what I would be trying to pull off once school started in a few weeks. What a horrible way to begin my junior year.

On a Saturday morning I watched through the kitchen window as Dad's car disappeared into the garage. A moment later Mom walked through the same door FD had walked through so many times in another life. She stood facing me in all her coiffed magnificence, her long, loose hair replaced by an obedient pageboy. Other than that, she looked the same as when she'd left seven months earlier. For a moment I imagined she was walking in from Sunday mass and had never left home at all.

"Hello, Clarice."

I ignored her and grabbed a Coke from the fridge.

"I see a few rules have fallen by the wayside. Is Coke an acceptable beverage now?"

"Guess so."

Mom set her purse on the counter. She faced me with the same cucumber cold composure she'd had the morning she claimed she and Dad would never get a divorce, the morning I'd blown my cover as Kit put it.

"Clarice, we might as well get a few things straight. For your father's sake, I want this to work out, but I will not tolerate any sass from you. I know you two have...have leaned on each other these last several months, but I'm warning you—do not force his loyalty."

"Like you would know what the word means."

Her mouth twisted in a sardonic grin. "So this is how you want to play it? Young lady, you might do well to remember our discussion about boarding school last year. Do you understand what I'm saying? Don't push me, Clarice."

I glared at her, my face a mask of defiance. Her threats couldn't hurt me. She was the intruder now. This was our home, mine and Dad's.

A door slammed. Dad squeezed in from the garage with a box of books and an exaggerated smile. "Ah. I see you two have said hello. Vi, these go in the bedroom?"

Mom flinched at his use of her nickname and kept her eyes on me. "Yes, in my office."

As Dad walked out of the kitchen I spun on my heels and followed him.

*

School started the first week in September. I slid under the radar of my social circle and concentrated on getting through classes. Assignments that had once come so easily now required massive effort. Had anyone noticed my dark circles I was ready with a story about a neighbor's barking dog keeping me awake at night. By the end of the first week, no one had noticed anything wrong, a testament to my performance as a live human being.

Latin class ran ten minutes over and I had to stop at

my locker. There was still a chance I could catch the early bus. The bell rang. I was halfway through the door when Sister Dorothea touched my arm. She waited to speak until the classroom was empty.

"I'd like a moment, Clarice. Sit down, will you?"

Glancing in the direction of my locker, I resigned myself to missing the bus and let the book bag slide down my shoulder. I sat in a front row desk. Sister Dorothea leaned against hers with a face full of concern. Her arms were folded beneath the habit, which gave her the appearance of not having any limbs at all. I used to laugh about it with Francie.

"Clarice, this is the third year you've been in my class. I can usually count on you for kicking off a good discussion. This first week of school you've hardly said a word. The few times I've called on you I've had to repeat the question because you've been so preoccupied. Is everything alright?"

My throat went dry. "Yes, Sister."

"I haven't seen you with Francie. You two used to be inseparable."

"We're...not as close as we used to be."

"I see. Everything okay at home?" She searched my face for an honest answer, her caring expression reassuring me that I could confide.

Oh yeah, everything's peachy. My mother had an affair with Father Big Celebrity Donnelly, got pregnant. She left me and Dad while she went to have the baby. My dad fell apart. She just came home and he thinks we can just pick up where we left off, like the whole thing never happened. I can't confide in a living soul about Father Donnelly or my parents. These secrets are eating me alive.

"Yes, Sister. Everything's fine."

"I know college is important to you, Clarice. You have nothing to worry about with your grades. Perhaps a little more social life might take the edge off the pressure you're putting on yourself. You have dark circles under your eyes and you've lost what, ten pounds over the summer?"

The barking dog story came in handy followed by another about jumping on the Mayo-Clinic-Grapefruit-Diet bandwagon to account for the weight loss. Her face told me she didn't buy either story for a minute.

"May I go now, Sister? I don't want to miss the bus and I still have to go to my locker."

"Yes, you can go."

I leaned over to grab my bag and got up. She came away from the desk and took me by the shoulders. "Clarice, I hope you know you can confide in me. I may be able to help. We could talk somewhere else where you wouldn't be seen. No one would have to know."

How I wished she would wrap her arms around me, take me home for a dinner of roast beef and mashed potatoes and green beans with people who hadn't poisoned each other with toxic secrets. After dinner she would draw me a hot bath and visit while I soaked. She would tuck me into bed between fresh sheets and sit close until I drifted into a deep, dreamless sleep.

The next morning I would wake and my life would be normal. Mom and Dad would pick me up in Mom's new Ford. She would be happy, not because of the Ford. She would be happy to see me.

Kit would be with them, never having been pregnant. We would still share a bedroom and the big Marlborough K would look down on us. FD would come over Friday nights to watch *The Twilight Zone*. He would be my friend,

Kit's friend, Dad's friend. Mom would be his real reason for coming over and she would flirt because she's Mom, but they wouldn't be lovers.

He would be a real priest. God wouldn't have abandoned me. I would go to UCLA, become a writer, marry a man I loved and live in a *Father Knows Best* house with three kids and two dogs. My life would have meaning. I would grow old and die surrounded by family.

"Yes, Sister, I know I can talk to you if I need to."

A look passed between us, both of us knowing I would never confide in her.

*

At home we had settled into our usual, pre-baby routine, the pre-baby designation usurping FD's pre and post arrival in our lives as the new line of demarcation in the family chronology. Sometimes I thought I might be going mad. The way everyone acted I wondered if I had gone over the edge. No one else had changed, at least not in how we acted with each other. I had to remind myself that these last seven plus months hadn't been fantasy, they had been very real. Mom, Dad and FD had been able to put it behind them. I was the one stuck in a time warp. One of us was in an alternate reality. It must've been me.

This particular afternoon I walked in from school to find Mom and FD in the kitchen in deep discussion about Kit. They glanced at me and kept talking. I grabbed an apple as my eavesdropping cover. From what I gathered washing the fruit, Mom had opened a letter addressed to Dad. Kit had invited him to Bogota to meet his five-month-old grandson.

For a moment I thought I'd heard a tinge of sadness in Mom. By the time the apple was dry familiar fumes of fury filled the air, even with Kit three thousand miles away.

"Walker will go to Colombia over my dead body, grandson or no grandson."

"Vivienne, the man wants to see his first grandchild. That's understandable. Why don't you go down there with him, bury the hatchet?"

"That's a great idea, Jack. Kit would love nothing more than my showing up on her doorstep so she could flaunt that damn maid. No thank you."

"I'm sure Walker won't mind going alone." FD was teasing her the way he always had.

"I'll say it again. Walker will go to Bogota over my dead body. I'm sure by now Kit has bored everyone within earshot with tales of her evil mother. Her father showing up alone would only make them believe if they hadn't already."

"Vivienne, forget about Kit for a moment, forget about Aida. You have a grandchild."

"Yes, and I have a right to see that grandchild. If I know that girl she'll do everything she possibly can to prevent that, even if they were to visit Carlos's uncle in Santa Monica. Kit would jump at the opportunity to humiliate me."

"I didn't know you even liked babies, Mom."

Daggers shot from those cobalt eyes. "For the love of God, Clarice Cavanaugh, where on earth did you ever get that idea?"

"I once heard you tell FD that if you'd had the Pill you wouldn't have had kids."

"Young lady, what I say to Jack is none of your business, and for your information we were talking about a hypothetical situation. When you eavesdrop all you get is misinformation. Now why don't you take that apple and go to your room."

I grabbed a napkin and started walking. "Do you know his name?"

"Whose name?"

"The baby... do you know his name?"

"Carlitos. We will be referring to him as your cousin Carl, if we refer to him at all."

Nobody went to Colombia to meet the baby. As far as Mom was concerned, Kit and Carlitos didn't exist. She never mentioned their names and Dad was careful not to either.

By now I would've thought Mom and FD would be finished taking on joint projects, the baby being the grand finale. I was wrong. Their next endeavor would be their last. It would also mark the beginning of the end for me.

FD arrived as usual for Sunday dinner. If the tacit agreement to bury the past had been designed to ease the strain of what those months had cost, it wasn't working. The tension between my parents felt thicker than ever. Pre-baby Dad had worried about Mom leaving. Post-baby there was no doubt. Dad was keenly aware of the devastating impact such an event would exact on his well-being.

Mom set the dining room table with French linen and polished silver on Sundays for FD's benefit. Tonight was the same, so I didn't see it coming. Dad's place at the head of the table was the only remaining vestige of his role as head of the family.

FD stood near the buffet and studied a wine label as he explained his choice in a professorial tone, as if it mattered to anyone but Mom. He had assigned himself sommelier—selecting, buying, serving the wine—and performed his role with great ceremony. I wondered if the wine he'd consecrated at the altar that morning had given him near the satisfaction of the spectacle that followed at our table.

FD popped the cork and took a long whiff, then wrapped the bottle in a tea towel and carried it with both hands to the table. For a moment he looked like a man with a newborn, the responsibility of carrying something precious and fragile informing every step. It was a shock to my system each time I remembered FD was a father.

Had he and Mom held their baby, experienced the wonder of bringing a new life into the world? Had they felt the joy of being a family before handing the baby over for adoption?

A clinking noise broke my daydream. The Waterford wine glasses had been a gift to Mom, who now followed the Wine Steward's lead as aptly as any seasoned acolyte on the altar. She lifted the glass and flicked her fingernail against the rim. A sickening smile confirmed that FD had chosen well and signaled her pleasure at the clear, high-pitched ring of fine crystal.

Dad and I exchanged glances to steel ourselves for the final nauseating phase. The lovers offered vivid descriptions of the Chateauneuf du Pape—the rich color, the scents of vanilla, red fruit, and cinnamon, the perfectly controlled blend of grape varieties, the full-bodied texture—all the while knowing such nuances were lost on Dad.

FD shuffled to my side of the table. With a wink he filled my glass half-way. "Your mother says teenagers in France drink wine at every meal. I expect you could handle a small glass with dinner."

"Mom would know all about drinking habits in France after her long stay with Aunt Bordeaux." I lifted my glass in an air toast to Mom. Her face turned as red as the wine.

Liquid gurgled as FD poured with one hand and squeezed her shoulder with the other. "Let me finish my official duties here, then Reese, we have something to discuss with you."

My fork hung mid-air. "Oh, no."

"Dear girl," he said with trademark grin, "you have no faith, that's your problem. Did it ever occur to you this might be good news? Vivienne, do you care to take it from here?"

"Last Wednesday I went with Jack on his weekly visit to Our Lady of the Angels convent in downtown Los Angeles."

"So? What does that have to do with me?"

"Be careful, Clarice." Her measured tone had an edge. "I was given permission to accompany Jack as he counseled these nuns. Now bear in mind, cloistered nuns have taken vows of silence, chastity, and poverty. They own nothing. Well, it just so happens one of these nuns has wanted to leave the Order for a very long time. She has no money, no family, that is, none to speak of. She literally has no home to go to. I doubt you can even begin to imagine what that must feel like, Clarice, not having a family to turn to."

I tilted my head with indifference. Dad kept his eyes on the roast beef, a reluctant participant in whatever he knew was coming.

"So Jack and I, and your father, of course, thought the least we could do, now that Kit's gone I mean, is offer her our home."

"A nun? Here?"

"She wouldn't be a nun anymore. That's the point."

"Won't she get excommunicated?"

"Jack is helping her compose a letter to the Vatican to request dispensation from the Pope. That may take years. In the meantime this is a matter between her and God." Mom lifted her glass and inspected the bottom for any that might drip on her dress.

"Well, if French kissing is a mortal sin, a nun breaking her vows must be a ticket straight to hell."

"Clarice Cavanaugh! You watch your smart-aleck mouth!"

"Vivienne—"

Mom took a slug of Bordeaux.

"Reese, this nun, Petra, has thought about this grave decision for three years. If Pope John Paul grants her dispensation, she'll still be in the Church. Either way, she has chosen to leave the Order. The best way we can help is to support her decision. She's stepping into the world after fourteen years of cloistered life. Can you imagine how intimidating that must feel?"

"Okay, so she's leaving the convent. And you guys want her to live here. Is that it?"

"Not quite. Your mother and Dad and I are in need of your help. We know you'll do all you can to help Petra adjust, which won't be too hard because she'll be bunking with you."

"ME? You're asking me to share my room with some old NUN?"

"I cannot think of a better person than you. Petra will need companionship. She'll need to learn about life on the outside, the music, the clothes, the behavior of a young single woman. And she's not old. She's only thirty-two."

"She's closer in age to you guys. Why stick her with me?"

"In chronological age, yes, she's closer to our age. You

have to remember she's been cloistered since she left high school at eighteen. Emotionally, that makes her closer to you. That makes you the perfect influence for assimilating her into our youth culture. Besides, you have a natural compassion, a sweetness. She'll need that most of all."

"I've changed. I'm not so sweet anymore." I tossed the fork across the Nortaki china plate.

"Ah, Reese, but you are sweet. I knew that the moment I met you. It's who you are at the core. That you cannot change. Accept it, dear girl, you're a very special soul. And we need you right now. So, what do you say, old friend?"

Old friend. Did he think I was born yesterday? The man had a remarkable ability to sound sincere even when he wasn't.

There was no point arguing about it. We both knew there was only one answer. The nun would bunk with me.

10

THE FINAL NAIL

I got to work on the bedroom. Mom bought new sheets and comforter. I cleared space in the closet. My movie magazine pictures of a shirtless Troy Donahue went into a desk drawer. I finished off the face lift with strategic placement of new throw pillows for pops of color. Mom and I had to admit the room looked inviting with sunshine flooding through the Venetian blinds. Stage set.

Sunday afternoon FD's car slipped into the garage. Dad and I waited in the kitchen for my so-called protégé. The trio emerged with FD in the lead with his big goofy grin.

"Ah! And here, Petra, is the incomparable, indefatigable Miss Reese Cavanaugh: Youth Ambassador to the Stars."

Petra and I faced each other. It was impossible to tell her age. She wore dowdy clothes, polyester pants and a baggy sweater that probably came from a donation bag like the ones we filled from our closets for the church. Petra had apologetic eyes and the biggest dimples I'd ever seen.

She might've been thirty-two, but didn't look much older than Kit with her short stature and flawless skin. Dad noticed right away she had the same youthful quality as FD, the one he said came from not paying a mortgage or having any stress. Fourteen years praying couldn't have had any stress either. Petra probably stopped aging when she entered the convent at eighteen.

The moment our eyes met, I sensed a certain simpatico, perhaps that of captives sharing an uncertain fate who understood the importance of pleasing our captors. Whatever it was, the feeling was instantaneous. I liked this woman-child who needed me to show her the ropes.

Mom gave her a tour of the house, ending in my bedroom, our bedroom now. FD met us there with her suitcase. "Well, this is the girl's dorm, huh?" He and Mom sized up the progress of their plan with nods of satisfaction and left.

I plopped on my bed and picked up a magazine as Petra lifted the suitcase onto her bed. There wasn't much to unpack. A few personal belongings, mostly underclothes, filled only half the space. It was a good thing Mom had bought her starter clothes.

I turned on the radio to fill the silence.

"What's this music? I really like it."

"The Beatles, my absolute favorite group in the world."

Her face was a blank.

"The Beatles? You must've heard of them. They're like, the most famous band in the whole world."

"No. In the House, we were only allowed to listen to certain pieces. We got to listen to The Sound of Music for an hour on Sundays. I like your Beatles."

"Well if you couldn't listen to music, and you couldn't talk and you didn't work...what did you do all day? Pray?"

She chuckled and sat on the bed, shoving the suitcase to make space. "We worked plenty...fourteen hours a day. Our Order made communion hosts for the greater Los Angeles area. The Sisters and I were up at five every morning for prayers. We baked all day until evening vespers and dinner. Then we put in another two hours packaging the hosts for distribution."

"That sounds like slave labor. And you couldn't talk all day? Or listen to music?"

Petra raised her eyebrows and shook her head. She didn't seem to have a single edge of bitterness. In fact, I got the sense this woman didn't have an angry or resentful bone in her body. Kit wouldn't have lasted a day. I wouldn't have fared much better. What an odd way of life, with no music or books, surrounded by friends, working in silence from dawn to dusk. At least the Sisters of Mercy at St. Monica's taught in a classroom all day, which sounded a whole lot better than forming little circles from flour. How had Petra kept from going batty?

As roommates go Kit had been my only experience. Bunking with Petra bore absolutely no resemblance to that. She and I spent every free hour together. While I was at school she completed assignments Mom had given her in typing, filing, letter writing and taking phone messages. I role played with Petra and soon she took over answering our house phone.

Mom sent her on chores to Pronto market for coffee and cigarettes to refresh her memory dealing with money. It astounded me that she had lived fourteen years without basic activities such as locking the front door, making small talk at the store, dealing with cash. A snack between meals made her absolutely giddy with pleasure.

In return for Mom's training, Petra cooked dinner—it turned out she could do much more than bake—and cleaned house, which I helped with on Saturdays. The laundry was also a joint effort. Tedious chores weren't tedious with Petra.

Mom finally had her maid. This one came with a bonus no paid servant like Kit's Rosa could offer. My mother made sure word got around church that Vivienne Cavanaugh had "rescued" a nun from the oppression of cloistered life. True to form, Mom portrayed herself as an advocate, bucking the system of ancient tradition to free a helpless victim.

This was a part of Mom that FD loved—her rebellious nature—especially within the context of Church authority. It didn't matter that beyond the insular Catholic world, questioning the status quo was admired behavior in freewheeling 1964. Not only was it a badge of honor; for a woman who considered herself a feminist and intellectual it was required. Society had finally caught up with Mom.

*

Every night Petra and I talked for hours after lights out. It fascinated me that she had stuck it out so long in the convent. I had to understand why. Otherwise there was no way to determine whether she was weak or strong, an aspect of character plaguing me in my own sense of self.

"What happened to make you want to leave?"

"I was twenty-nine years old and had no idea who I really was. I was terribly lonely. When Father Donnelly filled in for our old priest and brought in a counselor, Aunt Maria, she helped me see I could have a life different than the one I'd fallen into right out of foster care."

"Yeah, she'd be the person to do that. And her real name is Vivienne, not Maria."

"If not for your mom I'd still be in the convent, miserable and lonely. She saved me."

My role as her lifestyle consultant turned out to be a good fit. We peeled back layer after layer of the frumpy, sheltered nun, exploring who she was underneath. Mixing and matching, we hit pay dirt—an A-line skirt, flats, and a Poor Boy sweater, repeated in varying iterations. Armed with pictures from Kit's movie magazines and a can of hair spray, I styled Petra's short dark hair into a close relative of the ducktail.

Petra had adapted quickly to our world. In four short months, with her new look and marketable skills, she was ready for a life of her own.

In January we celebrated my sixteenth birthday with the usual family gathering, which included FD's priest friends. The New Year meant it was time for Petra to face the job market. Two weeks into the job search, she landed one at a yarn shop in Santa Monica—The Skein Game, which Mom and FD gleefully deduced carried an erotic overtone.

Dad perused the classifieds for apartments to rent. A furnished one bedroom duplex off Sunset Boulevard a few miles away filled the bill.

Moving day Petra and I spent the afternoon setting up her new place, both of us encouraging our high spirits to quell the bittersweet moment. I knew her joy was due not only to a newfound feeling of self-sufficiency. It was also because she had found the one thing she'd sought in cloistered life—connection with another human being.

The fact that I turned out to be that person was pure serendipity.

*

Petra's absence deepened the river of tension flowing between me and Mom. The respect, if not outright deference offered by Petra had nurtured Mom's delusion of being a selfless instrument of the Lord. Now she only had me, a sullen teenager whose bitterness reflected the ugly truth. Dad's steadfast façade was wearing thin, chipping away at his belief we could go on as if nothing had changed. It was only a matter of time before he would have to face what he already knew. In the meantime, I hoped the weight of ever-increasing depression didn't flatten me. I had to hang on.

By February I was miserable with Petra gone. Spring break was still two months away. It was hard not to dread long days at home with the tension between me and Mom. As unbearable as the thought was to me, I'm sure it was equally disagreeable to Mom. These were my thoughts as I walked in from school. She was in the kitchen stuffing Bell Peppers.

"Clarice, you're always home right after school. It was all I could do to get your sister here by dinner. Don't you have some club to go to or something?"

"While you were gone I gave up being banned from the house. Dad didn't have a problem with that."

Her back stiffened. "That's because your father was at work. Things are different now. You'll need to get more involved with school activities, not be such a recluse. My gosh, most girls your age are out and about with friends every chance they get."

I poured a glass of milk. "Aren't you the one who's always saying 'just because your friend jumps off a bridge doesn't mean you should'? Besides, I'm not bothering you. I get a snack and go to my room."

"It's awkward having clients in and out with my teenage daughter hanging around. There is an issue of confidentiality, you know."

"Would you prefer I climb through the bedroom window so Mrs. Ellery could see?"

"Don't be smart with me, Clarice." The façade was slipping,

"I'm just pointing out the obvious. This is my home and I have a right to be here when I want, clients or no clients. Maybe you should rent an office and stop seeing clients here."

Mom stopped stuffing and turned to me. "You listen here, young lady. I don't know what things were like when I was away, but I'm here now. Like it or not, I am still your mother and this is still my home. If you think you can whine to your father, I'd think twice. I'll tell him how impossible you've become, with a smart mouth to boot. Now, Miss Cavanaugh, if you want to live here in peace, I suggest you damn well do as I tell you, and I'm telling you to find something to do after school."

"You're right. You don't have a clue what things were like when you were away. As for living in peace, what peace can there be with you here? You've ruined everything!"

"That's it, young lady. I don't have to listen to this." She gritted her teeth. "You're a fool if you think you can compete with me, and if you don't believe me...go ahead, give it a try. Now go to your room."

That's exactly what I did. I slammed the door so hard it might've broken Kit's record. Mom wasn't going to come between me and Daddy. I would make him see Mom was the one who was impossible to live with, that his fairy tale fantasy of happily ever after was a bust.

Kit was wrong about Dad. So was Mom. He would defend me.

*

Saturday afternoon I found Dad puttering in the garage. I sat on a stool and twirled left and right, watching him organizing his work bench. "Dad, I need to talk to you about something."

"Shoot."

"This situation, with Mom, it's not working out."

He didn't answer.

"You have to do something. I've tried my best since she came home in August. It wasn't so bad with Petra here. I cannot stand living in the same house with Mom. She hates me. She says she doesn't want me around because her clients might see me. That's just an excuse. What she really wants is for me to disappear."

"Aren't you being a little dramatic, Peanut? Now where is that half-inch wrench?"

"Dramatic? Dad, how can you forget what she did to us?"

"That's behind us now. I've had to forget about it, and that's what you need to do. It is possible for the three of us to live here as a family, I'm convinced of it. But you have to make more of an effort. You have to cut your mother some slack. She's been through a lot."

"She's been through a lot! What about us?"

"Reese." Dad took a deep breath. His shoulders slumped. "Please, for my sake, and for yours, make more of an effort to make this work. This is what you and I talked about, everything going back to normal."

"Daddy, I've been making an effort and I'm telling you, it's not working. You have to do something! I can't live in the same house with Mom anymore."

He stopped fiddling with his tools, hung his head and spoke in a barely audible voice. "Then, Peanut, honey, you'll have to find somewhere else to live."

At first I thought I'd heard wrong. The room turned white and spun. I felt lightheaded, dizzy. I waited for him to say he didn't mean it. He just sat there with his hands resting on his knees, head hanging.

I burst out the door. Blood swooshed through my ears. I ran down the stairs through the yard to the gate and didn't slow down until I hit the ocean.

That night in bed I stared at the ceiling and visualized the big Marlboro K, trying to remember Kit and what life had been like before everything changed. It was well past midnight with no hope in sight for sleep. I thought about my test the next day in Honors English. I wanted to do well, wanted to show Brother McPherson I understood his saying we could find comfort in poetry, the secret language in which he and I communicated through Edna St. Vincent Millay, Yeats, Frost.

I focused on something pleasant to make me sleepy — the image of Dad playing his harmonica at our old house. He would straddle a chair in the dim hallway light until the music carried me far, far away.

Two o'clock, no luck.

Mom's sleeping pills.

I tiptoed down the hall to the bathroom. The bottle was almost full. I got a glass of water, then gently tapped the container to coax a pill into my hand. Ten tumbled out, little red Good-N-Plenty's cupped in my palm. I didn't move a muscle. Adrenaline electrified my body in a tingling sensation.

I felt strange, devoid of emotion, watching from someplace far away. Everything became crystal clear. How had I not seen what had been right in front of me? The secrets I'd been keeping for three years had drained the life out of me. My spirit was gone, my soul was gone, my body exhausted and numbed by depression. This was not a life or death moment. This was a moment of revelation. I was already dead, and had been for a long time.

My heart began to slow. The electric charge fizzled into a flat calm. I tossed the pills into my mouth. The plastic coated bullets stuck to the walls. I glugged the glass of water and poured another. A second handful went in. This time the pills clumped in gridlock. I gagged and gulped the glass of water. The third handful went down easily, as did the fourth.

The bottle was empty.

I crawled into bed with Cyrano and said three Hail Marys.

11

WANDERER

"Arrrghhhhh…acchhh."

A tube the size of a fire hose filled my throat. I coughed and flailed in panic. My right arm was tied to a bedrail with an IV connected to bottles hanging on a pole.

A nurse appeared. "Miss Cavanaugh, keep still. You're alright. You're in St. John's Hospital Intensive Care Unit. The tube is helping you breathe."

I thrashed and shook my head.

The nurse held my shoulder. "Breathe through your nose with me. In, out, in, out…okay, that's better. The more you fight it, the harder it will be to breathe."

I tried to focus on what she was saying. My mind felt so fuzzy, like someone was holding a pillow over my face. I wasn't dead. I was in the hospital. The nurse leaned close.

"Here, let me suction you. I know it feels like you're choking. Try not to swallow or push the tube out with your tongue." She vacuumed my mouth with a small plastic hose. "We'll remove the tube once we're sure you're breathing on your own."

She studied the beeping machine, green waves peaking and dropping with each breath. "A machine has been breathing for you. When the ambulance brought you to the ER, you were having trouble breathing on your own."

I felt trapped in the bed, uncomfortable, restricted. I tugged at the bedrail.

"The tube is giving you fluids and electrolytes intravenously. We tied your arm to keep you from dislodging the needle. You're fighting the ventilator again...keep breathing for me...in...out...nice and slow. That's a girl."

She brushed the damp hair from my cheeks and shined a tiny flashlight in my eyes. "You've been in a deep sleep for almost thirty hours."

A doctor stepped through the curtain. The nurse said something about pupils being equal and reactive to light. He watched the breathing machine. Panic returned. The green waves reverted to irregular jumps and starts. I remembered the nurse's instructions. The waves settled down.

"I'm Dr. Pasternak, Miss Cavanaugh. I'm going to take the tube out. You can help by not resisting. I'll do it quickly once I turn the ventilator off." The mechanical whooshing sound petered out. "Ready? Okay, here we go."

Out, out, out came the fat cylinder, inch by inch like some gruesome magic trick. I clenched the sheet, certain the tube must've been sand-coated. The foreign object came out in one final sting. The doctor watched my chest. "You'll have a sore throat for a few days." A woman called his name. He swatted the curtain aside and left.

The nurse untied me from the bedrail. Both hands flew to my neck to soothe the rawness in my throat.

"The ward clerk called your parents half an hour ago when you started waking up. They'll be in after they see the doctor. I'll order you some broth." She turned and left.

My eavesdropping ears picked up a hushed voice. "We were able to keep her heart rate up. It was touch and go there for a while. She's awake. Expect her to be foggy and confused. It's not brain damage; your daughter has been in a mild coma. It'll be a day or so before she's fully awake. If you hadn't called the ambulance when you did, we might be having a different conversation.

"Does she know she's not coming home today?"

"I'll let you tell her. We'll keep her here and monitor her vital signs for a while, then transfer her down to One North."

I must've fallen back to sleep. Mom and Dad were leaning over the bedrail. Mom's face was drained of color. Dad's was pale and haggard, a look I knew all too well.

"You've given us quite a scare, Peanut. I sure am glad to see those beautiful brown eyes."

Mom was silent. Whatever concern she'd felt was short-lived, irritation in its place. "What in the world were you trying to do? You scared the bee-Jesus out of us." They dropped into chairs squeezed against the bed. I avoided their faces and cringed at anguish in Dad's voice.

"Don't you know how much we love you, Peanut? What would I do if anything happened to you?"

"Of course she knows. She was just trying to scare us, isn't that right, Clarice?"

"I'm sorry if I scared you. I want to go home now."

"Well that's not going to happen. The doctor says you need to be evaluated. They're transferring you to the psychiatric floor."

"I won't go!"

"Oh you'll go, and don't try to make this out as anyone's doing but your own, young lady. You can thank your lucky stars that our health insurance covers it."

Mom's words had not one shred of compassion. Why would they? This is what she'd wanted all along—me, out of the way—and keeping her hands clean the same way they had been banishing Kit. This was the doctor's call, not hers.

What would he think if I explained I was doing exactly what my parents wanted? There was no other way to interpret their message. Mom had demanded I disappear after school until dinnertime. Dad had told me I would have to find another place to live. My overdose had given them a solution far better than any boarding school in Arizona. Blue Cross would cover my exile.

*

The next morning I changed into the clothes Dad had left on his way to work and followed a nurse down three floors. The words on the door at the end of the hall were big enough to read from the elevator:

PSYCHIATRIC UNIT
Visitors must check in at the nurses' station.

The door opened into a long hallway divided by a glassed-in nurses' station. We didn't stop. Residual grogginess kept me from feeling nervous. Two patients passed us dressed in regular clothes. They looked normal. Normal like me, which now meant crazy. At the end of the hall we stopped at another door, this one with a small window at eye level and a sign.

Locked Unit
No Admittance

The nurse tapped the glass. A red-haired woman with porcelain skin and a friendly face opened the heavy door and stepped aside to let me in. The ICU nurse handed her my chart and left.

"Hello, Clarice. My name is Shirley. I'm the day nurse. We've been expecting you. Let me show you around the unit."

The room was not any bigger than our kitchen,

furnished like a living room with a small table and four chairs on one end. I counted three patients—an older woman working on a jigsaw puzzle, another who looked to be Mom's age sketching by the window, and a young man who looked half asleep on the sofa.

Shirley stepped over to a nurse's desk and added the metal ICU chart to the pile of four. "It's alright, Clarice, we won't bite. These are your roommates, so to speak. Kate is on the open unit...you'll meet her later." Each patient turned and acknowledged me. None of them looked crazy either.

"Patients back here eat meals in the common room and days are spent doing different therapeutic activities. We have our own little world here in the locked unit. An Occupational Therapist comes back three mornings a week and an Art Therapist once a week. Once your doctor gives the okay, you'll be able to spend time on the open unit."

Shirley made it sound as if I would be here for months.

"Each patient has their own room back here." She motioned me to a corner room and extracted the biggest key ring I had ever seen from deep in the pocket of her uniform dress. The thing was as wide around as a soda can and heavy with metal. She unlocked the door.

It was impossible to mask my surprise. The bed with a peach coverlet faced a big window overlooking the front of the hospital.

"You'll be able to do your school work here," Shirley said, nodding toward a desk.

"I don't think I'll be here long enough for that. I'm going home in a few days."

Nurse Shirley started to say something. Instead she gave me a lopsided smile and suggested I write a list of things I needed from home "just in case."

We returned to the common room and sat down at the table. Shirley handed me a menu and explained I would make my own choices. Assuming the doctor ordered no restrictions, I could have anything on the menu, even steak every night if I wanted. Insurance is a wonderful thing, Shirley said with a conniving twinkle. Yes, I thought, every sixteen-year-old should go to sleep wishing she could wake up in the locked psychiatric unit of a private hospital so she could order steak every night.

The heavy door opened and clanged shut. A man in his twenties dressed in white entered.

"This good-looking guy is Ian, Reese. He's my partner in crime on the day shift. He's full of mischief, but plays a mean game of backgammon and he's not a bad listener either."

"Welcome to our little family. In a few days you'll like it back here so much you won't want to go to the open unit. You play backgammon?"

The next day after work Dad brought my books and assignments. My heart dropped at the thought of missing Brother McPherson's class and wondered what he must be thinking. I had never missed a single day of school.

I handed Dad my list: Cyrano, two pullover sweaters, jeans, tennis shoes and toiletries, which had to be kept with the nurse. As he looked it over, I grabbed the paper and added *Best Loved Poems of the American People*, a hefty volume Dad had given me for Christmas last year.

Shirley poured a cup of coffee and joined me and the other patients for breakfast. The phantom patient, Kate, spent her days on the open unit. I must've been making up calories from my ICU stay because I was starving. Orange peel and an empty bowl was all that was left after

I inhaled the cream of wheat. My eyes watered as the orange slices stung my raw throat. Shirley waited for the others to leave the table.

"Reese, at eleven o'clock Ian is going to escort you to the medical building across the street to meet Dr. Granzow for your first appointment."

"Who's he?"

"Dr. Granzow is your psychiatrist. He'll—"

"What psychiatrist?"

Shirley set her coffee mug on the table. She reached over and put her hand on mine. It felt warm, soft. "Hon, didn't anyone explain that you'd be seeing a psychiatrist every day?"

"No. Anyway there's no point in my seeing a psychiatrist. My mom said I was only here to be evaluated. That can't take more than a couple of days."

"Reese, hon. Nobody goes home from the locked unit in a couple of days. This is psychiatric intensive care. Seeing your doctor, participating in our therapeutic program, that's the whole point of being here. That's the way you're evaluated."

I met her warm eyes, tears burning mine. I hadn't wanted to admit Dad's bringing me clothes and schoolwork had been a sure sign I wasn't going home tomorrow. Staying locked up was one thing, talking to a psychiatrist was quite another. "I don't need a psychiatrist. I'm not crazy."

"Well, I don't know what you mean by crazy. You've been admitted to the locked unit directly from ICU because you made a serious suicide attempt. There has to be something causing you tremendous distress. Your psychiatrist will help you figure that out, help you find other ways to deal with your emotions. We're all here to help you get better."

I let out a shaky breath and turned to the window. The street was quiet, too early for visitors.

Shirley squeezed my hand. "Ian will walk you over at eleven."

I nodded without looking at her, wishing I could disappear.

Ian unlocked the door. The open unit seemed big and empty after being in tight quarters. We passed the nurses' station where I had come in from ICU and kept walking until we reached the back door. Ian unlocked it and I walked outside to a Staff Only parking lot.

I squinted in the morning sun. "Shirley said the doctor was across the street."

Ian grinned. "Yeah, yeah. She's right, but there's no harm in taking the long way around, get a little sunshine. You haven't been outside in a few days."

He saw my confused expression.

"Don't worry. Shirley knows my little trick. C'mon, let's enjoy the walk."

The sunshine felt good in the cool spring air. We paralleled the hospital and crossed the street to a three-story building in what would be the first of many trips to Dr. Granzow's office. Ian stayed with me in the waiting room where piped-in music and richly upholstered furniture made it look nothing like the waiting room at my dentist's. A few minutes later a man opened the inner door to his office. Ian nodded to him and left.

The room was low lit with overstuffed leather chairs. The severe looking man in his sixties with a long face and sunken cheeks retreated to a massive desk. He spoke in a German accent.

"Hello, Clarice. I'm Dr. Granzow. I'm going to be

seeing you while you're in the hospital. The focus of this first session is to get to know a little about you, what's going on in your life." He folded his hands on the desk. "Why don't you tell me about school, your friends."

I ran my hands along the cool leather arms of the chair and didn't answer.

"How do you get along with your parents?"

"Fine."

"It's alright to talk to me, Clarice. Everything we discuss is completely confidential."

Dr. Granzow lit a pipe, dipping the match into the tobacco pot several times between short puffs before taking a full drag and filling the air with pungent smoke. I frowned and swiped it away with a muffled cough.

He leaned back, pipe clenched between his teeth. The leather chair deflated with a noise that sounded like someone passing gas. "So...everything is fine at school and at home and with your friends. You overdosed for no reason. Is that it?"

There was no point in saying anything. One answer would lead to another question and another, each exchange pushing me further into a corner.

"Is this the first time you have tried to hurt yourself?"

Laguna Beach flashed before me, the sweet memory of swimming past the buoys with no one around, the ocean current taking me far, far away.

"You know, Clarice, if you want to get well and go home, we have to work together. I can't help you if I don't know what's causing you so much distress."

Nothing I could say would be true or right. The smell of tobacco made me nauseated. Or was it the secrets eroding my insides.

Dr. Granzow waited. I retreated deep into myself, into

my own bomb shelter where I lived in darkness. Twenty minutes ticked by. He sprang forward in the chair and laid his pipe in a clean ashtray. In a rough move he grabbed the top chart from a neat stack and began writing. Five minutes later he flicked the top closed and picked up another. Then another. He never looked up and his face was a blank.

A clock chimed on the quarter hour, the half hour, and finally the forty-five minute mark. Dr. Granzow checked his watch. He closed the fountain pen and walked to the door. Without acknowledging Ian, the doctor returned to his desk and picked up another chart.

Ian and I left the office and headed back to the unit, taking the long way around.

Saturday Mom and Dad came to visit. Mom sat in the upholstered chair next to the night stand. Dad set down the pile of things from my list and straddled the one at the desk. I was cross-legged on the bed.

"Well, if this isn't the cat's pajamas! It looks more like a luxury hotel than a hospital room."

"Maybe we should trade places." I retrieved Cyrano from the pile Dad had set on the bed and plopped him on my pillow in the same position he occupied at home.

The visit was awkward for all of us. Neither of them said anything about why I was in the hospital and I was afraid to ask how long I had to stay. Thirty miserable minutes later, Dad gave Mom the cue with some excuse about needing to stop by his office as long as they were in Santa Monica.

"Walker, will you leave us girls alone for a moment? We need to talk about womanly things, if you catch my drift."

"Huh? Oh, sure! I'll just be outside flirting with that

redhead."

Mom tapped a pack of cigarettes against her finger until one stuck out.

"You can't smoke in here, Mom."

Irritation clouded her face. She slapped the Old Gold back into place and dropped the pack into her open purse on the nightstand. The glare she gave me turned my stomach. "About this psychiatrist they have you seeing... I want you to think long and hard about what you tell him. A lot has happened this last year. It won't do any of us a shred of good having a stranger poking his nose into our personal business. What goes on in this family is a private matter among the three of us. Do you understand what I'm saying?"

Cyrano's ear felt velvety between my fingers. I slid the plush forward then back, enjoying the two kinds of softness. I wasn't about to give Mom the satisfaction of assurance. Let her worry for once, spend a few sleepless nights. Let her find out what it feels like to have gnawing in your gut day in and day out.

Mom exhaled hard through her nose. "Look, I don't know what to make of that little stunt you pulled with the sleeping pills. If you think feeling sorry for yourself is going to change anything, you'd better think again. You aren't the one who has suffered here, Clarice. You're not the one who had to go away then come home and reconstruct your life."

"Who's feeling sorry for who? Or, excuse me, *whom*?"

Her face turned red and blotchy. "I'm hardly feeling sorry for myself. What I am doing is thinking about what's best for all of us...you, me, and most of all, your father. We don't need our name dragged through the mud. I don't care if these people are professionals, the minute you tell anyone it'll be all over town. Gossip spreads faster than cheap lipstick. If you care anything at all about the welfare of this family, you'll keep our troubles to yourself." She leaned back, softening her voice. "Then when you come home, you and I can start over, try to do a little better. Can we agree to that plan?"

I held a horizontal Cyrano over my mouth.

"Okay, you want to give me the silent treatment. Fine." Mom got up and came closer. She gathered a clump of my hair and held it for a moment, then flung it across my face, making my eyes water from the sting. "Don't cross me, Clarice. Don't even try. You think you feel alone now? Just see what happens if any of this gets out. I'll make sure you never set foot in my house again."

She turned to leave. "By the way, a letter came from your sister. I wasn't aware you were corresponding. That comes to an end right now. I'll be damned if I'm going to have you two criticizing me."

"Mom! What harm is there in a letter?"

"Your father understands you are not to get anymore letters from Kit, or Petra for that matter. I'm going to give you the benefit of the doubt and assume you haven't aired our dirty laundry with her. I'm going to make sure it stays that way."

"I'm not a prisoner. You can't just cut off communication."

She smirked. "Let's just say this is a reminder of how miserable I can make your life. I'll save the letters for when you come home."

I listened to Mom and Dad chat for a moment with Shirley. The heavy door closed behind them with a bang. I fell back on the bed and cried.

Monday through Friday for two weeks Ian escorted me

to Dr. Granzow's office. We always took the longest route. Monday through Friday for two weeks I chatted with Ian both ways. I said nothing during my fifty-minute session.

I was the only adolescent in the locked unit, or the open unit for that matter. Everyone on staff was kind to me, especially Shirley and Ian. They teased me about ordering the same menu every day—half a roast beef sandwich with mustard on whole wheat and a hard boiled egg for breakfast, a vegetable salad for lunch, a five-ounce filet mignon and fresh green beans for dinner, plus the occasional custard before bed from the fridge in the day room.

For the first time in three years I had an appetite.

Dad contacted school about my "mononucleosis". Twice a week on his way into work he collected assignments from school and delivered them to me. The completed work I gave him in exchange would be dropped off at school the next time.

Mom joined him on Saturday afternoons for a visit, no doubt to keep up appearances more than to check on me. Our conversations were laden with tension and limited to everything other than anything important. FD joined them sometimes. His corny jokes gave us a reprieve from each other.

No one at school had a clue I was in the hospital. One Saturday Francie showed up at my house and ran into Dad on his way to the car with two of my blouses on hangers. Dad finally explained where I really was and swore her to secrecy.

Two weeks after zero progress in our sessions, Dr. Granzow took another approach and allowed me to participate in therapeutic activities on the open unit. The order stipulated I was to return at lunch to the locked unit where meals were served with plastic utensils instead of metal ones. I didn't mind. Shirley was my favorite person in the place and it was comforting being among familiar faces.

On the open unit I said little in group therapy. That changed with the Recreation Therapist. He invited me to play ping pong and I nearly cried for joy. Derrick won all our games in the beginning. Once the rust wore off, we split the wins fifty-fifty. The Recreation Therapist was a big athletic guy, the same size as Dad, with Elvis Presley hair he combed at regular intervals.

Playing ping pong reminded me of the countless hours Greg Stewart and I had spent hitting across the table, talking about everything under the sun, our game score inconsequential.

From what I gathered that was the same idea with the Recreational Therapist—get the patient to loosen up and talk. The meat of any conversation would be recorded in the chart and shared with staff. After a few days of friendly chit chat, Derrick began interjecting probing questions. He was proud of his degree in Psychology and the two additional years needed for his state license. I liked Derrick, and we did talk. There wasn't much to chart. I had become expert in the art of evasion.

One evening after dinner I was on my bed doing homework. Shirley popped her head in the door, which had to remain open. ICU staff had to be able to see patients at all times. She told me I had a visitor. Brother McPherson, large as life, appeared in the doorway. I almost didn't recognize him in khaki pants and a light green pullover sweater instead of his cassock.

"Brother McPherson!"

"Hello, Reese. I hope you don't mind my coming to see

you." He laid a book bag on the desk and sat down in the chair near the bed. "And please, call me Tim."

"How did you know I was here?"

"I got the story about mono from Sister Dorothea and Francie. Something told me there was more to it. Last night I called your Dad. He finally told me."

I felt heat rise to my face.

"How are you feeling?"

"I feel okay. I mean…I'm not sick."

"Right. Of course. I just meant—" It was his turn to blush.

"It's okay. We both know I'm here for a reason."

"I'd sensed for a long time that you were unhappy. I just didn't know how deeply troubled you were. I wish I'd known. A number of times you seemed like you wanted to talk after class. I hope you know you can confide in me."

I yanked Cyrano into my lap and stroked his ears.

"You know, Reese, I might understand what you're going through, what you're feeling, emotionally," he said, "and I'm a first class listener."

Brother McPherson leaned forward in the chair, hands on his knees, the same immaculate, soft–looking hands as FD. How I had longed to confide in him, dreamed of resting my head on his broad shoulder and letting him comfort me. I knew, just as I had with Petra, the truth would sound beyond credibility. I would lose whatever friendship I had with my beloved teacher.

"I'm sure you are a great listener. This is something I have to work out on my own."

He nodded and sat up straight. "Hey, I brought you something I think might cheer you up." Two hefty volumes of poetry came out of the book bag—Gerard

Manley Hopkins and William Butler Yeats. The third was a thin one of Robert Frost.

"Are these for assignments?"

"No. These are friends I turn to when I'm down."

"I didn't think holy men ever felt down."

"Oh, you'd be surprised."

"You turn to poets for answers instead of God?"

"He leaves a lot of it to us."

"Or in my case, all of it."

"I doubt that," he chuckled. "The Lord is there for you as much as me."

There was no point telling him God had abandoned me without explaining why. It might as well have been Dr. Granzow in the chair instead of Brother McPherson.

"I've bookmarked a few poems I think you'll find especially meaningful. Maybe we can talk about them next time. That is, if I'm welcome back." He fiddled with his fingernails. "You and I are kindred spirits, Reese. And now that I've confessed I'm still searching for answers, I'm going to keep reminding you what I keep reminding myself—they're not out there. They're in here."

Kindred spirits? Not likely. I suspect part of Brother McPherson's youthful demeanor resulted from having lived his twentysomething life sequestered from treachery, any fire and ice emotional experience acquired vicariously through literature. Sensing no response from me to his comment and perhaps feeling a little embarrassed because of it, Brother McPherson stood up and returned his chair to the desk. "The nurse said I shouldn't stay long this first time."

I thanked him for the visit and the books, then waited for the heavy outer door to clang shut with a click. I opened Yeats to the first bookmark.

To a Child Dancing in the Wind
Dance there upon the shore;
What need have you to care
For wind or water's roar?
And tumble out your hair
That the salt drops have wet;
Being young you have not known
The fool's triumph, nor yet
Love lost as soon as won,
Nor the best labourer dead
And all the sheaves to bind.
What need have you to dread
The monstrous crying of the wind?

Tim's visits became the highlight of long days filled with what increasingly felt like pointless activities—art therapy, school work, silent visits with Dr. Granzow, even playing ping pong with Derrick. It was Tim's evening visits in the soft lamplight of my room that offered comfort, an hour searching for answers to life in iambic pentameter.

One day after lunch Shirley motioned me to wait before returning to the open unit. The other patients had left the table. I had been regaling them with reports of beating Derrick at ping pong. The victory smile faded. Shirley had a serious look.

"Hon, Dr. Granzow reported to the nursing staff that you're not making progress in your session. It's been four weeks and you still refuse to talk."

I slid the pepper shaker back and forth between my hands.

"All of us share his concern, hon. For whatever reason,

you won't let anyone into that head of yours." She reached across and stopped the sliding salt shaker. "If you want to get well, you have to let us help you...with words. Do you understand what I'm saying?"

I nodded.

She let go of the salt. "Some new medications have been shown effective in patients with major depression. Dr. Granzow feels this might be a way to help you."

"What kind of medication?"

"Antidepressants, not the kind used in the past that made people dopey. These new ones elevate chemicals in the brain that are low in depressed patients."

"Dr. Granzow is punishing me because I'm making him look like a failure."

"No hon, that's not why. He believes he can relieve the depression so you can talk about the things you've been struggling to cope with on your own."

I threw her a questioning smirk and turned my face to the window.

"Hon. You can't live here forever. A pretty girl like you should be going out with friends, dating, going to football games and dances. This medication just might be the answer."

I already knew the answer—turn back the clock to a time when I didn't have my terrible secret, make me into a normal girl whose mother loves her. Could an antidepressant do that?

Yeats had been wrong in his poem. I most certainly did have to fear the monstrous crying of the wind. That monstrous crying was the sound of demons whispering their warning that my father would kill FD and go to prison if he were to learn the truth. One slip of the tongue, those demons repeated day in and day out, and you will annihilate everyone you love.

"I obviously have no choice in the matter. Dr. Granzow is going to drug me whether I agree to it or not."

I pushed the chair away from the table and went to my room, frightened, trapped. Later that day I had my first dose. For the next week I was so sleepy it was all I could do to eat. Homework was impossible, much less participating in activities on the open unit. During sessions with Dr. Granzow, I curled up on the couch until Ian escorted me back.

The doctor assured me the side effects would wear off in a week or two. They didn't. He lowered the dose. That didn't help. He stopped that medication and switched to another in the same class, eliminating the time gap between trials. The result was no different.

Tim's visits dwindled to fifteen minutes since I could barely stay awake. He would read to me in the soft light and construct conversations we might have had. I could see the sadness in his eyes every time he looked at me. If I fell asleep before he left, he'd leave a volume open to a particular poem. He was especially keen on Gerard Manley Hopkins.

Peace
When will you ever, Peace, wild wood dove, shy wings shut,
Your round me roaming end, and under be my boughs?

Poor Brother McPherson. If he only knew, he would stop trying to comfort me. Not only would I find no peace, things were as bad as they could get. Or so I thought.

There's no way I could've seen what was coming.

12

GOD RECONSIDERS

It was all I could manage to keep up with homework. There was no point in my parents visiting. Most of the time, I slept through without awareness they were in the room. Dad delivered my assignments to the nurses' station on the open unit during the week without bothering to come back to the locked unit. Mom and FD stopped visiting altogether. I couldn't say I blamed them.

Worst of all to everyone's frustration, including my own, there was no improvement in my mood after the third antidepressant. Dr. Granzow weaned me off medication.

My energy returned as the drugs left my system. I resumed group therapy with trademark silence and ping pong with Derrick. My rapport with staff was never the same. I became guarded even with Shirley and Ian, consumed with dread at what Dr. Granzow might have in mind for the next step in my treatment plan.

An excursion with staff wasn't uncommon, the goal to build trust outside the clinical setting. Derrick approached the doctor with the idea of taking me to a movie with him and his fiancée. Dr. Granzow wrote a one-time order.

The next Saturday Derrick and Janet picked me up. It was strange seeing him in a different setting, just as it had been visiting with Tim outside of school. Janet was a beauty with long, straight hair and a patrician nose. Derrick introduced her as his brainy-UCLA-graduate-student-fiancé. Outgoing and chatty, she put me at ease right away.

Guess Who's Coming to Dinner? was playing in Westwood. After the movie we piled into Derrick's car babbling about its wallop as social commentary. I forgot about the hospital.

"Hey, it's only eight-thirty. Anybody for a cup of java?" Derrick asked.

"Not me, baby. You forgot I have a seven-thirty meeting with my advisor in the morning."

Derrick snapped his fingers and inhaled out loud through clenched teeth. "Right. Well, I know you won't turn it down," he said to me. "Anything to stay out longer, huh? We'll come back to that little coffee shop next to the theater after we drop off the party pooper."

Derrick wrapped Janet in his arms for a long kiss, then he and I doubled back toward Westwood. He seemed nervous alone with me. That was odd. I had always been comfortable with both Ian and Derrick and couldn't understand why he would be tense.

Derrick started telling me personal details about his and Janet's relationship, how Janet was a devout Catholic and refused to have sex before marriage. I figured Derrick was just like Mom with her favorite subject, oblivious to the fact it was totally inappropriate for the sixteen-year-old patient in his care.

I grew increasingly uneasy with his tales of past sexual activities. I wished he hadn't brought up the whole idea of coffee. The Saturday night traffic on Wilshire slowed as we approached Westwood. Instead of moving into the left turn lane in the direction of the theater and coffee shop, Derrick made a right. The bustling, well-lit college town was replaced by a dark, deserted residential street. He drove to the end and switched off the ignition.

"Why didn't you go left into downtown? There's no coffee shop around here."

"I just wanted to talk." His voice was thick.

"That's why we were going to a coffee shop. Anyway, it's almost nine. I should probably get back." I stiffened and searched the neighborhood for signs of life.

"Hey, you and I are buds, right? The truth is, Reese, your doctor and the nursing staff hoped that by getting out for a few hours you might open up and talk. You're real good about keeping things to yourself, isn't that right?" He reached across the bench seat and tucked a strand of hair behind my ear.

I jerked away and squeezed against the passenger door. A lump closed my throat. "Actually, Derrick, I don't really feel like coffee. I think we should—"

He lunged sideways and grabbed my shoulders. I was so taken aback there wasn't much I could do. The expression on his face was pure evil. My back pressed against the door in retreat. He cornered me and shoved his tongue deep in my mouth.

I pushed back with both hands. "Derrick, get off me!"

"I've been waiting to get my hands on you, Reese. I know you like me. And you sure don't seem sick." His tongue was in my mouth again, his hand under my bra.

I wriggled side to side and dislodged him from my face. "Don't!"

His eyes darkened with anger. In rapid moves he pulled my hips toward him until I was flat. My head hit the door handle. With one massive arm pinned across my chest he unhooked his pants, then ripped mine open. He tugged until they were all the way off.

"Stop! I mean it!"

In one fast movement his hand was over my mouth. He rammed himself inside me, pushing, pushing. I thrashed and grunted until his hand slid off my mouth.

"HELP! Somebod—stop! You're hurting me!" He covered my mouth again and kept pushing. My head banged against the door handle over and over. I struggled for air.

One loud grunt with an extra hard thrust and everything stopped. His hand slid from my mouth and fell limp to the floor. The full weight of his body collapsed on me. I held my breath and listened to his panting slow down. He didn't move.

"I promise not to scream. Please get off. You're crushing me. I can't breathe." He didn't respond. I willed myself to stay calm, praying it was over. He lay quiet for several minutes. I thought he had fallen asleep. Then he lifted up and I was sure he was getting off me. Instead he started again.

I looked beyond the window clouded white with steam. The world fell quiet. I heard nothing. I felt nothing. My body relaxed and drifted with the current. Swells rolled in gentle sway beneath me. The first buoy bobbed in the water next to me, then the second, the third, the fourth, until I lost count. I had no awareness of the present, no sense of the past, no physical sensation other than floating, floating.

A crushing blow brought me back as Derrick's flaccid body hit my chest. I tried to inhale. My lungs refused to work. "You're smothering me, Derrick. Please, get off. I can't breathe."

He pushed himself off and dropped back in the driver's seat. Jagged breaths heaved his stomach. He cracked the window. Cold night air expanded my lungs.

175

The knot on my head was already beginning to swell. My entire body ached. Derrick pulled up his pants and zipped them.

I let the fresh air bring me to my wits and picked up my pants from the floor. It was then I noticed the blood smeared on my thighs.

The clock on the dashboard lit up when Derrick turned on the ignition. It was ten-thirty.

"Reese, I'm sorry. I had no idea you were a virgin. You've been coming on to me and—"

"Take me back."

"Sure, sure. Are you okay? I swear I didn't mean to hurt you."

"Take me back to the hospital."

"Yeah, okay, first listen. This is important. You need to promise me something. You can't tell anyone. This could cost me my job, or worse, my license."

I stared straight ahead.

"I'm not the only one who could get hurt. If anyone found out, your behavior would be seen as sexual acting out. Do you know where they send patients who can't be controlled?"

My mouth dropped. I squinted at him in disbelief. Was this a threat?

"Camarillo State Hospital, that's where. Believe me, that dungeon is a hell hole. They have kids from the criminal court system, mean kids. Rebellious patients get put in restraints and locked in isolation. Patients like you, depressed and uncooperative, get shock treatments. People die in that place, or get attacked by other patients because it's so understaffed. A nice girl like you? They'd eat you alive."

I didn't respond.

He slid the car into gear. "One more thing—take a shower and wash real good. Ask the nurse for a Tampax. You can use the cardboard tube as a plunger and douche."

The car rolled into the staff lot. "I'll sign you back in and—"

I was out the door and halfway up the steps before he could finish his sentence. I pounded for someone to let me in. Derrick stopped at the back door and talked to the night nurse. By the time he walked down the hall I was in the locked unit.

"How'd it go, the big outing? You look flushed."

"Hi, Amelia. It's freezing out there. The outing was fun. Janet's really nice and the movie was terrific."

"What'd you see?"

"*Guess Who's Coming to Dinner*. Sidney Poitier, Spencer Tracey, Katharine Hepburn."

"No one in report said it was a double feature. I guessed that was okay. You were safe being with staff. What was the other movie?"

"The other movie? Oh, some boring thing, a documentary about Africa I think. Anyway, I'm going to hit the shower and fall into bed. Goodnight."

Alone in my room I sat on the edge of the bed and tried to calm my nerves. I remembered Derrick's instructions and returned to Amelia for a Tampax.

She unlocked a cupboard and handed it to me. "Reese, you're shaking."

"I'm still cold. I'd better get in that shower, pronto. Goodnight again."

I peeled off my clothes as if they were contaminated and got in the shower without waiting for it to get hot. Bursts of water shot from my mouth as I spit out gulp after gulp. My fingernails scraped the skin raw from scrubbing my thighs so hard.

The bar of soap slipped. I bent to retrieve it. My shaking legs gave way and I slumped to the floor. I stayed there, sobbing. Water red with blood swirled the drain and disappeared.

*

In the morning every part of me hurt. My bottom lip was red and swollen. The knot on my head smarted with each stroke of the brush. Bruises like twin blue moons rested over my hips. A matched set of thumbprints emblazoned my arms. An ugly knot on my knee from repeatedly knocking the steering wheel throbbed at the slightest bend of my leg.

Adding to my generalized agony was the prospect of facing Derrick. I complained of cramps to Shirley and asked to stay behind. There had to be a better way to avoid ever again stepping foot on the open unit. Cramps had been all I could think of at the moment. I would figure out a better excuse. Once Dr. Granzow heard I had withdrawn from activities, he would assume the outing hadn't resulted in the desired outcome and write an order restricting me to the locked unit until my mood status improved. I would ask for another antidepressant trial if that's what it took.

The conscientious night nurse had reported my comments about enjoying the outing. Participation in group activities on the open unit remained a standing order.

Group therapy met in a room near the back door. The hallway looked a mile long as I hunkered behind Shirley. We were halfway down the hall when the nurses' station door opened and Derrick appeared.

It happened so fast there was no way to avoid looking

at him. I stopped cold. He stood in freeze frame with his hand on the door knob. Our eyes caught in mutual shock. Anyone passing might've wondered at the odd tableau. The hallway was empty except for my small posse, which had kept moving.

A heatwave of anger and utter humiliation shot through my body. I didn't flinch.

Derrick thawed into his professional role, the clipboard unsteady in trembling hands the only sign of emotion. "Good morning, Ping Pong Warrior. On your way to group?"

"Reese, they're waiting for you," Shirley called.

A doctor coming out of the nurses' station asked Derrick to move. Our silent confrontation ended. He stepped around me and proceeded down the hall.

That was the extent of my bravado. The next day I refused to leave the locked unit. The next day and the day after that I did the same, refusing to talk to anyone, even Shirley, a monotone yes or no from the bed where I stayed curled up my sole response. Finally I got my wish. Dr. Granzow wrote orders restricting me to the locked unit and started a new medication.

Tim's visits had become awkward the further I sank into depression. He was flummoxed at the rapid change in our relationship. He showed up anyway. One evening I didn't acknowledge him at all. After a while he kissed my cheek and left.

Instead of the usual book of poetry opened to a favorite, Tim had left a folded note on the bedside table. The verse written in blue ink was done in Tim's own hand.

Lost
Where do you go, hon, when you leave me?
To faraway fields of Lupin and Lilac?
You leave me here, alone, searching for you, calling out…
But being neither father nor lover
I cannot follow.
Come back to me, sweet girl,
Come back and let me make you safe.
Better yet! Let me be lost with you, wandering
Until we find respite from the storm — your storm.
For I too am lost, until you bring me home.

My blunted brain couldn't make sense of it. I stuck his poem in the drawer.

The final antidepressant was no more successful than the previous three. I forced myself to stay awake at night by sneaking coffee leftover from breakfast and lunch into my room and storing it in a water pitcher. There was no other way to combat the drowsy effect of medication.

I was determined to keep up with assignments and graduate with my class, start college with my friends. Though I had missed most of spring semester I had completed the coursework and was halfway through requirements for next fall. By now my classmates must've assumed I was one of those girls, shipped off to have my baby before "returning from Europe." There was nothing I could do about that. I felt bad anyway.

By late May my mood hadn't improved. Not only had God deserted me, medical science had been rendered ineffective. I could've saved Blue Cross the money and told them my illness was untreatable. Dr. Granzow had broached the subject of shock treatments to my parents.

Dad drew the line at "zapping my brain." He understood how much going to college meant to me.

Dr. Granzow's treatment plans had been exhausted with no significant improvement in mood status. He concluded I had remained "a danger to myself", legal grounds for continued hospitalization, which is exactly what the doctor recommended.

Mom supported the plan for long term treatment in a psychiatric facility, adding it would be impossible for her to provide "adequate supervision" to ensure my safety.

My parents and Dr. Granzow had run out of options.

So had I.

*

A streetlight reflected on the ceiling. I wondered if anyone had noticed an acoustic tile was loose. I ruminated on that tile all the next day into the evening. When the night shift came on at eleven, I said goodnight to Amelia and waited for her to complete first rounds. It would be two hours before she checked again.

I folded four paper towels and placed one under each leg of the desk, then started moving it away from the wall. Progress was painstaking with only a few inches before stopping to listen for Amelia. The journey ended with the desk directly beneath the loose piece in the ceiling.

I placed the chair on the desk and climbed up. The tile was two inches out of reach. Stretching on tiptoes I extended my arm as far as I could without losing balance. I locked the piece between my forefinger and thumb and slid it out of the grid.

The metal pipe glistened in full view.

I hopped down and tugged the top sheet off the bed. Once it was twisted tight on the diagonal I clipped a metal barrette on each end for added weight. I climbed back on the chair. The only sound was the whoosh of my heart. I was afraid of Amelia interrupting my plan, not about the decision itself. The same state of calm as the night of the overdose had come over me.

I flung the weighted sheet into the air.

CLANG! The barrette hit the pipe and bounced back, bringing the sheet rope tumbling over my head. I teetered. It was all I could do to keep from falling. There was no sound from the day room, though I was certain Amelia had heard the noise.

I tossed the sheet a second time. The barrette brushed the pipe with a ding and stalled at the top. It plummeted down on my side again.

I got down and retrieved two more barrettes. Once I'd knotted one end of the sheet into a bigger ball and clipped the extra weight to the tail, I returned to my gallows platform and made a third attempt.

It hit the pipe. For a breathless second the ball hovered over the pipe. Ever so slowly, it rolled to the other side. I tied both ends of the sheet into a noose.

I was ready.

The door opened. Amelia appeared. "Scott!"

She gaped in horror. I couldn't move a muscle. A second shout brought a male psych tech bursting through the door. He lunged at me in full throttle. The force of momentum sent us both flying through the air. I landed on the bed. He bounced off and rolled to the floor.

Amelia whipped to her desk and made an emergency call to the doctor. Scott was on the floor looking shaken. He leapt up and dragged me to a chair next to the desk. He shoved me into it, the power of his grasp crushing my still-bruised arm.

Amelia hung up and unlocked the medication cabinet.

Her hands trembled as she drew liquid into a syringe. The psych tech restrained me though I offered no resistance. Amelia swabbed my shoulder and jammed the needle in all the way.

Sleep, at last.

The next morning I woke in a fog. My head felt like lead, my mouth cotton. Leather restraints shackled my limbs to the bed. Shirley stood over me, her whole being drenched in sorrow. She pulled out the massive key ring and unlocked the cuffs. We avoided each other's eyes while she helped me out of my dog-themed pajamas into a fresh gown. I was not to get out of bed or dress in my own clothes.

Shirley sat next to the bed and worked on charts. Her face was slack with resignation. Thirty minutes later Mom and Dad walked in, both of them rigid with anxiety. I had never seen anything close to fear in Mom. It was unmistakable. Pancake make-up camouflaged dark circles. She comported herself with poise decked out in her customary cashmere sweater and scarf tucked into the canyon of cleavage below.

After she'd determined I was fine the fear transformed into anger. Shirley loaded up the charts with shoulders tight from the collective tension in the room. She threw me a nervous glance. Apparently Mom and Dad had one more option.

Dad stayed near the door with the whole room between us. Mom plunked into the chair vacated by Shirley. She glared at me with disgust.

"You've really done it this time, Clarice. You've forced our hand. Go ahead, Walker, tell her what happens now."

Dad's familiar expression was the same one facing me every day in the mirror—hopelessness. He spoke with raw anguish. "We just left Dr. Granzow's office. He feels there's nothing more he can do for you here. Liability concer—"

"For God's sake, Walker, just tell her."

Dad shot her a glance as close to anger as I'd seen since he'd stormed out of the room the day she told me I was going to boarding school. He scratched his neck like he did after taking off his tie.

"Peanut, there's no way you can come home now, not after last night. It's not just that. This Recreation Therapist, Derrick, reported to the doctor this morning that on the night of the outing you made veiled threats about hurting yourself. He feels awful about not reporting it sooner. Maybe what happened last night could've been prevented."

A sneer threatened to curl my upper lip.

"Dr. Granzow feels you need to be hospitalized a while longer."

"I have to stay here?"

"Even if Dr. Granzow wanted to keep you, our insurance coverage has about run out."

The feeling of déjà vu was so strong it would've knocked me over had I not been in bed. "If I'm not staying here, and I'm not going home—?"

"Dr. Granzow is transferring you to Camarillo State Hospital."

At first I didn't comprehend. The words bounced outside my brain, their meaning unable to penetrate. It slowly became clear. This was the end. I was to be locked away in the hellhole Derrick had described where patients were drugged and shocked and abandoned as prey for other patients. His lie would protect him forever. I would be out of the way. Out of everyone's way. *What did you think Mom would do? You're too dangerous to have around. You could ruin everything for her.*

"The insurance requires transport to Camarillo by ambulance. I told the doctor I'd like to drive you myself and he agreed to that. I'll take the day off work tomorrow." Dad turned and left the room without looking at me.

Mom stood up, shaking her head in revulsion. She was a stranger to me, both of us lost to each other. But I loved her. Even if she hated me I loved her. Deep down I knew she loved me too.

I was eight years old again, my fate in her hands. I needed her now more than ever. She alone could save me. "Mommy, please—"

For a moment heartbreak came through those stunning cobalt eyes. My beautiful mother looked at me, her little girl, pleading for help. She let out a shaky breath and fought the impulse. I knew my mother wanted to take me in her arms, protect me from my horrible fate, tell me I could come home so she and I could start over.

Please, Mommy. Do it. Do it now.

She took a step back and summoned the return of her usual cold demeanor, then swung around and walked out the door.

Three injections kept me sedated the rest of the day. That night a special duty nurse supervised my restless sleep. Through the fog I envisioned the hellhole hospital, trying and failing to piece together how it had come to this. The cumulative power of medication finally caught up with me. I fell into a drugged sleep, suspending fear of my future until morning.

Shirley helped me pack. We divvied up the unwieldy load of miscellaneous belongings—books and the box of poems from Tim, extra shoes refusing to fit in the suitcase, a paper Mache bust of myself from art therapy. Neither of us said much.

Dad carried my suitcase to the car, which he'd parked in the staff lot, the same lot I had crossed dozens of times with Ian, the same lot where I had escaped Derrick after his assault.

Shirley and I hugged without speaking, too much emotion between us for words. Dad started the engine. Shirley produced a slim volume from her pocket and handed it to me.

"Promise me you'll read it."

"It's not Kahil Gibran, is it?" I asked, referring to our conversation of what I considered sappy poetry.

"You're hopeless. No, silly. This is a true story. This man survived unbelievable horrors in a concentration camp during World War II. He suffered in ways you and I can't even imagine."

"And this will cheer me up?"

"I believe he has something to tell you. Promise you'll read it."

I looked at her in search of what, I didn't know.

"Find someone to confide in, Reese. It's the only way you'll get well."

I ached to tell her how much comfort she had given me, how much she meant to me. All I could manage was a weak smile through eyes sad with gratitude.

We drove out of the parking lot. Through a blur of tears, I watched in the rearview mirror until Dad pulled in front of a truck and Shirley disappeared.

At the next turn, I caught the book before it slid off my lap to the floor.

Viktor Frankl, *Man's Search for Meaning*.

Viktor Frankl would never know it. He was about to save my life.

13

THE SEARCH FOR MEANING

The late afternoon was picture perfect as Dad and I drove north on the Coast Highway past the Palisades, then Malibu, the glistening ocean a watercolor seascape. It had been three months since I'd last seen the ocean. I had almost forgotten the power of its beauty.

After all that had happened, it had still been hard leaving St. John's, harder facing the unknown. What good had it been getting ahead in my assignments now that I wasn't going home? At least school would be out for summer in a few weeks. Surely I would be back for senior year and graduate with my class.

Dad and I drove in silence. There was nothing left to discuss. In random moments I would forget our destination and enjoy riding again in the car with him, as if this were any morning on the way to school. In less pleasant moments I would remember this was the same road he and I had traveled the night we went looking for Mom in San Francisco.

That thought was laced with bitterness. Today's journey wasn't the two of us bound by a common mission. It was Dad driving me out of his life the way Mom had driven us out of hers, which is what had put us on this road in the first place.

An hour after leaving St. John's the winding ribbon of highway along the coast straightened out. We crossed into Ventura County and veered into flatlands, salty sea air overpowered by the stink of fertilizer on miles of lush farm produce. Dad's directions to the hospital led us away from the flatlands into the mountains. The road narrowed into zigzag switchbacks the higher we climbed in elevation.

The mountain opened to a totally different landscape. We turned to each other in shock. Dad visibly relaxed at our first sight of Camarillo State Hospital. Lush sprawling grounds with tree-lined streets and manicured gardens looked more like the campus on the boarding school brochure than a mental hospital. Low rise buildings of Mediterranean architecture were arranged in clusters around a massive central courtyard like the California missions I'd studied in school.

It wasn't until Dad turned off the main road into the driveway lined with pepper trees that we got a closer look.

Heavy metal grates over the windows transformed a welcoming campus into a macabre reformatory. My mouth went dry.

Dad followed the signs to a building with a bell tower and parked in front of Admissions. A group of patients crossed the enormous lawn with an attendant. Boys wearing football helmets jerked forward in spastic motion. The girls shuffled single file dressed in donation-box clothing, their hair uncombed, faces without expression. A bony woman leaned lopsided under an oak tree. She looked drugged, or dead, her eyes blank, mouth agape.

I clung to Dad's side in terror. We entered the Bell Tower Building through French doors into a cavernous lobby. The room was drab and sparsely furnished with a long desk and metal chairs along one wall.

Dad set my suitcase down, sending an echo through

the hollow room. I stayed near the door and waited. Dad proceeded to the desk, as if he were registering at a hotel and might come back to tell me there was no vacancy.

I sat down, dizzy with free floating dread. No plush leather sofa, no Sparklett's water cooler, the piped-in music and soft lamplight in Dr. Granzow's waiting room replaced by harsh fluorescence and the jarring sound of a heavy door blasting open and clanging shut in the distance.

How insular my world had been, my middle class life in the Palisades. Even my suffering had taken place in a private hospital with peach coverlets on the beds.

Dad instructed me to wait while he met with the doctor and disappeared into an office to the right of the lobby entrance. I drew the suitcase close, my sole contact with him. The woman at the desk eyed me with muted disapproval at the scraping noise.

An hour later Dad emerged from the office, his shoulders hunched like an old man instead of a robust one of thirty-nine. He rubbed his forehead and kept his head down. "The doctor—it's a she—seems sharp, real sharp. Gets right down to business. She's worked with adolescents for twenty years and seems anxious to help you."

He looked at me for the first time since our initial view of the hospital, the view from above that looked like a campus. "I know this isn't St. John's. You just do what the doctor says. Then you can come home and we'll get on with our lives, the three of us, just like we'd planned."

The words were delivered without conviction. I felt the heaviness in him, his body leaden with defeat at the failed effort to hold our family together. The dreams of his youth lay buried under secrets and compromise and tolerance of a life more lonely than the one he'd grown up with, the one he'd so desperately tried to erase with a family of his own.

I couldn't think of anything to say. Dad stood up and shook each leg of his slacks to loosen the wrinkled bunching. "That's about it then." I wouldn't look at him. He took my face in his hands for a moment, the sadness of all we had been through filling his eyes. He kissed me on the forehead and left without looking back.

I walked to the window in a stupor and watched the Ford drive away. "Goodbye, Daddy. I love you."

A severe looking woman of indeterminate age and diminutive stature stood facing me.

"Hello, Reese. I'm Dr. Pallone. Let's go in my office."

The room smelled old and musty, as if all the troubles revealed inside had taken up residence in the walls, under the rugs. There was not an inch of empty space on the desk. Metal charts in short messy stacks covered most of the surface, loose papers scattered the far reaches.

Dr. Pallone motioned me to one of two well-worn corduroy chairs in front of the desk. She sat in the other. The woman moved with conviction, as if used to operating without a shred of doubt. Everything about her was all business as Dad said, from the tight bun at her nape and black-rimmed glasses to her neutral expression. She spoke with deliberation in a rich alto.

"Do you know why you're here, Reese?"

"I'm crazy."

"Is that what you think? Or is that what you've been told?"

I shrugged my shoulders.

"I understand you made a pretty serious suicide attempt at home and were close to making another at St.

John's."

I studied the Persian rug under my feet. Sunlight had faded areas of rich red into a sickly pinkish white.

"What do you know about this hospital?"

That it's a hellhole where patients are drugged and attacked, or locked in solitary confinement for weeks, or given electric shock treatments and turned into zombies! "That it's for patients who need to be in a hospital for a long time. Crazy people like me."

There was no irritation in her tone like the edge in Dr. Granzow's. "I've been a psychiatrist for a very long time and dealt with a lot crazy people, to use your words. I'm here to tell you you're not one of them."

"You do know I've been locked up for months."

"You're sick. That doesn't mean you belong in a psychiatric hospital."

"What do you mean?"

She made a hand steeple. "Your father gave a detailed account of what's been going on at home, the events leading up to your suicide attempt. According to him, until six months ago you'd never shown any visible sign of depression. You were a straight 'A' student, had friends, plans for college. That sounds to me like a well-adjusted teenager." Pause. "Then your mother left."

What does she know? I scooted to the edge of the chair. I could feel her eyes on me.

"Your father told me about this priest, Father Donnelly. It seems he's been deeply involved with your family. Particularly your mother. Your father said they have, and I quote, 'a complicated and close relationship'. Does that sound right?"

I nodded quickly several times.

"How did your dad feel about that?"

"He didn't kno—"

Dr. Pallone waited several moments for me to finish my sentence before she did it for me. "He didn't know what was going on between them. Is that what you were about to say?"

I didn't blink. The pattern in the Persian rug became fuzzy.

"Your father told me that during the first three months of your mother's absence last year, he broke down emotionally and was unable to function. He credits you with taking care of him. It was you who did the cooking, laundry, grocery shopping, made sure he ate and paid the bills."

My heart skipped. Why had Dad told her all this?

"He described the two of you driving to San Francisco in the middle of the night, almost eight hundred miles in twenty-four hours. You drove. He said he was too distraught to be much help."

Everything was discombobulated. The doctor made it sound like Dad was crazy, not me.

"All the while this is going on you continued going to school every day and never breathed a word to anyone about your mother's disappearance or your father's condition."

I wrapped my arms and rocked in tiny up-and-back motion.

"Three months later Father Donnelly tells you where your mother is...and that she's pregnant...from rape." Pause. "Your mother had this baby and gave it up."

Dad told her about the baby! I rocked faster, backward, forward, my shallow breaths becoming a pant at the shock of hearing the truth spoken out loud for the first time. I couldn't contain the chaos in my body. Lightheaded and dizzy, everything tilted and swayed. I was passing out.

Dr. Pallone took hold of my shoulders and pushed me back to an upright position. "Close your mouth and breathe through your nose."

I did as she said. After a few minutes the pant slowed to normal breathing.

"Reese, you've been holding some pretty heavy secrets for a long time."

A lamp on the desk wrapped us in soft yellow light, the world beyond this room non-existent. I tried to grasp the enormity of my dark secret exposed to daylight. Someone knows. Someone other than me and Dad and Kit. A stranger. My face scrunched involuntarily as I tensed and held my emotions in check.

"For three months it had just been you and your father, living through this difficult experience."

Dr. Pallone disentangled the rat's nest of secrets one enmeshed layer at a time with care and precision. After each revelation she assessed my reaction before unraveling the layer underneath. Her words were spoken without sentiment, yet her compassion touched my soul, soothing the rawness of secrets uncovered.

The last truth would be hardest to hear.

"Then after seven months your mother comes home. You resent her. One day the two of you have an argument. But this isn't when you took the overdose, is it?"

I shook my head.

"No. You turned to the one person you had counted on to defend you, the person you had taken care of on your own for months...your father."

I could no longer hold myself together. The tears came, softly at first. The crying grew into sobs, uncontrollable, unstoppable, my anguish surfacing in audible wails. I snapped a Kleenex from the box and then another, unable to stem the flow of body fluids unleashed upon hearing the one truth I had not been able to bear.

I don't know how long the crying lasted. It felt like a long time, three years of pent up emotion released on the words of someone I had known less than fifteen minutes. Dr. Pallone waited without a word until the sobs sputtered out in ragged hiccups.

I let my head fall back in the chair, free of the massive weight I'd been carrying for so long. This woman, this stranger, had walked right into the fallout shelter and switched on the light.

Truth. What a beautiful word. Clean. Pure. Strong.

She leaned forward, closing the gap between us. "Reese, I think you're a very angry, very scared young woman, and I think you've been trying for a long time to tell everyone around you that you need help."

"It's my fault. I wouldn't talk."

"Your behavior did the talking. You had been trying to cope with the disappearance of your mother, deception from the family priest, your father's emotional breakdown, only to have him betray you when you needed him most."

Long pause.

"These adults were charged with your care. They let you believe keeping their secrets was protecting them from disaster. That's a terrible burden for anyone, much less a sixteen-year-old girl. You finally reached your breaking point. That doesn't mean you're crazy, and it doesn't mean you belong in a hospital."

A cold wave of anxiety crashed through my short-lived relief. There still one major piece of information missing. I knew the question. It was the same one I'd asked Mom and Dad that morning long ago in their bedroom, the same question I'd asked yesterday from my bed in St. John's. Twice I had asked the question. Twice the answer had crushed me.

But I had to ask it.

"If I'm not staying here, and my parents won't let me come home, where am I going?"

Dr. Pallone shifted to her other hip and answered in a business-like tone, an undercurrent of excitement barely detectable beneath the matter-of-fact delivery. "We have options other than going home or being in the hospital— Family Care."

Of course she would send me away like everybody else in my life had. I would be displaced once again after experiencing the first connection I'd felt since the early days with FD.

"Reese, this hospital is for patients who are severely mentally ill, people with psychotic disorders that make it difficult for their families to care for them at home. It's for violent patients who can't be free in society and adolescents referred by the courts. You don't belong here."

"Apparently I don't belong anywhere. I've proved I can take care of myself. I don't see why you can't make my parents let me come home."

"It's not that simple. Dr. Granzow didn't recommend long term hospitalization to punish you. He did it because he understands the danger of going right back into a situation so destructive you thought your only option was to kill yourself."

My wrung-out body was too drained at this point to care where I would be going. Dr. Pallone was sending me away. That's all I needed to know. I stared into space with my head back in the chair.

"We have good Family Care here in Ventura County."

"Is that some kind of foster care?"

"These are small supervised homes with other patients. They're licensed by the state and provide a safe environment in the community where you can see a psychiatrist and continue treatment."

"I'm going to foster care just because my parents are messed up?"

"Reese, it's time someone started protecting you instead of the other way around. For the time being that someone will be the state."

"Dad shouldn't have told you about San Francisco. You're using that against him."

"Secrets don't work that way. They don't keep you safe. Your father knows that now. He told me the truth because he wants you to get well. He knows these secrets have hurt you. He also knows he hasn't protected you in ways a father should."

"How long do I have to stay?"

"You'll be eighteen in a year-and-a-half."

"A year-and-a-half? I won't be able to graduate with my class at St. Monica's?"

"According to Dr. Granzow's notes you continued with schoolwork during your hospitalization. You'll do the same here. Our classes follow state curriculum. Once we get you into Family Care you can transfer to Ventura High and graduate on schedule."

I puffed my cheeks and let out a long breath.

"I know it's a lot to take in. You didn't create this illness, Reese, and you can't cure it without help. The feelings you're experiencing—anger, hopelessness—are powerful emotions. There are healthy ways to cope, but you can't deal with something you can't openly acknowledge. First things first. Now that we've exposed this dark secret to light and air, the healing can begin. You'll be able to look at things differently. That's a good start."

Differently is an understatement. The assumptions and beliefs I had walked into this office with an hour ago had been totally deconstructed and reconfigured. I had been looking at everything from upside down, my perspective distorted. Right side up was a different view entirely. Someone was going to protect me. For the first time, I felt a glimmer of hope that all was not futile.

"Now, here's the hard part. Placement in Family Care is going to take a while. This is a big hospital with thousands of patients to take care of. It's best to assume you'll be here for a few months at the very least. That gives you and I time to work. You'll be assigned a social worker who will get you on track with school and work on your placement. Does this sound like a workable plan to you?"

For the first time in weeks I smiled, a warm, genuine expression of gratitude. "It does."

"Good. Now let's get you admitted. You can skip the physical since you've been medically monitored for three months. A psych tech will escort you to the ward. You'd better dry your eyes. Walking in with a tear-stained face is not the way to start out around here."

Dr. Pallone got up and walked to her desk. She muttered something, more to herself than to me.

"You're going to be okay, Reese Cavanaugh."

*

A husky thirtysomething man dressed in white with slick black hair entered. The key ring swinging from his belt must've outweighed Ian's by at least a pound. He gave me a wary glance and grabbed my suitcase. I turned to say goodbye to Dr. Pallone, her head over a chart as she dialed the phone.

I followed the Keeper of the Keys out of Admissions and into the wilderness of hospital grounds. Raoul moved fast for such a giant of a man. We zigzagged our way through the cluster of rectangular buildings. I noticed each cluster had a number painted in block letters on the locked gate to identify the ward. I wondered how I would find my way back to Dr. Pallone's office without a map.

Raoul stopped outside the adolescent ward and rattled through his keys. An odd sound caught my attention from behind. Before I could move out of the way, something came flying at me. I slammed hard against the wall with the wind knocked out of me.

Dumbstruck, I struggled to catch my breath.

Raoul spun around. "ARCHIE! C'mon, leave her alone. Get up now. C'mon."

It was one of the helmet-headed boys I had seen from the car. Bushy red hair stuck out of the ill-fitting helmet. He had dropped to my feet with his nose over my shoes, vigorously rubbing them with his huge hands.

"I love you! I love you! You're so beautiful! Will you marry me?"

"Don't mind Archie," Raoul said. "He's harmless, aren't you, Archie." Raoul helped the boy up and shoved him in the other direction. "Go catch up with your group now. I'm sure Sandra is wondering where she lost you."

Raoul turned back to the door and unlocked it. I stepped inside and nearly gagged. The air was heavy with the smell of confinement—disinfectant, stale food, urine. Raoul motioned to a heavyset woman at the end of the hallway and ducked into an office with my suitcase.

"You must be Cavanaugh," she said. The woman looked older than Raoul in her shapeless blouse and polyester pants. "I'm Maggie, the tech in charge on days."

I leaned against the wall and brought my foot within reach to re-tie the laces of my shoe undone by Archie. "Yes, Reese Cavanaugh."

"Let me show you around the girls' dorm."

"What about my suitcase?"

"You'll get it back after it's cleared for contraband."

I trailed Maggie down a long corridor into the day room. It was a replica of the lobby with the addition of filthy walls of peeling paint. A tattered couch in the middle of the room sat facing a wall-mounted TV. A worn monastery table served as a desk at the far end of the room.

"This is where you'll spend most of your time when you're not at school." Maggie pointed to a central glassed-in nurses' station. "You'll line up there for meds, at the door you came in for the cafeteria and school."

We moved through the dayroom to one of two wings off the nurses' station. "There are thirty girls on the ward, split between two dorms. Your bed is this way."

The long rectangular room had military beds lining each wall covered with gray equally-military-style blankets like the ones in Greg's bomb shelter. The narrow space between beds was crammed with two metal lockers, one for each patient. I envisioned my private corner room at St. John's, the big window, the desk, the painting of a sailing ship on stormy seas, the peach-colored bedspread. I swallowed hard and caught up with Maggie, who stood waiting for me, hands on hips.

"This is yours. We'll get your name taped on the

locker. Other than that, no pictures or posters allowed." She paused to make sure I was taking it in. "Dinner is at five-thirty, free time until seven, homework till nine, lights out at ten sharp. Wake up is six-thirty on weekdays, an hour later on weekends."

She stopped for a moment and massaged her forehead. "Oh, and the TV is on from four to five-thirty and six to seven during the week. It stays on until ten-thirty on Friday and Saturday. You watch only if your name is on the grade list, C or higher."

I memorized the rules the same way I had memorized *The Raven* with every expectation of one hundred percent recall.

"On Tuesdays and Fridays, a staff member escorts patients in a group to the canteen. Again, only if your name is on the approved list. You'll be assigned a laundry day, which includes doing your bedding. You get one bath towel and one face towel and washcloth, so don't lose them. You miss your laundry time slot, that's your problem. There's a roster in the snack room listing ward chores, which rotate every week. Any fighting that gets reported is documented for your social worker and sanctions will follow. Any questions?"

Fighting? I did my best to muffle any hint of shock. Instead I sounded naïve, even worse. "What's the canteen?"

"Boy, you are new to the system. It's the commissary, the store here on the grounds. If you have any spending money you can buy snacks and toiletries and magazines, stuff like that. There's a pay phone outside. You only make calls to someone approved by the doctor. Calls are limited to ten minutes. Got it?"

"Got it."

We walked to the door as she rattled more rules. After saying goodbye to everyone at St. John's, driving up the coast, parting with Dad and my session with Dr. Pallone, I didn't think my mind could process one more thing.

"There are no locks on these lockers, so unless you want something to get stolen, don't buy it or have anybody bring it from home. Patients aren't allowed in the dorm between eight-thirty in the morning and nine-thirty at night except to get something. If you don't feel well we'll send you to the sick bay."

Maggie left me at the nurses' station. I wandered into the dayroom and kept my head down until I sat at one corner of the monastery table in back.

At dinner time I lined up with the other patients and walked single file behind Raoul in a different zigzag trail to the cafeteria. Screams rang out in the distance. I didn't look up or indicate I'd heard anything, but I shook inside.

One by one we queued up in the food line. The smell alone was enough to make me gag, the faint aroma of cleaning solution masking an underlying odor of old meat. Leftovers I had shoved down the garbage disposal looked more appealing than the concoctions in metal tubs.

Some kind of grayish meat clumps in gelatinous gravy nearly did me in when the line slowed. Creamed corn was next. I slopped a spoonful onto my plate. At the end of the line I grabbed a naval orange from a bowl of fruit, a small carton of milk from the iced bin and two boxes of raisins from desserts. Then and there I decided this was to be my diet. I would rather die of starvation than eat this rancid fare.

I had no idea where to go, so I tagged behind the girl in front of me and sat at the same table. A surly brunette with big hair and heavy make-up stopped eating and glared at me. The talking stopped as the other girls turned to me with a united sneer. The first girl spoke.

"Excuse me, asshole. Did anyone give you permission to sit at this table?"

"No. I just thought—"

"Well you thought wrong. If you know what's good for you, you'll beat it...and leave the orange."

I got out from the bench with my tray and searched nearby tables. Mean Queen sauntered around the table staring daggers. She grabbed the orange.

"Beat it, bitch."

I spotted a trash can in the far corner and headed there with eyes straight ahead. The milk I forced down felt cold in my empty stomach. I stuffed a box of raisins in each pocket of my jeans and set my tray in the dirty stack before making a bee line for the door. Raoul sat at a nearby table with other staff.

"Hey, Cavanaugh, you have to wait for the group."

I tilted my head in the direction of Mean Queen and Company, at the room of tables with no empty seat.

"There's a small courtyard if you go out the side door. You can wait there."

The barren patio had a concrete bench along the wall. The cold unwelcome hardness reminded me of sitting on the sand the day I came home to find Mom gone. I closed my eyes and tried to fathom how I would survive this place.

"Hi." A petite towhead blonde appeared in the doorway. "I'm Molly. You must be the new girl."

"I'm Reese," I said, hoping she would go away. She came over and sat next to me.

"Welcome to the Camarillo Hilton. Don't let Angela and her crowd get to you. They're all rotten bitches. I've been here eight months and believe me, the cliques in this place make high school look like a newcomer's club. What are you in for anyway?"

I didn't answer.

"Hey, it's okay if you don't want to say. Sooner or later everybody does though. I'm a hopeless alcoholic, can't be trusted on the outside. Yep. I know. I look sweet as can be, but I'm a purebred lush...drank enough rubbing alcohol to drown a horse. It didn't kill me though, just gave me ulcers and landed me in here."

"How old are you?" I tried not to sound shocked.

"Sweet sixteen and I've been kissed...plenty...and more."

There was no way to hold back the blush.

"Don't tell me you're a virgin. Holy crap." She eyed me up and down. "You a runaway?"

I shook my head pathetically.

"Done a stint in juvie?" Her eyes widened at my blank stare. "Juvenile Hall?"

I shook my head.

"Drugs?"

"No."

"You a cutter? You know, slice little designs on your arms or face?"

"No."

"Attack anyone with a weapon?"

"Of course not!"

"Well kid, then you're in deep shit. This place is survival of the fittest. You'll need something to stand on or you'll get squashed like a bug."

Molly's summary statement of my total inadequacy as a credible patient marked the grand finale of my introduction to Camarillo State Hospital. Four miserable hours later, I lay under the gray scratchy blanket with Cyrano clutched to my chest in sheer relief at being alone in the dark—and in sheer terror. I gave in to both and fell asleep.

*

"HEY! WHAT the—"

I bolted upright as ice water drenched my head. It was still dark. Three girls stood near the foot of the bed. Mean Queen from the Welcome Table spoke.

"Hahahahaha! Good morning, CLARice! What a dumb-ass name. We just wanted to give you a head start figuring out how things work around here. Go ahead, rat to Maggie and see what happens."

I held still and let the ice water run down my chest.

"Say, you look cold. You really should dry off. Oh, I almost forgot. You'll find your towels in the toilet...along with that stupid dog. We decided he needed his ears cropped."

Maggie walked in the dorm. "Harrison, Chisolm, Lupercio. What are you three up to?"

The girls dispersed in the other direction.

Maggie caught sight of me. "What happened here, Cavanaugh? You're drenched."

"Nothing, Maggie. I spilled some water."

"Uh huh. Sure. Well, it's six-thirty, time to get up."

Shivering, I lifted the blanket with care not to soak anything else and peeled off the wet nightgown. The whole dorm was awake now. I pulled on dry clothes from the locker with all eyes on me. No one said a word.

Drying my face with the wadded up nightgown, I kept my eyes forward and headed to the bathroom. Three stalls later I spotted Cyrano soaking in urine. I transferred him to the sink and filled it with hot water while I located his equally putrid ears and my towels in other stalls.

I carried the bundle of dog-in-towels to my locker. I was sure my quivering lip would give me away. As soon as Cyrano was secure I rushed across the day room into line for the cafeteria. My face was stoic as I passed Raoul behind the others.

If this ice water awakening had been about keeping a secret, Mean Queen and her cohorts would soon realize they were dealing with an Olympic-class competitor.

I had passed my first test.

*

After breakfast we were escorted across the vast courtyard lawn to the classroom. Two teachers rotated among us to help with assignments. I was given a workbook of general math for a high school junior. Once my transcripts arrived it would be clear I had completed my requirements at the Academy of St. John's.

I finished my work and still had two hours until it was time to return to the adolescent ward. I felt in my bag and pulled out the book from Shirley. *Man's Search for Meaning,* by Viktor Frankl. She had inscribed the inside cover.

Dear Reese,

During five years in a concentration camp, this man struggled every day to understand meaning in his suffering, a reason to go on living. He found it by refusing to allow men with no souls to crush his. He dared to choose hope for the future and that gave him freedom. No one can take that away. Regardless of circumstances in life beyond our control, we all have free will. You must find yours, Reese, and choose hope for a future of your own making.

Love, Shirley

My insides wept in shame. I could never have survived what Viktor Frankl had. In fact I had never done anything hard in my life. Faced with what had seemed like an unbearable situation—living in a mansion near the beach with a mean mother—I had succumbed to self-loathing instead of believing myself worthy of trusting that someone could help.

Was it possible I could be like Viktor Frankl, find strength in adversity? I expected there was one major difference between him and me. I expected he'd had a mother who loved him.

Still, if I had been willing to ask the question, I had to consider the answer.

14

TRANSFORMATION

Two days later, Raoul walked me to my first appointment with the social worker. After the cafeteria experience, I got the feeling Raoul was looking out for me. It was nothing obvious, maybe just a slight tilt of his head alerting me to an Archie love attack or the opposite from Angela, reigning Mean Queen.

We strolled across the lawn to a building on the other side of the courtyard from the adolescent ward. I asked Raoul about the social worker.

Griff Masterson was a nice guy, he said. Young, married, "Good lookin' like me!" More important, in terms of a good placement in Family Care Griff was my man. We entered the arched corridor and walked to his office at the end.

He was on the phone. He nodded to Raoul and waved me inside. With his head angled to cradle the phone in his neck, he scrambled from behind the desk and cleared a chair, mouthing reassurance he would be with me shortly. I wondered if he always did five things at once. He looked about mid-thirties with a runner's body like Greg Stewart's. Long legs stuck out the other side of the desk in front of where I sat in the chair.

Griff shuffled through a chart and jotted notes in rapid fire motion while he held the phone. I looked around the office, which had the same feel as Dr. Pallone's of having too many patients and not enough staff. His desk, like hers, was a wasteland of paperwork competing for attention.

The social worker hung up and introduced himself as he swept back dark honey hair from his forehead. "Excuse the chaos. Give me a sec." It must've been my chart that had been open.

His eyes darted back and forth at the same speed words appeared on the page when Mom typed.

"I just got off the phone with your doctor. Let's see what we have here...severe depression manifested by two serious suicide attempts, three months and four antidepressant trials at St. John's, dysfunctional family, Mom sexually involved with priest, desertion, illegitimate child, Dad emotionally labile, pregnant sister—"

"It sounds worse when you rattle it off like that." I hung my head and squirmed.

"Does it?" He tossed aside the chart. "So why don't you tell me how it is?"

I didn't respond.

"Okay, let's start with some good news. According to your transcripts from St. Monica's, you've completed core requirements for junior and senior year. How 'bout them apples?"

"I have?"

"Looks like you loaded up the last two years. A few electives senior year and you're finished with high school, young lady."

"Okay."

Griff leaned back with arms folded behind his head. "Boy, I'm usually hanging by my fingernails to see if patients pass to the next grade level and here you are, sounding disappointed."

"No, I mean, it's good news. It's just that I like school

and wonder what I'll do all day."

Griff rolled side-to-side in his chair. "I have an idea." He twirled around and rummaged through a stack of journals on the bookshelf. "I know it's here somewhere…ah!" He blew off a layer of dust and swatted the air to clear it. "This is the Ventura College catalogue. Once you finish your electives you'll be eligible to take classes."

"College? How would that work?"

"Not right now. Once we have you placed in Family Care, Voc Rehab will foot the bill."

I raised my eyebrows in confusion.

"Vocational Rehabilitation. It's a state program for patients in need of job training. Ever thought about what you'd like to do in this world?"

I focused on his feet, fully aware how inappropriate my answer would sound. "Write, teach English Literature."

"Ah, well, that's definitely beyond the range of Voc Rehab. A year of books and fees at community college is doable though."

"Really?"

"The state will support patients trying to get a foothold in the community. They're less likely to end up back here."

"Wouldn't my parents pay for college?"

Griff answered in such a matter-of-fact tone I wasn't sure I'd heard right. "Dr. Pallone is petitioning the court to grant you status as an emancipated minor."

"What does that mean?"

"It means you'd be considered a legal adult, free of parental authority. The request gets reviewed by a judicial board, but it's based on medial need…psychiatric welfare...it's a done deal."

"The court can arbitrarily take me away from my parents?"

"It's not arbi—" Griff put his pen down and looked at me. "It's not arbitrary, Reese. Would it surprise you to know that what your mom did by deserting you was illegal?"

"Illegal!"

"California's child neglect and abandonment laws consider desertion a criminal offense."

"My mom's not a criminal. It's not like she left me alone."

"According to state law, desertion results in willfully exposing a child to mental suffering. Legally that's abuse. If the deserting parent leaves the child in the care of a mentally incompetent adult who fails to protect that child by exposing her to grave physical danger, that's neglect."

"Incompetent adult? Physical danger?"

"Dr. Pallone said you and your Dad went on a wild goose chase to San Francisco. In his state of emotional distress, he used poor judgment putting a then-fifteen-year-old with no license behind the wheel to drive hundreds of miles in twenty-four hours. Your father exposed you to grave physical danger."

"Dr. Pallone didn't tell me any of this."

"She did explain about living under state care. She didn't go into the legal muscle she'll have in case your parents disagree with the treatment plan. That wasn't her focus."

"Even if my parents were to disagree, which they wouldn't, why take me away from them?"

"Reese, when I read the facts about your family a few minutes ago you got defensive, said it sounded worse than it was."

"The way you read it off like a shopping list did sound worse than it was. All that stuff didn't happen at once."

"You're not able to see this objectively. You're not expected to. That's why these laws exist, to protect children. Abuse doesn't always show up as bruises and broken bones. That doesn't mean it's not abuse."

I wanted to crawl under the desk in shame. They had gotten the wrong idea. Abuse. Neglect. Foster care. Griff was talking about someone else's life, not mine. Yet I knew this is what Griff and Dr. Pallone had seen from the outside looking in—not Mom and Dad as I knew them. They saw sickness, recognized it right away. It wasn't special or dramatic. It fit neatly into a category with legal terms to describe it, ways to proceed in dealing with it.

All this time I'd thought my suffering was unique, so shocking it would knock the sensibility out of Petra, Sister Dorothea, Tim. In truth I was one in a line that stretched as far as the eye could see in front of and behind me. Dr. Pallone hadn't needed me to reveal a single thing that first day. The list of facts from Dad told the story, my deep dark secret exposed in a timeline of events she read as easily as an EKG.

The night I took Mom's sleeping pills I never could've imagined the chain reaction it would cause. My family had been exposed without my uttering a word. No one could stop the momentum now. Too many people and agencies were involved, not the least of which was the State of California taking over as my parents.

Griff waited until I had come back to the present.

"Dr. Pallone isn't interested in punishing your parents if that's what you're worried about. She's interested in protecting you. Abuse qualifies as sufficient grounds for emancipation, which means you'll be authorized to consent to your own treatment. That's all this is about. She wants to make sure you don't go home."

It was all so confusing. The state was placing me in foster care and giving me the right to object? How could Dr. Pallone be so sure I wouldn't? Was I really ready to trust her? Look what happened when I'd trusted Father Donnelly. And Derrick.

Then again, I was going to have to trust someone at some point. There was little chance for love without it, and love was the most important part of my Life Plan. At least when I'd had a Life Plan.

"Cavanaugh?"

"Huh? Oh. Dr. Pallone said you'd know how long it would take to get into Family Care."

"I'm not going to lie to you. The hospital is stuffed to the gills. I have a long list of patients waiting for placement and only a handful of homes. Nothing is going to happen overnight."

"Okay."

"Don't get discouraged yet." He picked up the catalogue and leaned across the desk. "See if one of these vocational programs appeals to you." He raised his eyebrows and grinned as encouragement to stay positive and keep moving forward.

I rolled my head with an acquiescing sigh and took the catalogue.

*

I finally received my first letter from Tim. In a quiet corner of the day room I sat down to read it.

June 20, 1965

Dear Reese,

I hope you've settled in okay at the new hospital. Camarillo is a beautiful drive up the coast and only ninety minutes each way. Still, that chunk of time makes it harder to visit. I was hoping for this weekend, but Brother Dominic has the flu, so yours truly will be taking the senior boys on summer retreat to Lake Arrowhead. God help me.

Life around here is crazy as always. We got through finals. I have your term paper on "Shared Symbolism: Catholic and Protestant Poets." You got a whopping A. Big surprise

I have a poem for you; it's not my own, but I don't want to tell you the author or the title because it may change your reaction to it. I find it comforting and thought you might too. I hope to see you soon. Hang in there.

Love, Tim

I have desired to go
Where springs not fail,
To fields where flies no sharp and sided hail
And a few lilies blow.
And I have asked to be
Where no storms come,
Where the green swell is in the havens dumb
And out of the swing of the sea.

Gerard Manley Hopkins. I knew the poem, and the title: *A Nun Takes the Veil*. Tim was right—I liked the poem better without it. Folding the letter into small squares, I headed to the nurses' station for permission to go in the dorm so I could hide it in my locker. Maggie nodded her okay.

I tucked the letter and poem in a large envelope and shoved it back under my dirty clothes. I heard muffled cries from the bathroom. Listening to make sure, I crept to the door and poked my head inside. At first I couldn't decipher the tight group in the corner. Angela and two of her cohorts had another patient pinned against the wall.

A washcloth stuffed in the poor girl's mouth muffled her grunts and cries. The two girls had hold of her arms while Angela punched the girl in the stomach, then grabbed her by the hair and banged her head against the wall.

"Had enough yet? Huh?" Angela squeezed the girl's mouth on each side. "If you ever again—"

I couldn't move. Angela saw me. "HEY! Cavanaugh, beat it…NOW…unless you want to be next!"

The girl pinned to the wall pleaded to me with her eyes. I retreated and let the door fall shut, feeling woozy and ashamed in equal order. The muffled cries resumed. I ran out of the dorm.

At dinner Angela brushed me as we exited the food line. She hissed a warning not to stick my nose where it didn't belong or I'd be sorry. I maintained a neutral expression and said nothing. She took the orange from my tray and exited the line.

I had passed Test # 2.

*

The afternoon sun felt good as I walked into Griff's office. He was sorting through charts at his desk. He always seemed disorganized, yet he knew right where everything was. Yes, life on the ward was fine, which jived with what the staff had reported. I'd been hard at work on my senior electives with not much else to keep me busy except writing letters and reading. Most of my time in the hospital classroom was spent helping other students.

It was hard to believe I wouldn't graduate with my class. No cap and gown, no celebration. This milestone would slide by in unremarkable fashion, a notation on my transcript. Somehow that seemed fitting. I was no longer the little girl who'd watched her father drive away in his Ford, leaving me in a strange and frightening place. The world of giggling girlfriends and worrying about grades had been concerns of a different lifetime.

Griff snapped his fingers to get my attention. "Cavanaugh?"

"Sorry. What was that?"

"I asked if you'd found something in the catalogue. Short of a master's degree in English Lit, did any of the one-year vocational programs interest you?"

"One did," I said. "The Psychiatric Technician program."

"Psych tech! I'd have thought you'd never want to see the inside of another mental hospital."

"It appeals to me more than radiology tech or veterinary assistant. Besides, I think I might be good at it. I can finish my bachelor's once I get a job."

Griff rested his chin in both hands with a silly grin. "Boy, you do think big. And long term." He snatched the catalogue from my hand. "Psych tech, psych tech. Here we are. Let's see, it looks like you'll need some pre reqs— English 1A, chemistry, speech, physiology—that'll do for a start."

"What if I'm not in Family Care by the time fall semester starts?"

"I've had second thoughts about waiting. Dr. P's on board. I'm going to get your Voc Rehab paperwork rolling. Once funding comes through, I can get you enrolled at VC. You can catch the second summer session."

"College? Now? While I'm still in the hospital?"

"I'll arrange rides. We have staff who live in Ventura."

I didn't know what to say.

"Alright, now get outta here and let me get to it. Oh! I almost forgot. How would you feel about grounds privileges? Go anywhere you want on your own…the commissary, the library."

My grin was as big as the day FD had lavished me with the Christmas dresses.

"No one else on the ward has privileges at the moment. You'll take some guff over it."

"I've gotten good at taking guff."

*

It was late afternoon, the air stifling in the ward. I sat tucked in a corner of the day room with my book.

"CAVANAUGH!"

Hearing my name at bullhorn level gave me such a start that Edna St. Vincent Millay tumbled off my lap to the floor. I went to the nurses' station where Dolores, the psych tech, slid open the glass partition.

"You have a visitor. Raoul went to fetch him in Admissions. You can talk in the snack room with the door open for thirty minutes, that's it."

Who would be coming to see me except Tim, who always came directly to the ward? I walked down the long hallway and waited at the door. Five minutes later Raoul opened it. I stared at my visitor, struggling for recognition. It wasn't a him. It was a her.

"Reese!"

I backed up instinctively. The voice registered. "Petra?"

"Hahaha. Yeah, it's me!" She came forward and threw her arms around me in a bear hug.

"Oh my gosh, look at you!" I moved back enough to take a good look, like an elderly aunt noting changes in growth.

We stood facing each other in mutual shock, hers no doubt at the clinical surrounding and me at the specimen that was Petra. Her hair had grown long. Heavy bangs covered her forehead all the way to the rim of her square rose-colored glasses. Around the guru neck of her white tunic was a strand of wooden beads in a variety of colors.

All that would've been enough of a statement without what she wore on the lower half—cotton pants in psychedelic oranges and blues that tapered to her calves where they widened into voluminous bells.

"Is there somewhere we can talk? I think I'm becoming the main attraction," she said, conscious of patients staring.

I led her to the relative privacy of the snack room.

"Holy moly, hon, this place is nuts. They had to search my bag and me before they'd let me in. The windows are barred. The doors are locked. What is this, San Quentin? What are you doing here?"

"Long story."

She looked at me a long time in search of the old me, the one she remembered. "You know what I mean. Why in God's name are you in this scary place? You haven't answered a single letter."

"The insurance ran out at St. John's and Mom intercepted my letters."

"Hon, your mom told me you couldn't have visitors. My gosh, don't you think I would've visited before now? Uncle Walker wouldn't tell me anything more than you'd been transferred to another hospital. I thought he meant another hospital like St. John's. But Camarillo? Norwalk State Hospital has been all over the newspaper with reports of patients being abused—as in beaten and drugged. Why didn't you go home from St. John's?"

"I'm...it's just depression. And this place is free. I mean it's for patients who need to be hospitalized a long time and don't have enough insurance. My doctor here is real good," I said in a feeble effort to steer the conversation away from the setting.

"Do they have you doped up?"

I cocked my head. "Do I look doped up?"

"No, but how is being locked away in this God-forsaken pit helping you? Isn't this kind of extreme just for being depressed?"

"My doctor just doesn't think I should be home right now. Hey, want some juice? We have orange, tomato—"

"Hon, I don't want any juice. Look, if you can't be home, you don't have to be here. Come live with me. I've moved to Santa Monica...to an apartment near the yarn shop with Dodi. She won't mind your rooming with us until we can figure something out. You and I could get a place together."

My mind ran amok at her logical suggestion, knowing it was impossible. "Right. I'm sure my doctor would discharge me right away to a wild hippie woman. One look at you and they'd see Flower Child written all over."

Petra burst out giggling. "What if I dug out my old nun's habit? That would convince them!"

This time we both laughed.

I explained about the plan to find a Family Care home, about how Dr. Pallone and Griff were helping me. Assured that I wasn't a prisoner, Petra moved on with the news she had come to tell me.

"The reason Aunt Maria and Uncle Walker haven't been coming to see you isn't because they don't care, it's because they've separated."

"Separated?" My mouth dropped.

"I found out a few weeks ago. I dropped by the house for a quick visit and saw the For Sale sign in front. I couldn't believe it. Uncle Walker had already moved out."

"What happened?" *Had Dad finally learned the truth about FD and the baby? Had he shot him? Was he in jail?*

Petra went on to tell the story as Dad described it to her when she reached him by phone at work. One day he had come in the kitchen from outside and didn't shut the back door all the way. Mom was working on a scrapbook of FD's career, bits and pieces spread all over the table. For years she'd been saving newspaper clippings about his role in the community—getting fat donations for the Church, his commendations from Cardinal Mahoney, and so on. The door blew open. Clippings flew everywhere.

Mom had gone crazy, yelling at him about what a stupid buffoon he was and how he was never interested in climbing the career ladder like FD had in the church. Petra said she figured maybe Dad had gotten tired of always playing second fiddle to FD. They had a big blowout and Mom told Dad she wanted a divorce. Dad agreed right on the spot. Mom told him she wanted whatever they got for selling the house, plus her car and all their savings. Said she deserved it after spending twenty years making a home, giving up her career to raise a family."

"Wow. What's Dad going to do? Move to Santa Monica closer to work?"

"He said on the phone he was going to quit his aerospace job and move up the coast, find something less stressful."

As Petra talked, I realized how much I'd missed her, missed the sound of her voice.

"There's more, hon. Brace yourself."

"What else could there possibly be?"

"Uncle Walker told me FD was leaving the priesthood. He wants to marry Aunt Maria."

"What? He always talked about becoming a bishop someday!"

"Apparently he's willing to give all that up to marry Aunt Maria."

"Whew. How can that even work, leaving the priesthood? I don't think he knows how to do anything in the real world. He can't even change a stupid tire."

The thought of his worldly incompetence sent us into giggles again.

"Hey, maybe Aunt Maria could teach him secretarial skills. Look how it worked for me."

That brought another wave of giggles. The news hit hard beneath the laughter. I was struck by a crushing realization. My big secret, the one I had been willing to die for, the one that had landed me first in St. John's and now Camarillo, had been revealed at last. Mom herself had exposed it!

The world hadn't come to an end. Dad hadn't shot FD. All my suffering had been for nothing. How could I have swallowed Kit's ridiculous fantasy? She had used me for her own ends to stay in the Palisades and keep Mom off her back.

Dad hadn't needed protection from the truth. He'd probably known it all along. Maybe telling Dr. Pallone about their baby had finally opened his eyes, made him see there was something worse than losing Mom. Maybe he realized he'd lost her already, along with both daughters because of her conniving and manipulation to keep her affair under wraps.

My whole life had changed overnight because I'd believed one stupid story from my sister. Could Kit have known I would carry it as far as it had gone, keep my secret no matter what it would cost me?

"You okay? You haven't said much."

"Yeah, I'm okay, just taking it in."

Our half hour visit was up. Petra shuffled through a humungous burlap purse. She opened my palm and placed a velvet box in it. "I got you something. Think of it as an early birthday present."

"This is July. My birthday isn't until January." I opened the gift. It was a gold ring with a tiny stone.

"Garnet, the birthstone for January."

I gazed at Petra. How happy I'd been during those few months she lived with us. We had come to love each other like sisters. This ring was a special gift for a special birthday, something a mother might give a daughter. Or one sister might give another.

I hugged Petra tight. "I'm proud to have an honest-to-God hippie sister. I'll wear the ring forever."

Raoul opened the locked door. Petra and I stood in the arched corridor resisting our goodbyes. Out of nowhere something slammed me against the wall. Petra jumped back in horror.

"Reese! Reese! Pretty Reese! You have a new friend. Am I still your friend?" Archie was on his knees, his helmet off kilter as he rubbed my shoes.

"Of course you're still my friend, Archie. Get up and meet my...sister. C'mon. Aren't you supposed to be with Hector?"

Archie's eyes widened. "Gotta find Hector, gotta find Hector, gotta find Hector." He took off toward his unit in lop-sided motion. Petra looked at me wide-eyed. We burst into giggles.

This time there was no tension in our goodbye hug. Petra turned away. She waved the peace sign overhead, bellbottoms swaying around her feet.

*

A letter arrived from Mom.

July 28, 1965

Dear Clarice,

I hope you are getting well and cooperating with the doctor. I am still convinced the hospital is the best place for you.

By now Petra has told you about the divorce. This shouldn't be a surprise and should affect you very little. We'll stay in the house until it sells, then Jack and I will find a place and your father will move up the coast.

Jack has submitted a request to the Vatican for release from his vows. We'll wait to marry until that's official, but as you know, that takes time. Since you'll be staying in Ventura County once you're out of the hospital, it shouldn't matter to you where Jack and I end up living. I'll be packing your belongings and giving them to your father for safe keeping.

I assume you're still in contact with Katherine. I'm sure I can count on you to give her the news.

Take care of yourself, Clarice.

Mom

I ran my fingers over the letter, blue ink swirls of cursive, the exaggerated strokes of Ls and Fs as familiar to me as her face. I could feel my mother's presence on the page, even imagine a whiff of Chanel #5.

Had Mom felt anything for me as she'd written these words?

In spite of everything, I still yearned for my mother. In moments of happiness, it had been enough just to be in her presence, surrounded by the electric field of energy where anyone within range could experience the strange and mysterious charge attracting us to her light.

It had always bewildered me that someone with such magnetism could also possess equally strange and mysterious attributes of repulsion. There had been no way to predict which Mom would show up on any given day. My secret-keeping ability hadn't been honed by discipline. It was collateral damage from a lifetime of apprehension. I had made it my business to avoid Mom's wrath. Kit had taken pleasure in triggering it.

No wonder the world had looked at Mom and Kit and seen strength—two unyielding personalities vying for dominance with me and Dad in subordinate roles keeping peace. Outside the context of my family I had no idea who I was. Even that identity had been issued in comparison to Kit.

All this time I had been banking on some fictional character as the road to self-discovery by proxy. Instead the search had become a process of elimination, ruling out who I wasn't rather than discovering who I was.

Mom and Kit had been checked off the list ages ago. I didn't have, nor did I want, Mom's charisma with the control to manipulate, or Kit's force of will energizing rebellion. Whoever I would become, I wanted a kind of strength neither of them had—strength of character.

I knew I didn't have it, not yet. Otherwise I would've

defended the girl Angela had attacked in the bathroom, but I could recognize it in those who did, people like Shirley, Dr. Pallone, Petra—a spinster psychiatrist, a paid employee, and a-nun-turned-hippie.

I hadn't figured out the qualities they shared amounted to strength of character. I had experienced it as empathy, genuine concern for my distress that made them reach out with tender mercy. That doesn't sound earth shattering. Yet I had tried to conjure a memory in which Mom had expressed interest in anyone who didn't serve her needs, a friend or neighbor she might have consoled. Nothing. My cool detached mother was above the crowd as if she had filtered her emotions to extract self-interest from altruism, insensitive to feelings and needs beyond her own, separate and apart because of it.

Maybe it wasn't that Mom couldn't express empathy, rather she didn't have it to express.

Maybe she was incapable of love for me or anyone else. Maybe she was lacking the one trait needed in forming an attachment between mother and child, the core emotion passed down from one generation to the next that linked past and present in a continuous line of humanity—the capacity to care for someone else.

Dad's desperate need to please Mom had nothing to do with love. It had to do with hate, self-hate—deep regret for not having had parents who instilled in him the moral fiber to stand up for what he believed was right; bitter disappointment that it had been another man with whom his wife had fallen in love; disgust with himself for failing the children whose job it had been to protect. Dad was Edgar Linton in *Wuthering Heights*, a constitutionally weak man who desperately loved his wife despite her love for another man and who loses everything because of it.

Father Donnelly was the last person in whom I could've found character strength. Presenting himself as a man of God, he turned out to be the most morally bankrupt of all, the personification of human frailty. He not only betrayed my father by cheating, he let Dad believe Mom's desertion had been his fault.

My pedigree didn't look good for developing virtue if empathy was the core requirement. Yet I knew I had it in me. I knew it was empathy I'd felt the day Griff categorized my suffering as abuse and I had taken my place in an endless line of those who had suffered in ways similar and different from my own.

At the time I'd been both ashamed and comforted by the banality of my plight, mortified that I had perceived my life as spectacularly awful, at the same time consoled that others had suffered like me. I had been part of an invisible community. I did belong somewhere after all. That seemed as good a place as any to join the human race.

The absence of this life-sustaining emotion from the very people who brought me into the world meant that any hope of my finding love in the future would require a monumental leap of faith—belief that I was, in fact, capable of being loved.

Maggie called me to the nurses' station. I folded Mom's beautiful blue-ink swirls and slid the letter into my pocket.

*

I took advantage of grounds privileges with long walks after appointments with Dr. Pallone and Griff. I had just left his office. Griff had done his social worker magic, enrolling me in three of my pre-req classes at Ventura College for the second summer session beginning the first week in August. A psych tech living in Ventura who worked nights would drop me at the college on her way home from work in the morning. An evening shift psych tech who also lived in Ventura would pick me up from campus later in the afternoon on her way to the hospital.

As summer school got under way I lived in a different world five days a week. At night I studied and did homework in the day room. Weekends varied only in the addition of Tim's visits Sunday afternoons.

Sessions with Dr. Pallone remained a central focus. In the safety of her office I was able to cope with feelings of overwhelming sadness—the pain of estrangement from my parents and the reason for it; feelings of loss over everything familiar, including a bedroom that would no longer exist once the house sold; deep disappointment at not graduating with my class or starting UCLA with Francie.

In the safety of her office I was also able to confront my behavior and understand the forces that had shaped it. Insight, that's what Dr. Pallone called it. The net effect of our work had been far more beneficial than any antidepressant Dr. Granzow ever prescribed.

I still had plenty of bad days. The image of Derrick would break through my consciousness when I least expected it. I had kept that particular ugly truth from Dr. Pallone. I knew I should have told her, could have told her. I also knew I wouldn't. The sense of futility that had kept Mom's secret locked inside would do the same with this one. No one could help.

The way Dr. Pallone had invoked legal emancipation over my driving to San Francisco, there was no telling what she might do about Derrick. The humiliation would be unbearable. Staff at St. John's, especially Shirley and

Ian, would believe it had been my fault after Derrick convinced them I had encouraged him with my 'sexual acting out'.

I'd had enough shame for a lifetime exposing one secret. The very act of recounting that despicable night would be like going through it all over again, not only speaking the words out loud in front of someone else, knowing it would be documented in my chart for the whole world to see. That was not going to happen.

This was one secret I would take to my grave.

Those bad days made it impossible to see life beyond the one I was living in the Land of Inbetweendom. In the end my telling Dr. Pallone about Derrick wouldn't change the one truth that made my future impossible.

I was damaged goods, tainted in every way a girl could be tainted.

Loneliness, that's what the future held for me.

*

Summer rolled into fall and still nothing opened up in Family Care. At times the adolescent ward felt so much like home I almost hoped nothing would. In those moments I would forget about my old life. The people who had been so important to me a year ago seemed smaller than the ones I lived with every day.

Angela's voice carried through the day room all the way to the back, where I sat at the big monastery table writing a letter to Kit.

"It's completely stupid that watching TV is based on finishing homework. Tomorrow's Saturday. I can finish it then. *Star Trek* is on at eight-thirty! I can't miss it."

"Rules are rules, Lupercio. You have thirty minutes to either finish or quit squawking."

Angela skulked toward the table. I focused on my

letter and pretended I hadn't seen her. The screeching metal sent a chalk-board shiver through me as she yanked out a chair on the opposite end. I didn't flinch and kept writing.

She slammed the Algebra book on the table with such force I was lucky to lift my pen before it squiggled over the page obliterating the words with a wild design. Sound effects came next. The loud pop of bubble gum punctuated dramatic huffing and puffing. She leaned on one elbow, noisily shuffling pages of math homework.

I waited for the jarring to stop, then resumed my letter. *Life here is about the same and…* Tongue-clicking chimed in behind the gum-popping, huffing, puffing, tapping and kicking in an orchestra of agitation. I tilted my head in her direction without making eye contact.

"What the hell are you looking at, Cavanaugh?"

I ignored her. *I see my doctor every week and she's really—* Shhhlapppp.

Muttered curses attended the general wriggling as Angela pounded the pencil down on the homework sheets. Again I halted my writing in time to avoid vibrations from the extra kick to the table leg. I remained still for a moment in case she hadn't finished the tantrum.

Without looking at her I threw out a line in hope she might take the bait. At least I might be able to join forces long enough to finish my letter. "Don't you hate Algebra?"

"Jesus, that's putting it mildly. What the hell does chasing freaking x have to with anything? Except missing *Star Trek*."

I resumed writing. She resumed kicking. I stopped again. This time I lifted my eyes. "If you want I could take a look at your homework."

"Yeah, right. Miss Valedictorian of Camarillo State Hospital. You think I'm stupid? I can figure this stuff out by myself. "

I shrugged and went back to my letter. *My social worker, who by the way is very el-hunko, is trying—*

Her voice was so soft it took me a second to realize Angela was speaking to me.

She frowned at the sight of her cohorts staking out turf forty-five minutes before *Star Trek*. "I guess it wouldn't hurt to take a look. But I don't need no help."

I lifted rather than slid my chair down to avoid attention. The kicking and huffing and gum-popping stopped. In a jerky movement, Angela shoved the homework in front of me. She ripped out a sheet of notebook paper and busied herself.

It was first year Algebra, not third, though she and I were the same age. I finished the first three problems. Angela slowed her doodling. I leaned over to explain an easy method. Her expression registered somewhere between a threat and a plea. The message was clear.

I scribbled calculations down one column then the next and on to page two. Twenty minutes later the homework was finished. Angela eyed me with suspicion, then added a scowl saying I'd better not quit halfway through. She drew the pages over and studied them one at a time with a look of utter confusion at page after page of elaborate computation.

"These better be right, Cavanaugh. If you're settin' me up you'll be sorry."

"They're right."

Angela bit her lip. She surveyed her friends squeezed on the couch, no doubt pitting distrust of me against desperation to join them. Angela loved canteen days, her twice weekly outing to load up on candy and chips. That privilege would be history if she were caught cheating.

In harsh rubbing movements she began erasing random numbers, not enough to change any answers, just enough to fake a tentative appearance. Eraser flakes flew across the table. She brushed off each page to scrutinize the smudges before going on. Satisfied the work replicated the usual caliber of her assignments, Angela straightened the papers into a single pile. She repeated her scowl at me, then pushed away from the table.

I watched her march to the nurses' station. Angela not only handed Maggie the homework, she did so with a 'so-there' smirk. She retreated to the couch with a final glare at me as the girls scooted over to make room just as the *Star Trek* credits began rolling.

I had passed Test # 3.

*

Christmas Eve morning I woke up cold and lonely. There would be no school today, just as there hadn't been yesterday and wouldn't be tomorrow. At least seventy percent of the patients on the ward had gone home on overnight pass to be with their family. Angela was not among them. Neither was I.

The place felt eerily deserted. The cavernous echo now so familiar had grown to a howl. There was little sign of Christmas. The only pine trees were those drawn by patients taped to the snack room door. Ornaments in red and green crayon looked colorless in a dayroom with half the fluorescent tubes burned out in the overhead lighting.

Loneliness left me brooding. Even near the window I could barely see over my own shadow to write. A note on the glass in Maggie's writing said at ten o'clock those of us left on the adolescent ward would be escorted to the auditorium. A local parish auxiliary had donated Christmas gifts. Patients who hadn't gone home would be allowed to choose one.

There had been no sign of a gift from Mom. Petra had promised to visit on the 26th. Still, Christmas would hardly be Christmas without a present. I had nothing else to do anyway. Had there been something worth doing, my wretched mood had depleted my energy. At ten o'clock I pulled on a sweater and got in line.

The auditorium was arranged in rows of long tables, each table displaying unwrapped gifts, eight per table— crafts, knit socks, book bags, hair accessories. My mood improved just walking into the brightly lit room thick with patients from other wards mulling over the loot. Mom always said shopping was one activity that brokered no impatience. What she really meant was I had better not complain while she tried on clothes. Now it was my turn. I would indeed take my time investigating the plethora of choices, savoring the thrill of knowing one of them would be mine.

I paused to examine a western blouse with a stylized yoke and yellow piping along the pockets. My eyes were drawn to a lump of dark material next to it—a velour shoulder purse. How I envied the purse collection Kit had amassed with babysitting money, little numbers in 1960's Op Art color combinations, big bags with silver buckles. Any chance of borrowing one had been out of the question.

I held the purse, hardly able to believe my luck. The patchwork design was a paisley pattern in alternating tones of black and aubergine. I ran my hand over the fabric, the double thickness of plush velour luxurious under my skin. The metallic snap made a satisfying click when I opened it to inspect the inside compartment. Mom's words rang in my ear. 'Newness is the best scent in the world, better than Chanel #5.' There could be no mistaking the sweet smell.

The interior lined in black satin had pockets along the seam on both sides. Cool satin swallowed my fingers as they checked for depth. Sliding the fabric strap over my shoulder, I let the purse drop to my hip. Perfect.

This was it. This was my Christmas gift.

The supervising attendant ushered me out of the crowded tables to wait by the door. In the center aisle facing the stage I became mesmerized by light reflecting on gleaming wood. In mechanical steps I walked up the stairs and crossed the stage to the podium. My hands closed over the dark wood rails. I looked over the buzz of activity below. A sudden realization hit me, bringing the tingle of euphoria. I thought I was lightheaded from skipping breakfast. I waited for the feeling to go away. It didn't.

That's when I knew. I belonged at a podium. Honors English hadn't been just a class. It had been my salvation. This would be my meaningful work, opening that door to someone else.

"CAVANAUGH! Off the stage!"

My moment ended. I left the stage and joined my group waiting by the door. We passed around our gifts and evaluated them in comparison with our own choice. What I couldn't show them was the new pencil marks in the composite drawing of who I was, who I would become some day. My revelation had added definition to the sketch.

That was my real Christmas gift.

*

Some birthdays you never forget. For me it was the bleak January morning I turned seventeen. The day was like any other, unremarkable save for a card from Petra and another from Tim with mention of a gift he'd deliver in person the next Sunday. No one would wish me Happy Birthday because no one knew it was my special day. That made it unforgettable, a birthday marked by tears rather than joy.

January also marked the two year anniversary of Mom's disappearance. The resulting chain of events that turned my life upside down still seemed hard to believe. Looking back from my vantage point two years later, I ached for the girl I had been at fifteen. I couldn't have known the road I traveled would lead down a treacherous path into darkness, nor could I have known I would miraculously make it from there to here.

It had been nearly ten months since my first day of hospitalization last March, seven of which had been in Camarillo. Dr. Pallone's plan for placement had snagged on the slow-moving wheels of the system. I had begun to think a placement would never come through. Griff said the good news was the state had been issuing new Family Care licenses every month in an effort to accommodate the hospital. The bad news was each home had to pass muster, prospective "parents" trained. The bottleneck resulted from a shortage of state inspectors to license the homes along with inadequate staffing to educate owners on safety laws and requirements for legally dispensing medication. There was nothing to do except wait and move forward with school and in therapy.

The afternoon sun made a feeble offering on my way back to the ward from my appointment with Dr. Pallone. I jiggled like a toddler in need of a toilet to stay warm until someone unlocked the door. Raoul said Maggie had something for me at the nurses' station. It was a Fed Ex package. The contraband search had left the birthday wrap torn. Inside were two Oxford blouses, one in yellow, the other in pink. My mother's imagination in gift giving apparently didn't venture beyond androgynous clothing that would end up long forgotten in some church donation box. Stuffed between the blouses was a note explaining a year's subscription to *Seventeen Magazine* would be arriving six weeks later.

I let out a rueful chuckle. *Seventeen Magazine*, the perfect gift for a depressed teen in existential crisis rotting in a psychiatric facility. Those tips on dating and clothes would come in handy. How about tips on how to cope when Mom walks out of your life to have another man's baby, or better still, an article along the lines of Rape: Who Can You Turn to for Help. Those were just the topics a magazine targeting All-American girls wanted to publish.

I nodded to Maggie and kept walking, assured of her reciprocal nod granting permission to enter the dorm. Two hooks eighteen inches apart in the back of my locker served as hangers. I opened the blouses and secured them in hopes the fold wrinkles would smooth out on their own. No ironing on the ward. I was about to close the locker door. Something was off. I scanned the shelves.

My Christmas purse was missing.

15

THE ROAD AT MY DOOR

A letter arrived from Kit.

January 20, 1966

Dear Reese,

Belated Happy Birthday! I hope it wasn't too awful being in the hospital for your special day and for Christmas as well. Just think, in another year you'll be free and can do anything you want.

Carlitos was such fun over Christmas. At almost two he's old enough to understand what Feliz Navidad means…toys!

Things here aren't so great. Carlos and I haven't been getting along. He's at the ranch all week and on the weekends he wants to be with his buddies and play with Carlitos.

I miss my friends, I miss California, I miss speaking ENGLISH!! The only friend I've made here is Sonia, this older American woman. She loaned me a bunch of books. They've changed my life, Reese. That's part of the problem. They've opened my eyes.

I know this is not the life for me. I want to really live. It turns out Carlos is just as traditional as his family. He loves it here, loves the way men can do anything and women can do zip. I will never have freedom in this country, or in this marriage.

There's a great poem, Howl, by Allen Ginsberg. It's all about rejecting middle class society, seeing it for what it really is, the hypocrisy and all. And this cat, Kerouac, Jack Kerouac, I've been reading his book. It's mind-blowing! There's no God, no guilt, no private schools or pressure about college. He dropped out of Columbia University (!) to embrace life on his terms, the exact opposite of the brainless drones we grew up with, kids who never questioned.

I'm not sure what I want in life. I just know I don't want to end up like Mom, stuck in a dull marriage, taking care of kids I never wanted in the first place. For what? To see it all go down the tubes twenty years later when I'm an old woman?

I've decided to come home, return to the U.S. Carlos insists the baby stay with Aida, at least until I get on my feet. I'm going to write to Daddy and ask if I can move in with him, wherever that is now, until I get a job and my own place.

Anyway, it's not a done deal yet, only a start. Beyond getting out of Columbia, I have no clue what direction my life will go. At least it will be MY life.

That's my rotten news. We're quite a pair, the two of us, you in a nut house and me on the brink of divorce. I guess Mom won't be bragging about either of us anytime soon.

Love, Kit
P.S. The enclosed photo is Carlitos on his pony, Poncho.

Kit and Carlos getting divorced? My sister's life had gone off the rails. At least now I knew the general direction I needed to go.

*

Life in the hospital carried on as usual while I continued to wait for placement. Every Friday night Angela pulled up a chair next to me and doodled while I did her math homework. By the time *Star Trek* came on at eight-thirty, Angela was front and center on the couch. It was common knowledge among the patients, I'm not altogether sure the staff wasn't on to our little arrangement. It didn't matter.

Angela needed me and I needed her. Molly had been right the day she told me I was in deep trouble on the ward with my pathetic lack of street cred. In the end I had something better—brains. The irony wasn't lost on me that it had been Mean Queen who'd taken the bull's eye off my back in validating book smarts as a stand-in for street sense.

Sunday afternoon I had a visitor. It had been a whole month since Tim had been able to get away to visit. He and I embraced like the long lost friends we had become since last spring at St. John's.

"Ah, Reese. You look wonderful, hon!"

We settled on my bench under the towering oak and talked nonstop, me about the classes at the college and Tim about the ones he was teaching at St. Monica's.

I mentioned Family Care as little as possible and kept details fuzzy, which wasn't hard since I didn't know anything. It's not that Tim would've judged me. The more he knew about the plan the more questions he would have about why I wasn't going home. Sitting on the bench listening to him describe his jaunt to UCLA for a catalogue, how he'd mapped out English Lit courses in the best sequence, he sounded as excited as I would've been a lifetime ago. It was time to bring up reality.

"Hon, what are you saying? I thought you were taking these classes to get some of your freshman breadth requirements out of the way. I assumed the talk about staying in a care home after discharge from the hospital was one possibility. Not the only possibility. I don't understand why you would want to complete this vocational program and stay in Ventura County instead of starting your bachelor's degree at UCLA."

"It's not like I'm going to China. I'll be an hour-and-a-half away."

"I know, it's just—" Tim shook his head in confusion. "I imagined you and I having the long conversations we've always had, just on the beach instead of...you know...here. I was sure you'd be home in time for spring quarter, summer for sure. I don't understand why you would waste your time finishing this one year program. Is that why you want to stay in Ventura County?"

"It's not exactly a waste of time. I'll need to support myself once I leave Family Care. With my psych tech license I can get a job near UCLA, or maybe UC Santa Barbara, and transfer."

"A job? Why wouldn't you live at home, or in the dorm?"

There was no way around it. I told him about the divorce—omitting the little detail about Mom and FD— and how the house was on the market. I had no home to go to anymore, so it was just as well I would be going into Family Care.

"Oh, hon, Reese. I'm so sorry."

He pulled my head to his chest. After a moment of hesitation, my shoulders relaxed. I sensed Tim's need to comfort me yet I felt a growing unease. I tried to make light of it. "I guess that officially makes me an orphan."

Tim squeezed me close, whispering shushing sounds and stroking my hair. He wasn't about to make light of it. Then again, this was all news to him. I'd been adjusting for months.

"Hon, you've been through so much. And now, at barely seventeen, you're going to be on your own in the world, cut off from family, no home. You must feel like the rug has been pulled out from under you. There will come a time when you'll soar free. You'll find your home. Being in this place I don't imagine you've felt safe for a long time."

"Safe doesn't mean the same thing it used to. I'll take this dilapidated dungeon any day over fancy St. John's when it comes to—" I stopped myself.

He chuckled and pulled away so he could look at my face. "What? You're being sarcastic, right?"

Sadly I wasn't. I couldn't tell Tim that the places I'd thought would be safe, should be safe—my home, a private hospital—had turned out not to be, and the one place I had been certain was dangerous had offered me safe passage to adulthood.

I steered the conversation a different direction. "You've been such a good friend to me during the most difficult time in my life, Tim. You and I will go on being friends whether I live in Ventura or the Palisades. Or China."

He spoke softly into my hair as he held me. "I'm very glad to hear you say that, hon. I don't feel nearly as lost and confused when I'm with you. Questions about my faith, uncertainties over the future...everything feels lighter when I'm with you. I care very deeply for you, Reese. I have for a long time. Your happiness means everything to me."

"Talking to someone really helps. Other than Dr. Pallone and Griff, I don't talk to anyone about anything, at least not anything that matters." I broke free of his hug with a mischievous smile. "Maybe you should be a patient too. I know a good shrink I could recommend."

The laughter broke the stubborn unease I had felt since the moment we sat down, a tension I'd never felt before with Tim.

"Hey, you haven't opened your present yet." He reached into the pocket of his jacket and produced a beautiful aqua colored box with white ribbon bow. The box inside that one needed both hands to pry it open. I lifted the necklace out. A gold Saint Christopher medal the size of a dime dangled on the end of a glittering chain.

"Tim! It's the most beautiful thing I've ever laid eyes on!"

He wriggled in pleasure. "I got it at Tiffany's in Beverly Hills…it's 22 karat gold."

"No! Tell me you didn't! But—"

"Instead of sending me a Christmas package this year all the way from Ireland, I convinced my folks to be practical and send a check."

"You spent gift money on me?"

"I knew right away it had to be something special. Brother Dominic has a very stylish sister who regularly brings care package to the clergy house. I consulted her and this is what she suggested for a very special friend."

I kept my eyes on the gift. Any unease I'd felt earlier returned as full-fledged discomfort. I guided the necklace back in the box and snapped it closed. "Tim. I can't keep this."

"I want you to have it. Saint Christopher is the patron saint of travelers."

"I can't, Tim. Anyway, even if I could keep it there's no way to have something this precious here. It would be stolen in no time. Then I'd really feel awful." I held the box and waited for Tim to take it. He reached over. For a moment we both held the box. I felt trapped in his gaze, those intense green eyes that now searched mine, for what I don't know. It seemed like so long ago that I'd walked into class and laid eyes on Brother Tim McPherson.

"Tell you what. I'll hold onto it for safe keeping...for now...with the understanding that it's yours and when you leave this place you'll wear it."

I let go of the box. "Okay."

The rest of the visit we spent wandering the grounds, clinging to the minutiae of UCLA's freshman curriculum in full awareness it was a diversion from for the real subject.

*

On the ward I stayed extra busy to avoid thinking about Tim.

The school teacher, Joanne, agreed to let me volunteer in the classroom with whatever time remained after my classes and studying. Angela and company refused any assistance in that setting. The ward was a different story. She led her pals to the monastery table, the same three pals who hadn't been interested in class. Angela said they needed a little help if there was any hope of passing algebra and English. It wasn't a request for help. It was an order.

If our tacit agreement over algebra homework had earned me chops on the ward, my status as academic concierge practically made me a guru. Angela spread word that I would help anyone she asked. No one dared approach me without prior permission from my gatekeeper.

It was around this time I noticed Angela watching me, whether she was in front of the TV or with her friends styling each other's hair. Even though I pretended not to notice once in a while our eyes made contact. This odd acknowledgement gave us some kind of bond. I wasn't sure what Angela made of my endless studying, except that my days had purpose—well, if not purpose at least a short term objective.

In me I believe Angela saw a world beyond the adolescent ward. I think she knew reaching the pinnacle as reigning Top Dog in a state institution only to age out and be transferred to an adult version of confinement was not the same as making something of her life. The more I got to know Angela, the more I saw her shrewd intelligence, as well as sensed defeat.

A knife attack on her teacher had topped a history of incorrigible behavior and severe depression. That's the rumor I'd heard anyway. Whatever had landed Angela in a state hospital, I think she knew life beyond these walls was not in her future. I finally understood why she had singled me out in the beginning. It hadn't been personal. Angela had to denigrate anyone passing through rather than inhabiting her insular world.

I suspected beneath the bravado Angela and I weren't so different. We may even have suffered in similar ways. That experience has no boundaries in social class, though whatever advantages offered by mine had not likely been available to her. I could've told her the fancy psychiatrist and private hospital of my world had not only failed me, it had inflicted irrevocable damage. A state employee in the public institution of her world had saved me.

My guess was Angela craved purpose in life every bit as much as I did and thought in watching me she might find hers. I had noticed her eavesdropping the day I told Maggie about Viktor Frankl's life as a death camp inmate, how it led him to discover the importance of finding meaning in all forms of existence, even the most brutal ones.

Whatever it was that transpired in the course of our eight months together, Angela had changed her tone. She couldn't be outright friendly; her surly demeanor never wavered. The message came through anyway. One morning after breakfast, I needed a book from my locker for a patient I was helping in the classroom. I had taken to stuffing Cyrano under the bed since his urine bath my first morning. Any trip to the dorm included a quick check to make sure he was there.

I opened my locker and reached for the book. I stood to close it when something caught my eye. There it was on the bottom shelf.

My Christmas purse.

*

Three weeks went by without a word from Tim. That meant either he'd felt rebuffed at my not accepting his gift or he was every bit as confused as I was by the aura hanging over us. I had played and replayed our visit a dozen times. Nothing jumped at me that might've cleared the confusion. Something between us had changed. I had to find what that something was before we saw each other again.

It wasn't that I was clueless. I knew he liked me. Most of that stemmed from a shared love of poetry, which neither of us had in common with anyone else. It had become the cornerstone of our relationship. It had never made me uneasy and didn't now.

I thought if I could identify each feeling separately, by a process of elimination the answer would emerge and end my confusion. The most obvious feeling was that I missed him. I enjoyed our time together. It had to be more than that.

It also didn't feel weird that our friendship had gone beyond the classroom. Over the course of a year I had grown very fond of Tim. It had never been about physical attraction, handsome as he was. Like most girls in class I'd had a bit of a crush on him, nothing even close to Francie's groupie adoration. I didn't feel obligated to him in any way. He had always enjoyed loaning me his books. I was grateful he had continued making the effort to visit with an hour drive each way. Appreciating Tim didn't equate with obligation to him. No matter how hard I searched I couldn't find the basis for my icky feeling. But there was one.

It came to me in a sucker punch. Subconsciously I must've been attracted to him in spite of my claim otherwise. Maybe I had been sending signals without even knowing. Given my history with Derrick it's understandable I would resist admitting to myself any kind of physical draw.

That had to be it.

Tim had sensed vibes, thought I was asking for more than friendship. Questions about his faith had come up in conversation more than once recently. Could the two be related? Had he thought about leaving the clergy for me the way FD had left the priesthood for Mom?

An epiphany shook me to the core. I must've led him on, the same way Derrick told me I'd led him on at St. John's. Derrick had interpreted friendliness as flirtation because somehow I had given him the impression I wanted more than a patient-therapist relationship. That's why Tim had given me the expensive necklace. I had led him on. He had been confused enough to let me.

I felt sick. A lifetime with Mom had infused in me the very behavior that disgusted me in her, words filled with ambiguity, actions weighted with innuendo. I had become Mom.

Tim's tenderness was nothing more than the product

of mixed signals. I had been crossing wires as far back as Greg Stewart. It hadn't been out of thin air he felt rejected the morning he called after the dance, the night after our toothy kiss. Greg heard something in my voice. Why else would he have rejected me in kind unless he thought I was no longer interested in him? We were best friends! How could I not be interested?

It was my fault the relationship with Greg ended.

It was my fault Tim sensed more than was there.

It was my fault Derrick wanted me alone in his car.

*

The letter arrived late on a Friday afternoon. Maggie waved it in the nurses' station window to catch my attention. We chatted for a few minutes. Along with Angela, the staff had changed toward me though for a very different reason. I was on the path to being one of them, which afforded status the same way the pact with Angela had.

I polished an apple I'd brought back from lunch and headed for my usual place at the table. The fact that Tim hadn't visited in the three weeks told me he was embarrassed about the gift and was backing off. He and I would have to work our friendship back to a comfortable place.

I stuck the apple in my mouth and held the letter taut with both hands to flatten the folds. Keats. The poem was by Keats. I knew immediately.

Down by the salley gardens my love and I did meet;
She passed the salley gardens with little snow-white feet.
She bid me take love easy, as the leaves grow on the tree;
But I, being young and foolish, with her would not agree.
In a field by the river my love and I did stand,

And on my leaning shoulder she laid her snow-white hand.
She bid me take life easy, as the grass grows on the weirs;
But I was young and foolish, and now am full of tears.

My eyes were drawn further down the page. My mouth dropped open. The apple fell out, rolling across the linoleum.

"...and so I've gone to your parents for their permission to marry you. We need it in writing since you're under age. I can happily report I now have such written permission in hand. We could wait a year until you're eighteen but I don't see the point. I love you Reese. I want to take care of you, give you a home, make a home with you. I've been a fool not seeing it before now, how lonely I've—"

Marry me? What is he talking about? My mind whirled trying to understand what was happening. Why didn't Tim come to me instead of going to Mom and Dad? Even if they still had legal authority, why in the world would they agree to my marrying Tim? I'm barely seventeen!

I felt lightheaded.

Oh my God! It's happening again! My parents have found one more way to wash their hands of me. They didn't get the chance to make FD my legal guardian and send me away to boarding school. It hadn't been enough to let Dr. Granzow ship me off to Camarillo. Signing away legal authority as my parents wasn't reassurance enough that I was no longer their problem, not when they could be rid of me permanently in marriage to Tim!

I bolted to the nurses' station, my words garbled and sluggish, like an album playing on slow speed. I willed myself to sound calm. "Maggie, I need to see Dr. Pallone."

"Sure, Cavanaugh. Hold on a minute. Let me call over and check."

She made the call and returned to the window.

"No can do, Cavanaugh. She'll see you Monday for your regular appointment."

I walked in a stupor past the day room into the hallway. Raoul came out of the storage room. I was desperate to get out of there, desperate to be outside where I could breathe and think.

"I need out, Raoul."

"Sure, Cavanaugh. You sign the sheet?" He turned to unlock the door.

"Uh huh."

I clenched my fists and waited for the clicking sound of the lock. Before Raoul could pull the door open, I pushed past him from behind and squeezed through it. The outside corridor was empty. I stood for a moment and looked around, unsure where to go. Griff.

I ran down the corridor, picking up speed with each stride. At the great lawn I zigzagged through patients in transit. I reached the corridor leading to Griff's office at the end. The sound of my heartbeat drowned everything out save the thud-swoosh-thud of a quickening beat.

At the end of the corridor I never even slowed down. I shot past Griff's office and kept going, running, past the cafeteria, past the commissary, the clinic, past the Bell Tower. I darted between buildings, zigzagging my way to Admissions. Once I caught sight of the driveway my feet took on a life of their own, running faster, faster. In the distance, I could see the road leading down the mountain to the highway.

I reached the parking lot, the very one where I had watched Dad drive away. I crossed it in minutes, jumping the barriers marking each space like hurdles in a track meet.

My chest was heavy, my brain empty, my body in overdrive. *Run, Reese, run! Run like you've never run before!*

Somewhere behind me I heard a voice. I turned for a quick look. Raoul was running after me, shouting and waving his arms. He was breathing hard. His bulky body heaved to and fro as he gave chase. Broken commands reached me in bits and pieces as he labored to catch me.

"CAVANAUGH! Stop!"

I ignored him and kept going.

"Cavanaugh...STOP! If you go...beyond the gate...you're AWOL...I'll have to...call security..."

I kept running. Running like I'd never run, running from Mom and Dad and FD and Tim and Dr. Pallone and Griff, running from everyone helping me, everyone hurting me, tired of trying to decipher a world where nothing was what it seemed, everyone a chameleon and me color blind.

Another quick glance over my shoulder. Raoul had dropped back. He was staggering to a stop.

Keep running, Reese! Keep running!

A fog horn sounded. No. It was the hospital alarm going off. Patient AWOL.

I came to the gate at the end of the long driveway. It was open. I flew past it onto the winding drive that would eventually take me to the main road, and from there Pacific Coast Highway.

I rounded the first switchback and disappeared from sight.

A voice rang out. Raoul must've started again. It wasn't Raoul. It was Griff.

I quickened my pace on the downhill grade, running, breathing, running, breathing.

"CAVANAUGH! Stop! I can outrun you! Don't make

this any worse."

He had just rounded the switchback, too far behind me to catch up.

My body became weightless, fueled by a lifetime of surplus adrenaline, nascent energy waiting for this moment, waiting for me to break free. Nothing could stop me now.

Why hadn't I run from this place the very first day? Run from Mom and Dad who wanted so desperately to be rid of me, run from Tim and his need to take care of me, run from Dr. Pallone and her plan to send me to a strange home.

She had been in such a hurry to cut me free from my parents. No one could free me. I would rot for the rest of my life in a prison far more difficult to escape than any federal penitentiary. Exposing the Big Family Secret hadn't made me whole because I could never be made whole.

I heard footsteps behind me. Griff was gaining, his voice loud and clear.

"Cavanaugh! You're jeopardizing everything you've worked for! STOP! Talk to me. Just talk to me! That's all I ask. I won't try to take you back."

I pressed ahead, rounding the next bend. I could hear traffic on the Coast Highway below, an abyss calling me home. The surge of power quickening my body suppressed all rational thought. What did I care about privileges and goals, grand plans, the future, all concocted through rose colored glasses by somebody else. For the first time, I was running for me. I was running for Viktor Frankl. For his family. For every little girl ever torn from her mother's arms. For those who could not run.

Griff's voice grew louder. He was closing the gap

between us. "Cavanaugh... c'mon...stop, Reese. I just want to talk."

Movement caught my eye. Griff. He was almost up with me. I darted left to break his rhythm. He trailed behind as we carved into the mountain for another switchback turn.

I heard Griff panting. He appeared at my side. His legs hit the ground in smooth, giant strides. For a moment we ran in perfect unison. My body transcended asphalt in effortless moves. I was flying.

In a burst of extraordinary energy, Griff sprinted ahead of me as we raced full throttle down, down the mountain. I fell in behind him. He pulled further ahead. I kept running.

All of a sudden he stopped and spun around. He stood facing me with feet wide apart, arms out to the side. Caught in the force of my own momentum there was no way to slow down, no way to avoid him.

I crashed into Griff. His body felt like a concrete wall. The blunt force knocked the wind out of me. In one deft move Griff locked his arms around me.

"LET GO OF ME!" My arms were pinned. I struggled to push back and kick him. His restraint was a vise grip.

"Reese! Stop fighting. It's me. It's Griff."

"LET ME GO! I swear to God. I'll bite you. I'll tear you apart!"

"Whoah...whoah, Reese...sshhhhhh. Settle, girl, settle. I just want to talk. Let's quiet down...shhhhh."

He held me tight in his arms. My muffled threats drowned in his chest. I could feel his heart as it mimicked my own.

"Reese...listen to me. We can turn around right now and no one has to know how far you've gone off grounds."

He relaxed just enough for me to pull back and kick him. "Let me go!"

He squeezed me again to stop a second kick. "Reese, calm down. I just want to talk."

"No! You're going to hurt me! You're going to rape me!"

In a sudden move Griff let go and stepped back with his hands in the air. It happened so fast I lost my balance. I stumbled forward. Regaining my equilibrium I came to a halt and bent over, hands on my knees, gasping for air. Griff stayed back.

"Rape? What are you saying? It's me...Griff,"

I stayed bent over in a fight to fill my lungs.

"Who's hurt you? Someone here? Tell me, Reese." His voice had an edge of urgency that sounded nothing like the free-wheeling guy making wisecracks in his office.

"No."

He stepped closer. "C'mon, it's me, your pal...Griff. You can tell me."

"No one." I shut my eyes, trying to separate past and present.

"Was it someone at St. John's?"

"No one's hurt me." My breathing started to even out.

"Reese, you thought I was going to hurt you a minute ago. You said the word rape. Someone has hurt you. Who is it?"

"No one."

Griff waited a moment. He came closer, careful not to touch me. Our heads nearly met as he bent over on his knees again.

"Why were you running away? Cavanaugh? What's happened?"

His heartfelt appeal weakened my façade. This was Griff, a man who had done everything in his bureaucratic power to help me and in doing so had offered more guidance in nine months than my father had in seventeen years. I straightened up. "Nothing's happened."

"Well, something must've to get you so riled up that you'd go AWOL, jeopardize everything we've worked for all these months. Where were you running to? The Highway?"

I couldn't hold the anger any longer. "I thought this might be my parents' lucky day and I'd get hit by a Mack truck. They could quit thinking up ways to get rid of me. At some point they're going to run out of people to give me away to. Enough is enough. I get it."

Griff looked at me in confusion. I felt emotion pushing past the anger.

"Yes...Miss Goody-Two Shoes Cavanaugh has a voice after all. Better call in the muscles, put me in restraints. God forbid I say no for once. No! No! No! No!" My protests were garbled in uneven sobs. I staggered back, swatting at the air to keep Griff away.

"Reese, I'm not going to hurt you. And I'm not going to let you run away or get hit by a truck. I don't know what's happened but you're safe now. You're safe with me." Griff stepped closer. "You're safe." We stood without speaking as my crying slowed. I wiped my face on the sleeve of my sweatshirt.

"That's it...nice and slow."

A security patrol car sped toward us and screeched to a halt in the middle of the road. The guard rolled down the window. "Everything under control here, Masterson?"

"Yeah, Spivak, I've got it. Thanks."

"You're quite a ways down the hill. Want a lift?"

"That's okay. We'll walk. You mind radioing in and telling Dr. Pallone I found Cavanaugh? We're heading to her office. Be there in fifteen, twenty."

"Will do." With a nod to Griff and a suspicious once-over at me, the guard flipped a U turn and doubled back to the hospital. Griff and I watched the car disappear around the first switchback.

"What do you say, Cavanaugh? Shall we head back? Go see Dr. P?"

The list of damages rolled through my brain in a wave of nausea. I'd ruined everything. Ventura College. Family Care. There was no way I was going anywhere now. Maybe I'd end up in a cell block with violent patients and beat up by some crazed Angela clone. Whatever my fate, it was sealed the moment I stepped off hospital grounds. There was nothing to do now but face the music.

Griff didn't move, clearly hoping I would cooperate now that he'd sent Security away. I looked at him for a long moment.

In that face I saw Derrick in his car, pleading with me to protect him from losing his job, his license, his fiancé. In that face I saw FD after the Dodger game as we waited for the tow truck, asking me to believe he was a man of God who had never been in love. In that face I saw my father, crippled with fear at losing the woman he loved, begging me to protect him from a truth he couldn't bear.

Keep this secret, Reese, or you will destroy me. That's what each of them had said in so many words. I had protected three powerful men. And it had broken me. Here was Griff, asking nothing more than to help me.

I took the first step. Neither of us spoke. Griff was probably afraid he would open a Pandora's box in a non-secure area where he might have to physically control me again. I got the sense delivering me safely to Dr. Pallone would be accomplishment enough.

His vigilance felt reassuring. My emotions were teetering on the edge of containment. I could go either way, especially now that I had nothing to lose and was tired of running from myself. Running from the truth. Something had to change.

Day staffers leaving the parking lot gaped at us with curiosity to identify who had gone AWOL. The evening crew had arrived earlier for report. My escape had been serendipitously book ended by that twice daily change of shift carving patient coverage to the bone.

Griff and I cut across the parking lot to the Admissions building, to Dr. Pallone's office. Raoul appeared, trailed by patients returning to the adolescent ward. I lowered my head and turned away, nudging Griff to hang back until they'd passed.

Fingers began pointing. "Cavanaugh! Hey, it was Cavanaugh who went AWOL!"

Someone yelled. "Stop your gawking and keep it moving!" It wasn't Raoul's voice I heard. It was Angela's. Positioned with her back to me she kept the line moving with a slight shove forward as each patient filed by, a traffic cop thwarting Looky Lou's rubbernecking to check out the scene of the accident.

Dr. Pallone met us at the door. She motioned me inside while she and Griff spoke in hushed tones, not so hushed that I didn't catch the word 'rape'. Dr. Pallone closed the door and leaned against it for a moment. Just as she had that first day, just as she had during every session since, she walked past her desk to the chair next to mine and sat down in her usual calm manner.

I crossed my legs and faced the other direction.

"Sounds like you gave Raoul and Griff quite a run for their money."

I responded with silence. She waited. By now her lengthy pauses didn't throw me like they had at first. I knew she would wait at least a full minute for me to say something.

"Reese, what's happened in the last hour to trigger this?"

"Nothing."

This time a thirty second pause.

"Griff said you went AWOL. He said you wanted to send your parents a message. What were you trying to say?"

In a mocking laugh I faced her squarely. "That they could stop trying to get rid of me. I got the message. Again."

"What do you mean...'again'?"

"I'll tell you what! They gave me away again. Only this time instead of handing me off to Father Donnelly, they went one better. They might as well be passing around a bottle of gin the way they keep throwing me at one man after another."

"Who have they passed you to?"

"Tim! Out of the blue he asked their permission to marry me. Marry me! And did my mom and dad say 'Oh, no! Reese is only seventeen and needs time to get back on her feet'? No! Get ready for a bolt from the sky. They said 'Of course you can marry her. We'll put it in writing in case there's any doubt you've promised to take her off our hands.' That's what they said!"

"When did this happen?"

"Well since I'm the last one to know I couldn't tell you. I just got Tim's letter announcing the happy news. The fact that they have no legal authority to give me away must've slipped their minds. That really wasn't the point, though, was it? I thought I'd save them the trouble of a wedding and let a Mack truck give them what they really want."

"Is that where you were headed? The Highway?"

Silence.

"Griff said he had to restrain you when he caught up with you, said you kicked him."

I scoffed. "I didn't hurt him. I was scared, that's all."

"Scared of what?"

"I thought he was going to hurt me."

"Hurt you how?"

I turned away.

"Reese, what were you afraid Griff was going to do?"

I threw my hands in the air. "How did I know he wouldn't rape me? Girls get raped all the time, you know."

"Has Griff ever done anything to make you think he might harm you?"

"No."

"Then I'm wondering why you would think that."

I shrugged.

"I'm wondering if it's because someone else has hurt you...someone who raped you."

"I guess it all depends on how you define rape. I mean, technically, having sex with a girl under eighteen is statutory rape and my good 'ole parents have just sanctioned that one...in writing! 'Go ahead Tim, have as much sex as you want with your seventeen-year-old bride.' That kind of rape?

"Or maybe it's the kind of rape my Mom had where everyone does absolutely nothing about it, like it's perfectly normal for a woman to greet her husband at the door and say, 'Hi honey. How was your day? My day was peachy. By the way, I was raped. No, it's okay. We don't need to report it to the police. My rapist is going to get a firm talking to from Father Donnelly.' THAT kind of rape?

"You see I'm a little confused here, Dr. Pallone. There are so many kinds it's hard to tell which kind is Real Rape. Even if I could tell, what difference does it make? If my mom got pregnant from rape and no one thought that was worth reporting, rape without getting pregnant must not matter at all. Telling the police is probably just a legal thing, like being emancipated, stupid paperwork that ends up causing total humiliation and results in nothing."

"Rape is a crime of violence, Reese. There are consequences, for both rapist and victim."

"Consequences? You mean like someone losing his job? All he would have to do is deny it. So why in the world would anyone say anything to anyone? Silence, that's my power."

"Isn't silence how you got here?"

I rolled my eyes. "That was different. That was supposed to give me what I wanted, my crazy dream to live at home with my parents until I turned eighteen, like everybody else. Now I don't even have a home. Or parents, if you want to get technical about it."

"I know it's been difficult being away from home. It's the only home you've known. You just need to trust me a little while longer."

"Trust you? Why should I trust you? That's been my big mistake in life. I swear, I must be as gullible as they come. To think I actually believed Kit's story about Daddy shooting FD if he found out about the affair, or that I actually believed Mom that everything would be fine if I just played along. I even believed Daddy would stick up for me after what we'd been through. Kit told me he wouldn't. I was brilliant enough this time not to believe her.

"I'm through trusting everyone else. I'll decide for myself from now on. Instead of locking me in a mental hospital or marrying me off to a man ten years older than me, a holy man, I might add, has anyone ever thought to ask me what I want? No, quiet little Reese doesn't have a voice. I DO have a voice and I'm saying enough with everyone threatening me if I do this, don't do that. I'm done keeping everyone's secrets."

"Who has threatened you?"

"I meant in general."

"It sounded like more than your parents. Is someone else asking you to keep a secret?"

"Hey, I'm tired of doing all the talking. You know everything about me and I don't know anything about you."

"What do you want to know?"

"Are you married?"

The fleeting expression on her face was impossible to read behind glasses. "No, I'm not married."

"I figured. You'd rather be working, like Mom. Come to think of it, you're a lot like my mom. You're probably sick of me too, can't wait to send me away to Family Care so I'll be somebody else's problem."

Silence.

"Would my keeping you in the hospital accomplish anything? Other than disavow you of the belief that you're being abandoned again because you're unlovable?"

I clicked my tongue. "You always think you know what's in my head."

"You drew a parallel between your mom and me. She rejected you again by agreeing to marriage and I'm rejecting you by sending you to Family Care? Is that what you were feeling when you went AWOL?"

"I should never have trusted you. Family Care! Why should I trust a houseful of strangers? What makes you think I'll be safe? Even with people I know I can't tell the good guys and bad guys apart. They look the same, so honorable, so eager to help. They've all used me, even the ones I'd never dreamed—"

Dr. Pallone tensed like an animal onto the scent of prey who halts in his tracks before going in for the kill. "Who did you never dream would use you?"

I split my ponytail into halves and yanked them to tighten it. "The reason I went AWOL was because I wanted out of here."

"I know."

"I mean it. I want to go home!"

"I know."

"You can't keep me here against my will. I've done nothing wrong. I've never done anything wrong." My body shook. "I want to go home. If I'd known the last night I slept in my bedroom would be the last night ever, I would've remembered it better. Now I'll never have the chance. I want to watch *Twilight Zone* with FD on Friday night and take Mom coffee Saturday morning and sit at the foot of the bed."

The words poured forth in waves of longing. "I want to graduate in a cap and gown and have my picture taken with the rest of my class. If I'm not in the yearbook it'll be like I never even went to St. Monica's, like I never existed." I bent over and held my head.

"Reese..."

"No! You can't help me. No one can help me. I hate this place! I hate this room and these stupid books! They don't have any answers. What do they tell you, Dr. Pallone? Do they give you fancy words so you can label me? What will you call this? Labile? Poor impulse control? Maybe I should give you a stronger one... like... like... volatile!"

I jumped up and paced back and forth in front of the desk, my mind spinning out of control. I searched the room for an outlet. The bookcase. I lunged toward it and stuck my arm behind a row of books until my cheek pressed against binding. With a guttural cry I swept my arm along the shelf.

Books and journals teetered on the edge for a moment before crashing to the floor. "Is that volatile enough for you?" I wheeled around and attacked the next row of books. Scraps of paper tucked between the pages fluttered in the air like captive birds set free.

My energy settled into high gear, unleashing anger left untapped in my thwarted escape. I embraced the next row with both arms and drew the books to my chest. As they crashed to the floor I jumped out of the way to avoid getting hit. The domino effect kicked into motion as the remaining volumes pummelled onto the topsy-turvy pyramid. Books and journals scattered the floor as I cleared the next shelf and the next, standing on tiptoes and sputtering in frustration at the shelves beyond reach.

Someone knocked at the door. I didn't move.

"Everything okay in there, Dr. P?"

"Everything's fine Audrey."

"Why'd you lie to her? I could throw that vase through the window and chop us both to shreds with shards of glass! Don't you want to call Raoul to lock me up, put me in restraints? Aren't you afraid of me?"

"Are you afraid? Afraid you'll hurt yourself?"

Failing to catch a single emotion whizzing around in my brain, I crumpled to the floor. I didn't even hear her cross the room and crouch in front of me. She took my hands and brought us to a stand together. In all the months I'd been here, Dr. Pallone had never touched me. I was grateful she did now.

She was in control. I was safe.

She waited a long time after I collapsed in the chair. "Reese, you're talking about feeling trapped, being held against your will...alluding to people who've hurt you, people you never dreamed would. You kicked violently when Griff restrained you. You referred to being passed from Father Donnelly to Tim like a bottle of gin...said you couldn't tell the good guys from the bad."

"So? I am being held here against my will. I did fight Griff because he had me pinned. My parents have passed me around like a bottle of gin. And no, I can't tell the good guys from the bad. So what?" I fidgeted with a loose thread on the arm of the chair. "Who I've trusted or haven't trusted doesn't matter. My life was ruined the moment I snuck down the hall that night and saw something I shouldn't have."

"Tell me what you saw that night."

"I have told you."

She spoke in a soft voice, its warmth drawing me to her. "Tell me again."

I didn't answer. The image embedded in my brain popped up every time I pushed it down. A powerful feeling of déjà vu threw my normal heartbeat into a skipping rhythm.

A surge of electricity shot through me. My senses

heightened. An engine idled in the distance. Faded colors in the Persian rug grew bright. The vague moldy odor I'd grown used to in her office smelled like sharp cheddar. The texture of nubby upholstery on the chair could've been knotted yarn. Something was happening to me, a sensory explosion I was powerless to control.

"Reese, tell me again about that night."

Long silence.

My eyes darted back and forth. I drew myself up in the chair. The silent stillness transported me to a strange place where past and present merged in a singular blur. I became unaware of Dr. Pallone's presence.

I stared at the colorless winter sky. Memories flitted in bits and pieces across my vision, disappearing like soap bubbles as I tried to catch them. Vague shapes slowly came into view, nothing I could decipher. The longer I stared, the clearer the shapes became. One by one they formed images, the images passing before me like disjointed scenes in a movie.

I spoke in a high staccato voice. "She was hurt…crying and moaning. He was on top of her. She struggled. He wouldn't get off. He wouldn't stop."

"Who, Reese? Who wouldn't stop?"

"Derrick. He was hurting Mom, crushing her." My breathing quickened. "I begged him to stop. Derrick was too big to pull off her. No. It wasn't Derrick. It was someone else. It was FD. FD was on top of her."

Dr. Pallone said something. Her voice was so far away. The room closed in. Rapid breaths turned into shallow gasps. I couldn't hold down the panic rising in me. Someone had to help me. I wasn't watching from the living room hallway. It wasn't FD crushing Mom. It was someone else someplace different, a tight space with no air. And it wasn't Mom. It was me. I shut my eyes. The image stayed.

"I begged him to get off. I couldn't breathe...he was crushing me. He wouldn't stop. I promised I wouldn't tell anyone, if he would just let me go!"

Sweat dampened my back. I sat on the edge of the chair and writhed, as if held against my will. "He got mad...put his hand over my mouth. I couldn't breathe. Let me breathe! I'm going to die! Oh God...please help me! Help me!"

I wrapped my arms tight around me, rocking forward and back in short, fast movements. Dry sobs blocked my airway. Someone touched my arm.

"Acchhh...let go of me." I repelled the hand in a violent thrash.

A voice. Dr. Pallone. She was speaking again. I could feel her presence. She was close. I couldn't open my eyes to see her. She spoke louder.

"Reese. You're here. You're with me. Dr. Pallone. I want you to sit up and open your eyes."

The rocking stopped. I opened my eyes. Everything was jumbled. I couldn't figure out where we were, or make sense of what just happened. I felt numb, detached from my body.

"Inhale slowly."

I did as she said. The hammer in my chest lifted. Air returned to my lungs. I slid back in the chair with stilted motion.

"Do you know where you are, Reese?"

Everything was hazy. I felt disoriented. The room seemed familiar yet foreign. Dr. Pallone looked different, younger somehow. She wasn't wearing her glasses. They were upside down on her lap as if they'd been knocked off.

"Your office I think. Yes. Your office."

"Do you remember where you were before coming to my office?"

"I was in the ward. No. I was someplace else...with Griff. We were running together. No, not together. I was running from him...he was chasing me. He caught up. We struggled. I got scared." As everything came into focus my body began aching. I thought it was from running so hard. It wasn't. My muscles ached the same way they had ached that night. "No. I must've dreamed I was with Griff."

Dr. Pallone leaned close. "You weren't dreaming, Reese. You were right here, next to me. I asked you to tell me about the night you discovered your mother and Father Donnelly. Do you remember what you told me?"

Silence.

"Yes." I covered my face.

"You told me someone raped you, Reese. You re-lived the memory. It's called a flashback. You re-lived the experience."

I kept my face covered. My sense of time was all mixed up. It could've happened five years ago. It could've happened yesterday.

"Silence isn't power. The memory you just revisited is going to come back. Remember how we talked about how silence is the way you give power to your secret. After a while you're not controlling the secret. It's controlling you. The best way to deal with a secret is to take away its power, face it as many times as it takes."

Silence.

"Who's Derrick?"

"I can't tell you. He'll get in trouble. It was my fault."

265

"Getting raped was not your fault, Reese. What makes you think it is?"

"I acted...like Mom. I was friendly. I gave him the idea that...I liked him. The same way I gave Tim that idea. I brought it all on myself."

"Have you given Griff that idea too?"

"No!"

"No. Your getting raped had nothing to do with how you acted or how you dressed. Sixty-year-old women get raped. Five-year-old girls. Rapists are violent criminals. This is not your fault." Long pause. "I'm going to ask you again, Reese. Who is Derrick?"

The last rays of sunlight were shrinking from the Persian rug. I had come full circle. The first day she met me I'd been locked up inside. Now once again I had fallen into darkness. Once again, she led me into light.

"Derrick Gillespie, the Recreation Therapist at St. John's."

Dr. Pallone fell back in the chair with a heavy sigh. Neither of us spoke. This time the silence wasn't waiting for an answer. In that bubble time was suspended. I felt connected to her in a way I had never felt connected with anyone, bound by the intimacy of a terrible secret shared at long last.

I don't know how long we sat there. It could've been ten minutes or an hour, I couldn't be sure. A tap on the door broke the spell. It was Audrey, saying goodnight. Dr. Pallone didn't get up or signal the end of our time. She waited for me to say something.

"Should I go back to the ward now?"

"No. You stay with me for a while. I have some work to finish and you have some cleaning up to do. First let's go to the vending machine. I think we could both use a soda."

We picked our way through the scattered books and papers, closing the door behind us.

And with that my final secret was revealed.

16

THE WAY HOME

Monday morning a detective from the Santa Monica Police Department met with me in Dr. Pallone's office. She sat next to me as I gave a statement describing the night of the movie with Derrick and Janet, including the name of the night nurse on duty when I returned. The detective said it was possible I'd have to testify in court. Dr. Pallone promised that if that turned out to be the case, she herself would go with me.

That afternoon two police officers walked into St. John's and confronted Derrick. As it turned out, he went with them to the station without incident. After reading my statement he confessed to everything and was taken into custody.

*

I left a message for Tim at the clergy house that I needed to see him. Two days later I met him at my bench under the oak. Tim searched my face for some reaction to his letter. The speech I'd prepared in my mind evaporated the moment we sat down. Tim spoke first.

"Hon, I know this seems sudden. The truth is…I've felt this way for a long time. You're an old soul in a young body, that's why we've understood each other from the start. You must know how much I love you. And I think you feel the same."

"Tim, I don't feel the same." He flinched. All the words I had chosen for a gentle explanation had throttled him in one blunt sentence. "What I mean is I do love you, but not like that. I love you as a friend. You've been my only friend for almost a year. I honestly don't know how I would've gotten through this without you."

"Hon, friendship will turn to love. You need to let yourself adjust to the idea of me as your lover, your husband. I resisted thinking of you that way as long as I could. Then I realized the only time I feel right is when I'm with you."

"But Tim, why would you go to my parents? Why didn't you talk to me first?"

"I thought they might object. I wanted them to see what an honorable guy I am."

Poor Tim. He could've been the Boston Strangler and they wouldn't have objected.

"When you told me you weren't going home I knew I had to be honest with myself or I'd regret it the rest of my life. It hit me how much I wanted to take care of you, give you a home."

"I don't want to be taken care of by a husband. I'm seventeen years old."

He dropped his head. I was beginning to think I was with Dr. Pallone by how long it took him to respond. "Then I'll wait until you're ready. We can date, or live together. That's what people are doing now instead of getting married right away. Either way I'm leaving the clergy. I want to make a life with you, whether that's now or when you're eighteen."

"Tim, you're not hear—"

"I need you, Reese, and I think you need me. I may be ten years older, but emotionally, intellectually, we're the same age. You've taken away the loneliness I've felt since leaving Ireland. You are my home."

Again I was at a loss for words. Dr. Pallone had helped me understand I hadn't been sending Tim mixed messages any more than I had invited rape. I had played a part though. Tim had misconstrued the confidences of a lonely teenage girl. Grounded in the belief no man could love me, I had rejected signs that his growing affection had crossed a boundary. And because of those missed signals I was now losing my friend.

"What I'm going to say may sound harsh. At first what I felt for you was a schoolgirl crush. The more we got to know each other the more my feelings changed. Our friendship became very special to me...but that's all it was... friendship. That's all it's ever been. The safety I felt with you was based on that certainty. It never occurred to me that you might feel something stronger. Maybe this crisis of faith you've been having, your ambivalence about life in the clergy, has nothing at all to do with me. It would make sense that imagining a life with me would help you imagine life beyond the clergy. Maybe your feelings have nothing to do with me."

"You've been around shrinks too long, hon," he said with irritation. "I know my feelings."

"Tim, I have cherished our friendship. I couldn't marry you even if I wanted to. It's not our age difference. It's that you deserve more than I can give. All you know of me is depression. This isn't me, not the real me. I don't know who that is yet. If someday I'm lucky enough to find a man who can love me, I want the me he loves to be a whole person, a confident, self-assured woman who's fully formed, not the lonely, unhappy girl you've known. Does that make sense?"

"I have no doubt one day you'll be healthy. We can look back on this as a difficult time. But it's also the beginning of our shared history. My loving you now proves that I want all the parts of you, the depressed and the healthy. If I love you now as you are, I know I'll love whoever you become. You'll still be you. A person's core doesn't change."

His Irish green eyes pleaded with me to trust this would all feel right sometime in the future, just like the St. Christopher necklace I would accept once I changed my mind. I reached for his hand and closed it with mine, our fingers intertwined as one. My heart broke for him, for me. I knew if I cried now it would be that much harder to do what I had to do.

I kept our fingers locked tight. "Tim, you're my teacher. You're my friend."

He started to say something. I placed my finger over his lips. Our eyes held each other's in sadness, the sadness of saying goodbye to a childhood friend moving away, both of you knowing the departure marks the end of a precious moment in time, hating to let go of the present for a future you cannot see.

I kissed Tim on the cheek, then unlocked our fingers and walked away.

*

The anniversary marking one year since my first night at St. John's came and went. Another three months rolled by with still no word of an opening in Family Care. I was soon to have a similar date with Camarillo.

Archie and I waved as I crossed the great lawn where he sat with his group. I was on my way to Griff's office. He had kept me in funding all this time for the Psych Tech program at Ventura College. I had completed the coursework with only clinical rotations left, which would have to wait until I was in Family Care and could manage long hours in various facilities. I was excited to get started in the hopes of finishing the program with my class. I knew that was an uncertainty, like most things in my life, and tried not to dwell on it.

Griff's door was open. He was buried behind his Field of Chaos, as I referred to his desk. He greeted me with an inscrutable grin, hardly able to contain himself.

"What are you looking so mischievous about? Did Voc Rehab double my funding?"

"Better than that, much better. Today's your lucky day, Cavanaugh. I just got a call from Pauline Haberley at the Care Home we've been crossing our fingers for."

"Don't tease me, Griff."

"You'd better start packing. One of her patients is being discharged next week."

I dropped in the chair hearing news I'd begun to think would never come. "Wow." The idea of never again seeing Dr. Pallone came to me like a kick to the stomach. It had been such a long wait that I hadn't thought what it would actually feel like leaving any of them—Griff, Maggie, Raoul, Archie, Angela.

"You'll like this place. Only three other girls. It's close to the beach and your new psychiatrist, whose office happens to be in the same building as Voc Rehab." Griff leaned back and crossed his feet on the desk. "Not so easy cutting the ties a year later, huh? It was never meant to take this long. I know you've gotten comfortable here."

"To my great surprise. Just once I wish I could leave a place when I want to leave."

"You're only batting sixty percent finding a good home, Cavanaugh. You came to us from a crazy home and I think we agree this is your second. Third time's a charm. This is going to give you the chance to plan your future.

That's a great thing, you know. You actually get to choose where you go from here. You have no idea how rare that is. Dr. P and I both recognized a rare opportunity to turn someone's life in the right direction, someone who could follow through and make it happen."

"I know. And I'm more grateful than I can tell you. It's just...after all this time it seems so sudden. There's no time to prepare myself."

"You're prepared. Believe me, once you're gone you won't look back. You'll be so busy with a new home, a new doc, new people...freedom...that you'll forget you ever knew us."

I gave him a crooked smile. "Not likely Griff, but nice try. Anyway, you always said I needed short and long term goals. It's hard to tell if moving from a locked unit to a state home qualifies as a short one or a long one since it took a whole year. At this rate I'll be sixty before I have my master's degree. By the time I write my first novel it will have to be translated into Braille."

He wadded a piece of paper and tossed it at me.

I thought back to the first time I met Griff, thinking him disorganized, wondering how he could possibly accomplish anything. There was so much I wanted to say to him beyond the banter, so much he'd done for me without even knowing.

Griff had provided me with what Dr. Pallone referred to as 'an emotionally corrective experience'—a healing relationship with a man. I had asked her how I would ever trust if I had gotten it wrong with a parent, a priest, a therapist, a teacher. How could I have known a year ago that the one man who hadn't asked me to trust him would turn out to be the one I could.

I tossed the wadded ball of paper back at Griff. "Who

will I have to light a fire under me if you're not around?"

He caught it and laughed. "Who knows? Maybe you'll come back here some day and take over for Maggie."

*

Word of my placement spread through the ward like a California wildfire. Maggie, Raoul and the rest of the staff were excited for me. My fellow patients were both happy and envious. Archie was the one person I wanted to hear it from me instead of through the grapevine.

I didn't see him behind me walking to the cafeteria the next morning. In a flash he was zooming toward me. I managed to find a wall just as Archie dove for my shoes. The psych tech caught up. I asked for a moment.

"Reese! Pretty Reese! Don't go away! Don't go away!"

"Archie, get up. C'mon, I can't talk to you when you're on my feet."

He faced me, the helmet cockeyed atop his pile of red hair.

"This helmet, Archie. What can we do about this helmet?" I adjusted the thing, surprised at the quivering in my lips.

"Are you going home to your parents, Pretty Reese?"

"Nah, not to my old home anyway. I'm going to another place kind of like the hospital, but smaller."

"Take me! I want a family too."

"Sorry, Archie, this place is girls only. That leaves you out. Hey, you remember the day we both felt sad because our mom's hadn't come to visit?"

"No. I want to go with you."

"I said how lucky you were because everybody here knows you and likes you. They're helping you get better. Right? You don't bang your head as much or spin in circles until you fall over. The people here have helped you a lot because they care about you like family."

"Will the people where you're going be your family now?"

"Something like that."

"But I'll still be your boyfriend. I'll always be your boyfriend."

Over his shoulder I saw the psych tech heading our way.

"You'll always be my friend, Archie."

The psych tech took him by the shoulders into the cafeteria. I watched until I could no longer see the blue helmet.

*

Saturday morning I was too excited to eat breakfast. Maggie gave me permission to stay in the dorm packing and cleaning my locker. When the last of my clothes had been stuffed in the suitcase, books and letters piled in a box, I sat on the bed now stripped of linen. The dorm was deserted.

Had it really only been a year since the day Maggie stood here rattling off rules. It seemed like a lifetime ago. The terrified girl who had walked in the dorm bore little resemblance to the woman who would walk out.

"CAVANAUGH! Your ride's here!"

I took a final look around the room, then picked up my suitcase and headed to the nurses' station. Maggie introduced me to George Haberley, a friendly looking man with a thatch of silver hair. While he signed the paperwork I searched the dayroom. She was at our table in the back, polishing her nails.

She barely looked up, her usual tough chick expression daring anyone to interrupt.

"Hey, Angela."

She kept polishing.

"I figured I wouldn't be needing this anymore." I set my Christmas purse on the table.

She stared at it for a moment, then looked up, nail-polished hand in mid-air.

"See ya, Lupercio." I was already heading back to the nurses' station, but I heard her.

"See ya, Cavanaugh."

Maggie and Raoul shook their heads in disbelief I was really leaving. We hugged without a word. I led the way to the parking lot then waited for Mr. Haberley to point out his car.

It was a Chevrolet.

We made a left at the gate and wound our way down the switchbacks away from Camarillo State Hospital.

17

A NEW DESTINATION

I checked the clock and counted how many progress notes I still had to chart. My shift at Ventura Community had been uneventful, a quiet Saturday. After three years working the psych unit I had earned my Monday through Friday schedule. This was a rare weekend shift. I'd had enough of those at my first job, a locked unit at the county hospital. The inpatient setting at Community felt like a vacation in comparison, so I didn't mind trading the occasional weekend shift for a friend.

A well-built guy in jeans and a corduroy jacket came through the door. I guessed late twenties. He had a confident stride as he approached the nurses' station. He introduced himself as Daniel Berensen and said he was here to see his friend Russ, a recent admission to the open unit.

I felt him watching as I scrolled Russ's chart for the names of approved visitors. Daniel thanked me and started down the hall. Ten seconds later he was back.

"The thing is, I'm a little nervous. I'm not even sure Russ will want to see me. Do you think you could check with him first?"

"Of course."

He followed me to the dayroom. "I feel a bit awkward. I know Russ is depressed. I don't know what to say to him and I sure don't want it to be the wrong thing." He and Russ were doctoral candidates in chemistry at Cal Tech.

Daniel had noticed his friend's low mood. Struggling with the pressure himself he had no clue how to help.

Someone called his name. Daniel turned around to face Russ. Without breaking stride he pulled Daniel into a guy hug, both of them patting each other in reassuring slaps. They didn't notice me slip away to the nurses' station. The two friends sat in the day room and talked for an hour.

Daniel visited Russ every evening for the next week. He chatted with me either as he arrived or before he left. Three days of this and I found myself watching for him. Daniel didn't fit my stereotyped image of a dorky chemist with thick glasses and a pocket protector. He was warm and engaging, and from what I could tell, interested in everything. Even poetry. One evening he arrived for his visit with a thin volume of Robert Frost for his friend.

Our passing chats grew from sixty seconds to ten minutes. The day Russ was discharged, Daniel was there to give him a ride home. He invited me to dinner and a movie the following week. *Deliverance* hadn't been the ecology film Daniel thought it was, and it sure wasn't on the Top Ten list of first date movies. We still laugh about our inauspicious beginning.

For two years, I repeatedly pushed him away. He never once failed my test. Daniel fell in love with the me who still suffered bouts of depression; the me who was excited about finishing graduate school; the me who worked late into the night on my debut novel.

The me who moved forward in baby steps as I learned to trust a lover.

Tessa was born two years after we married. My life took on some semblance of the one I'd dreamed of as a kid, only a grown-up version, rich, textured. As the thirteen-year-old girl who thought life was over after having discovered a terrible truth, I never could have dreamed such a life could be mine.

At last I belonged.

Yet when I least expected it, pangs of loss would catch me off guard. In those moments I yearned for Mom, for the warmth of her charisma in the few precious memories I'd salvaged from the rubble—the way she glowed at Christmastime as she transformed the house into a fantasy wonderland; how she sang to herself every Friday afternoon with the Mixmaster whirring cake batter for FD's *Twilight Zone* visit; the sight of her on the living room floor surrounded by the pattern pieces making my dress for the freshman dance.

She had failed me in every way a mother can fail a child, but I loved her.

*

Hot Devil Winds slammed into town in late afternoon that day in September. I was at the dining room table with a glass of lemonade writing lecture notes for my first class at the Southern California State University when the call came.

Daniel answered. Dread came over me at the look on his face, a mix of anxiety and protectiveness I'd not seen since we had rushed Tessa to the emergency room with a spiked fever. I knew it had to be more than Kit calling to cancel dinner. Had something happened to Dad?

Daniel handed me the receiver as he mouthed the words *I'm right outside.*

The voice on the line sounded familiar. Still, it took a moment to register. My breath caught. It was FD. His voice was strained, an octave lower than the one he'd used as Father Popular Donnelly. He bypassed the small talk and got to the point. Mom had ovarian cancer. The disease had progressed rapidly. Hospice Care was tending her at home. Mom was near the end.

I steadied myself against the wall. It had been thirteen years since our last contact, her letter about the divorce while I was in Camarillo. There had been no subsequent letter, no forwarding address.

"Reese? Will you come?"

I ran my fingers over my forehead. There was no way she could hurt me now. I was loved, my own family a shield against her powers of destruction.

"Yes. I'll come."

"There's something I need to tell you before you see her." His voice became tentative. "I don't expect you to understand. I'm not sure how to say this without it sounding worse."

"Say what?" My heart fluttered.

"When your mother and I moved to Laguna Beach, she wanted a fresh start. She thought it would be easier all around if we presented ourselves as a newly married couple."

"No one's going to hear it from me that you were a priest, if that's what concerns you."

"It's not that. People know. It's just that, well, she never thought she would see you or Kit again. You were so angry and Kit had washed her hands of Mom. She couldn't bear the thought of people asking about her painful past."

Her painful past. I shut my eyes and took a deep breath. "Did what?"

"Presented ourselves as a first-time married couple. With no children."

My mouth fell open.

"Hello?"

"I...I need a day to decide whether or not I want to see her."

"I understand. Reese. If not for her, do this for yourself. There isn't much time."

For the next twenty-four hours I did everything possible to shove down the feelings. I immersed myself with frenzy in preparation for my class. I read extra stories to Tessa. I relined the kitchen drawers.

How could she do this? What kind of mother denies the existence of her children? She could've said we lived in another country, or even the truth, that we were estranged. I had friends who weren't close to their mothers. They didn't claim they were dead!

I would not be undone by my mother. She would not do this to me again. I would be strong. I would be *strong.*

That night I fell into restless sleep. At two in the morning I was wide awake. Daniel had a busy day ahead; I tried not to flop around. In the stillness Dr. Pallone's words came to me. *Pushing feelings down is how you give them power. They're feelings. They can't kill you. The way you take the power away is to let yourself feel, learn to tolerate the pain without acting on it. Then the feelings don't control you. You control them. You're not locked in the bomb shelter, Reese. Walk up the stairs into light.*

Tears trickled over my face to the pillow. I let the feelings flood me, the agony of one last rejection. Beneath the hurt, beneath the anger, another feeling emerged, a feeling more powerful than those I'd sought to quell. I couldn't ignore it. I couldn't restrain it. The feeling rose from some deep primordial place that transcended reason.

Love.

I loved my mother and needed to tell her before she died.

*

I parked across the street. Mom's house was in an upscale neighborhood on the opposite end of town from the beach cottage on the cliff. I wondered why they had chosen to come back here, to this of all places. Was it because here their fantasy had become reality in a baby whose flesh and blood was their own?

I gathered my strength and walked to the door. Before I could ring, FD opened the door. He looked exactly as he had the last time I'd seen him at St. John's—trim, clean-cut, the look of a man you would trust if you were in need of insurance. Or spiritual guidance.

For a moment, I was thirteen again, standing in the doorway of our house meeting this glorious man for the first time. I had given him my heart and soul the first sixty seconds because he'd bothered to ask me how I preferred to be addressed, winning me over completely with that singular display of affection.

Now I was the one outside the door, facing the man who had ruined my family, almost destroyed me, and very nearly robbed me of my God. It took years to understand I had not been abandoned at all. It was only the humans who had done that.

As FD and I stood on the porch facing each other, a half smile was all it took to bring him forward. In one giant step I was in his arms.

"Thank you for coming, Reese."

Floor-to-ceiling glass offered a panoramic view of the Pacific Ocean from the Palos Verdes Peninsula to Mexico. The hospice nurse led me down the hall to the back of the house. She said Mom was heavily medicated, conscious intermittently but lucid. We reached the darkened bedroom. I stood in the doorway, waiting for my knees to stop shaking.

The nurse turned and left me alone with Mom. She was asleep in a hospital bed, shallow gurgling sounds with each labored breath the only evidence of life. I stepped closer. The sight of her took my breath away. Instead of the beautiful mother I had known, a network of sallow wrinkles covered her face, the tissue-thin layer translucent over spider veins. Even under the sheet it was obvious the contours defining her voluptuous body had collapsed in a moonscape of bony peaks and deep valleys.

I let out a shaky breath in search for some sign of familiarity.

She didn't look as if she'd wake any time soon. I spotted a chaise and dropped down to wait for her next moment of wakefulness, wondering how Mom would react to seeing me after all these years, wondering whether I would know her at all. Who was this woman who had given me life then denied my existence? Was that the ultimate price for choosing FD, fabricating a new identity in a self-imposed Witness Protection Program, always on guard for inconsistencies in her back story?

Had she been so miserable with us that choosing a life of lies was worth it? I knew what that kind of existence felt like, freedom of authenticity no longer an option. I had to remind myself that whatever the price, she had been willing to do whatever it cost to be with Jack Donnelly as real husband and wife instead of the make-believe version she had lived so long.

In denying our existence Mom had buried herself along with us. Vivienne Cavanaugh was nothing more than the nagging vestige of a former life.

Who are we if not the culmination of our past? It may not define who we become, yet the past shapes and influences us on the way. Hadn't I learned that in therapy and seen it in Viktor Frankl—that we can't always control the circumstances of our lives, or the choices made by others who have control over us. It's how we exercise free will and respond to that over which we have no control that defines who we are.

Mom groaned. Late afternoon light slipped through the shutters. I tiptoed to the bed to see if she was awake. Mom opened her eyes, those cobalt eyes, faded luster still captivating. The Mom I had known was still there. We studied each other, her measuring the changes in me, my recovering from the sight of her. I wondered if we might find anything salvageable in our twenty-nine year history.

She lifted her head. It fell back on the pillow. "Clarice."

"Shhhh. You just rest."

"Clarice…" Any words she might have wanted to say refused to cooperate with her drug-addled brain. I pulled a lemon stick from the pack on the side table. She followed my eyes as I slid the swab across her top lip, then the bottom, repeating the move until the jagged skin was soaked in moisture. She placed her cold hand over my warm one on the bedrail. The veins in her neck pulsated with her effort to speak.

"Clarice, please listen. I never meant to hurt you kids. Or your father."

The honesty of her words caught me off guard. I felt the sudden urge to hug her. I held my breath and waited for the feeling to subside. "I know, Mom."

"You must know deep down that I've always—"

The bedroom door flung open. FD switched on the light, bursting our bubble with his well-honed levity. It was only in this moment I realized that that was how he guarded against real feelings. It was all performance art.

He approached the bed with the same arrogance of ownership he had demonstrated the day he negotiated Kit's smoking, as if he were Dad and Kit his daughter. I wondered why he'd barged in now, just as Mom had woken. Was he afraid of what she might say on her deathbed?

Mom didn't acknowledge his presence. She kept her eyes on me. Her mouth formed a straight line in resentment at his interruption. With a slight shake of my head, I let her know I had heard what she said without her needing to finish. FD nudged me further up the bedrail where eye contact with Mom was impossible. I squeezed her hand and let it slip from mine.

I returned to the chaise and waited while the nurse cleared the IV port. Mom groaned at her touch. As the morphine found its pathway through her body, she closed her eyes and settled. FD said he'd leave us to each other and return momentarily.

Mom opened her eyes and twisted in search of me, breathing hard as she strained. I resumed my place along the bedrail where we could see each other.

A warm smile came over her face. I knew that smile. It was the smile of Vivienne Cavanaugh. I felt transfixed by the tenderness in her expression. That's when I was certain. I was in the presence of my mother. It was Saturday morning. She was just waking up as I walked in the room with her coffee.

Mom lifted her hand toward the bedrail. I took hers in mine, feeling every one of its twenty-seven skeletal bones. It took every ounce of willpower I possessed to hold it together in what would be the last words we would ever exchange. I willed the tears to hold back and my voice to stay calm. She motioned me to come closer.

"I need to tell you, Clarice." A cough sent spasms running the length of her body. She closed her eyes, waiting for the next breath. "I…"

"Mom." I lifted my free hand to her face. It was burning, dry. I stroked her cheek. FD was heading down the hall. "Mom, there's no need to explain anything. I know you loved me. I know you never stopped loving me."

She held my eyes, grateful yet questioning, searching for something more.

I leaned close and whispered in her ear. "And I never stopped loving you."

She exhaled heavily. As FD walked in, she let her hand slip from mine. With a final glance at me, she closed her eyes.

That night Mom slipped from consciousness. She died the next morning at dawn.

*

Pepper trees lining the long driveway had grown since the last time I'd seen them. At the gate, I stopped and let the car idle in front of the new sign. The California State University system had finally added a new campus in Ventura County after years of funding delays. Land had become too expensive to justify building a campus from the ground up, especially when the state could convert an abandoned facility it already owned: Camarillo State Hospital.

Transforming the place had required structural upgrading and cosmetic work. To me it looked the same as it had twelve years ago. The 1930's Mission Revival architecture had been preserved, its oppressive façade subdued with whitewash and flower beds.

Memories overshadowed my awareness as if I had

stepped back in time.

The Bell Tower building where I had spent so much time with Dr. Pallone still housed administrative offices. Hers had no doubt been renovated, artifacts surrounding the woman who had saved my life thrown into a construction dumpster.

My eyes surveyed the scene. Instead of patients who had wandered the grounds with no place to go, students with backpacks and busy lives crisscrossed the quad. I traced the sidewalk from the adolescent ward to Griff's office and the cafeteria, smiling at the memory of Archie with his red hair and blue helmet accosting me. Students sat kissing on the bench where Tim and I had had our final conversation.

HONK!

I jolted and checked the rear view mirror. Turning into the parking lot where the sign read Faculty Only instead of Visitors, I remembered feeling utterly alone the day my father pulled out of this parking lot and drove away.

As I went through the motions gathering my things, it was impossible to stay focused on the present.

I didn't need help from signs directing students to the auditorium. I opened the door and stepped inside. A low hum filled the air as students chatted and shuffled into their seats. The institutional smell of confinement had been suppressed by fresh paint and wood polish. I crossed the stage to the podium, just as I had the day I chose my Christmas purse.

Cavanaugh...get off the stage!

I glanced at the class. Their faces were as fresh as mine had been when I was a patient standing here with the dream of teaching, wondering what it would feel like to be here for real. A student burst through the heavy door at the last minute. The reverberating echo of clanging metal was the same one I'd heard in the lobby where I'd sat waiting to meet Dr. Pallone.

The auditorium fell to a hush, all eyes forward. My knees buckled.

Walk up the stairs, Reese, into the light.

I stood tall, shoulders relaxed. "Welcome to Early Nineteenth Century Literature. My name is Reese Cavanaugh."

ACKNOWLEDGEMENTS

No book comes to life without the support of key individuals. Thank you to Rosemary Kind of Alfie Dog Limited in England for her support in ushering the book into print.

I am grateful to the following friends for comments on early drafts—Penny Bazant, Lisa Bigeleisen, Fran Christiansen, Dianne Kelley, Josie Martin, Tracey Miller, Frances Morrison, Kathryn Padgett, Linda Sorensen, Leslie Thompson, Peter Windsor; and to those who critiqued the final rewrite—Katharine Mallin, Nick Watts, Lawrence Sorensen, Shirley Waxman. Special thanks to my dear friend Deirdre Morse for her enduring support through multiple drafts.

Thank you to Miki Klocke for her photographic talent, and to Ann Hammond for the inspired painting on the cover.

I owe a debt of gratitude to Viktor Frankl for his psychological memoir, *Man's Search for Meaning*, and to Gabriele Vesely-Frankl, Ph.D. of the Viktor Frankl Institute of Logotherapy and Existential Analysis in Vienna for her comments on the manuscript.

I am enormously grateful to my son, Michael, for his unwavering conviction that ROAD was a story worth telling, and to my daughter, Christine, for her support in my telling it. I can never adequately thank my husband, Larry, for believing I could walk the long road with him and build the life we have together.

ABOUT THE AUTHOR

(Photo courtesy of Miki Klocke www.MikiArtisan.com)

In her debut novel, Lori Windsor Mohr draws on her experience growing up in Southern California, where she suffered from severe depression. She believes writing about suicide is one way of fighting the stigma still associated with depressive illness. After earning a Master of Science in Nursing at UCLA, Lori worked with suicidal adolescents. Twenty years after hearing their stories, she was inspired to tell her own.

Lori is the mother of two grown children and currently lives in Ojai with her husband and three dogs. Her short stories have been featured in breed journals, including *Family Dog*, Alfiedog.com, and *Pug Talk*, where she was a staff writer for six years.

Visit Lori at www.LoriMohrAuthor.com or email her at LoriWindsorMohr@gmail.com

Alfie Dog Fiction

Taking your imagination for a walk

For hundreds of short stories, collections
and novels visit our website at
www.alfiedog.com

Join us on Facebook
http://www.facebook.com/AlfieDogLimited

Made in the USA
San Bernardino, CA
25 November 2015